STRONGER, FASTER,

Arwen Elys Dayton spends months doing research for her stories. Her explorations have taken her around the world to places like the Great Pyramid at Giza, Hong Kong and its islands, the Baltic Sea, and many ruined castles in Scotland.

Arwen lives with her husband and their three children on the West Coast of the United States. *Stronger, Faster and More Beautiful* is Arwen's first novel published with Harper Voyager. You can visit her and learn more about her books at arwendayton.com and follow @arwenelysdayton on Instagram and Facebook.

stronger,

faster,

and

more

beautiful

ARWEN ELYS DAYTON

HARPER
Voyager

Harper*Voyager*
An imprint of HarperCollins*Publishers* Ltd
1 London Bridge Street
London SE1 9GF

www.harpervoyagerbooks.co.uk

First published in Great Britain by HarperCollins*Publishers* 2019
2

A catalogue record for this book
is available from the British Library

ISBN: 978-0-00-832240-3

This novel is entirely a work of fiction.
The names, characters and incidents portrayed in it are
the work of the author's imagination. Any resemblance to
actual persons, living or dead, events or localities is
entirely coincidental.

Set in Maxime

Printed and bound by CPI Group (UK) Ltd, Croydon CR0 4YY

MIX
Paper from
responsible sources
FSC™ C007454

FSC
www.fsc.org

To the next generation
and the next and the next
(and hopefully the next)

We have got to the point in human history where we simply do not have to accept what nature has given us.

> —Jay Keasling, professor of biochemical engineering, University of California, Berkeley, in *Wired*, 2009

A few years from now . . .

PART ONE

MATCHED PAIR

Human!

Stop!

. . . is what I'm thinking. As if I've already become something else, a different species, and I'm tired of hearing all of his worn-out, human-person logic.

The man is reminding me that Julia's heart will be combined with my own heart, so it's not like I'm "taking" hers. It's a synthesis. The new heart will fuse both in a way that's better than either of the originals. A super-heart, I guess you could call it.

He is reminding me of this, and every time I say "But—" he cuts me off by continuing his explanation, only more loudly. Now he's almost yelling, though he's just as cheerful as he always is.

Did I mention that he's my father? And he's only repeating what my doctor has explained so many times. Although, let's be honest, my doctor explains the same things very differently. She discusses recovery rates and reasonable percentages and acceptable outcomes. She tells me about other patients, though of course, my case and Julia's case—the case of Evan and Julia Weary, semi-identical twins—is unique, so we are, as she likes to say, "medical pioneers." I've come to think of us as the season-finale episode of a show about strange medical cases. Tune in for the outrageous conclusion!

I'm in my hospital room, but I'm sitting in a chair in the corner, because it's dangerous to stay in the hospital bed, which can be wheeled away for CAT scans or blood draws or surgery, or whatever, so easily. You have the illusion of control if you're sitting in a chair.

Julia is in the adjoining room. She's on the bed, of course. And though I can hear our mother in there with her, she's only saying a few quiet words to my sister, and my sister is not saying anything in reply.

"This is fortune smiling on us, Evan," my father says, using what has become one of his favorite phrases. He looms over me, because I'm sitting down while he's standing and also because he's six foot five. "Years from now, you're going to look back on these weeks and wonder why you ever hesitated. Julia would want her heart and yours to be joined."

Whenever he senses me becoming skeptical about what we're going to do, my father finds a new angle to convince me. This is the new angle for today: Julia's fondest wish is for our twin hearts to become one.

"But I'm the only one who will get to use the heart," I tell him. "It's not like we're turning into one person and sharing it. I get the heart. She gets nothing."

He raises his voice another notch as he says, "Would you rather put hers in the ground? Alone and cold? To rot?" Even he can hear the hysteria that has snuck into his argument. He lowers the volume to something like normal conversational level and adds, "You know she wouldn't want that. She does get something. She gets you, alive."

"I'm the one who gets that!"

"She gets it too, Evan."

I hope that's true.

"You sound out of breath," my father says. "How about we keep our voices calm?"

This is an infuriating suggestion since he's the one who's not calm, but his observation is accurate; I'm having trouble catching my breath. I concentrate on forcing air in and out of my chest.

I notice that we're only talking about Julia's heart, even though she'll give me so much more—her liver, part of her large intestine, her kidneys, even her pancreas. It's too depressing to keep mentioning all the pieces of both of us that aren't working right, so my parents and I have begun using the heart as a stand-in for everything.

I look up at him wearily. "Dad, why do we keep talking about it, anyway? You already decided."

"You decided too, Evan."

I sigh, and though I try to sound as angry as possible, he's right. I did decide.

· · ·

When the nurses show up to do tests, my father leaves. He doesn't like to stick around for the nitty-gritty, which used to annoy me but now is a relief. If my father is present, he considers it an obligation to insert as many positive comments as possible into whatever uncomfortable hospital procedure is happening. It's not ideal to have to make appreciative noises about the weather and baseball scores when a male nurse is putting a catheter into your penis, for example.

With my father gone, I hardly have to say anything.

Nurse: "Does that hurt?"

Me: "A little."

Nurse: "Is this better?"

Me: "A little."

Nurse: "Can you roll over onto your back now?"

I don't even have to answer that. I just have to do it.

. . .

Later, I'm left alone in my hospital room. This is the last day. It will happen in the morning. Julia and I have just barely made it to our fifteenth birthday. And now comes . . . whatever is next.

I am not immune to daydreams. I imagine slipping on my clothes, walking out of the hospital, and asking my mother to bring me somewhere peaceful to die. My favorite fantasy locations are on a beach overlooking Lake Michigan, or on the moon base, while staring up at the small blue face of Earth.

Yes, I know there isn't any moon base, but I'm not sneaking out of the hospital either.

The daydreams are tempting, but here's the truth of it: death sucks more than life, almost no matter what. There. I've admitted it. I want to live. Blech. It feels wrong.

I get off my hospital bed and go into the connecting room, Julia's. My heart races as soon as I'm on my feet, but if I move slowly, I can keep it from getting out of hand. Julia's room is kept nice and quiet and mostly dark, though it's still daytime, so cloudy light comes in through the slatted blinds over the window. Her ventilator hisses and clicks. Her bed is surrounded by IV stands that are providing her food, her water, her drugs. Dripping, dripping, dripping away.

"Hey," I say, out of breath when I reach the edge of her bed.

Hey, she says. Not out loud, of course. But I know she says it.

Julia is gray and her cheeks are hollow, but she's still beautiful. Her hair is red, like mine, but hers is much longer and it's been fanned out across her pillow (by our mother, probably), as if she's posing for an illustration in a book of fairy tales. Here is Snow White, awaiting the kiss of a prince to wake her. Here is Sleeping Beauty, for whom the rest of the world has been frozen. I slide myself onto the bed next to her and lie there as my heart and lungs slow down, listening to the sounds of the machine that is breathing for her.

"Hey," I say again.

It's so boring here, she tells me quite clearly, though, again, not out loud. The time when Julia can speak out loud is over.

"I've realized that being a medical pioneer is mostly about surviving the boredom," I tell her.

Julia sighs, silently of course. Then she tells me, *When the doctor calls us that, I imagine us in a covered wagon with one of those old-timey black doctor's bags.*

"Why do people think being a pioneer is good?" I wonder aloud. "Isn't it better to be waaay at the back of the line, after all the kinks have been worked out?"

This is going to sound mean, Julia tells me, *but I never even liked* real *pioneers. In those Little House books, I kept wondering why they didn't stay in New York or Chicago, where all the fun stuff was happening.*

"You're a snob," I tell her. "They were brave."

Yeah, they probably were, she admits. Then: *You're going to be brave too, Evan.*

"Yuck. You sound like one of those greeting cards with the fancy cursive."

I got sappy there for a second. Sorry. It's from being in the hospital. She changes the subject. *Where have you been all afternoon?*

"Tests. Oh—this is exciting—they took a sample of my poop. New test. I guess it was to see what my large intestine is doing."

What were the results of this poop test?

"It was poop. They confirmed that."

Well . . . that's a huge load off my mind, she says.

"After the test they plopped me back onto the bed."

I'm flushed with relief that everything's okay.

"It would have been so crappy otherwise."

We both laugh. Me out loud. Julia, you know, not out loud. Annoying puns are kind of our thing. I scoot over until my head is against hers.

I forget what that's like, she says.

"What? Tests?"

Moving.

"Oh. Right." Even though I'm here with her so much, sometimes I forget too.

We're both quiet for a while, but I know what Julia's thinking about. She's remembering that time when we were five years old, and she beat me twenty-four times in a row running down the street outside our house. I can feel her gloating.

I tell her, "Look, you beat me that *one* time—"

It was twenty-four times, Evan.

This is an old argument.

"Fine. You beat me on that one *day*. But I never let you beat me again," I remind her.

What neither of us says is that we didn't have many races after that day when we were five. Running became too difficult for either of us, and the following year, it was apparent that very few of our organs were growing at the proper rate.

Relax, Evan, she says. *You've won forever now.*

I don't answer her because that's a horrible thing to say. If we were having one of our competitions to see who could say the most despicable thing, she would totally win.

Oh shit, are you crying? I didn't mean it. I was only joking!

I put my hand over Julia's heart, and then I put Julia's cool, limp hand over mine. It's possible that I am crying, but there's no reason to dwell on it.

In that calm way of hers, Julia tells me, *We shared a womb, Evan, and a crib, and a room for the first six years of our lives. Now we'll share more things. It will be okay.*

. . .

Possibly you have never heard of semi-identical twins, so let me explain. Semi-identicals happen when two sperm fertilize the same egg. (I really hope you already know what sperm and eggs are, because I don't want to be the one who has to tell you.) At some point after this cellular three-way, Mother Nature realizes that something is not right, and the egg splits into two, which in our case meant that it split into me, Evan, and her, Julia. But it's not quite as simple as that. There are some mixed-up DNA signals with semi-identicals. Some become intersex (boy parts *and* girl parts), and some have other glitches in the embryo-formation process. We had none of those issues—our problem is that our hearts and livers and several other organs never learned how to grow to full size, even though the rest of us made a go of it.

I'm taller than you are, Julia helpfully points out as I float toward sleep.

She's taller by about an eighth of an inch, by the way. Fifty percent of our DNA is identical—from the egg we both shared.

And the other fifty percent, from the sperm, is not identical, but it comes from the same person (our father, unless our mom has really been hiding stuff from us). So we're as closely matched as any boy and girl can be.

But around our thirteenth birthday, Julia's organs started lagging behind worse than mine did. At first, for months and months, she was just tired. Then she was just asleep. Then it wasn't really sleep anymore, and she was in the hospital and the machines were brought in to keep her alive. And now she is on this bed, silent to everyone but me. *Vegetative* is what they call it, as if she is a stalk of wheat or a spear of asparagus. This sucks so deeply that there aren't really words. This is as close as I can come:

That's me in the middle, drowning.

. . .

I fall asleep next to Julia and I wake up when I hear voices in my own room. At first I think it's nurses who've come to give me a second rectal exam—just to make sure—but that's not who it is. It's my mother, and a man—not my father. This man has a different voice entirely, smooth and deep and sort of . . . *stirring*, I guess you could say. Except that he's using it to argue with my mother, and almost immediately I know exactly who the voice belongs to.

Don't keep me in suspense! Julia says, startling me. I didn't think she was awake. *Who is it?*

"It's that weird minister Mom's been talking to all month. I've heard his voice when she's talking to him on the phone."

Oh, yeah. She keeps mentioning things "the Reverend" says. I didn't even know we were Christian until Mom started having all these Jesus feelings.

"I'm not sure Reverend Tadd even *is* Christian," I whisper to her, still trying to hear what they're arguing about.

His name is Reverend Tadd? Julia asks skeptically. *Is that his first name or his last name?*

"I don't know. But I do know that he's an asshole. The way he speaks—it's like Jesus was his roommate at summer camp and if you're lucky he'll introduce you."

How does Mom even know him?

"She wanted someone to 'guide her to the right choices'—about us, I guess. I heard her tell Dad. They argued and Dad won, but Mom said she still needed to talk to someone. And talking people out of medical procedures is, like, Reverend Tadd's *thing*."

"Wait! You look angry." Our mother's voice rises suddenly on the other side of the door. "We've had beautiful discussions, and I said you could come bless them, but I don't want you to argue—"

The door from my room to Julia's room flies open a moment later, and the man is *in* the room with us, trailing our mother. He approaches the hospital bed, one hand raised, with a finger directed upward, as if he has a personal, finger-pointing connection straight to heaven and he's calling in a favor.

"You!" he says, his eyes locking onto me where I lie next to my sister. I'm not ashamed to say he's scary, because he is scary; his eyes are wild and his face is screwed up with outrage, but he's also . . .

Much younger and better-looking than I thought he would be, Julia says calmly.

That's exactly what I was thinking. The Reverend is young, perhaps only in his late twenties. He has thick, wavy black hair that falls over his forehead, and piercing dark eyes that are alight with passion.

Before our mother can stop him (which, to be honest, she is making only a very feeble attempt at) he's on his knees at the side of the bed, his eyes beseeching me. I'm startled by his sudden presence, but it's hard to be too startled when Julia is with me.

"You," he says, bowing his head over his hands briefly, as if to let me and Julia know that he's not too proud to beg—in fact, that he *relishes* this opportunity to beg.

"Reverend," our mother says, without much force. "It's been decided. And this is family business."

Ignoring her, he looks at me and says, "You know there's still time."

I should be cringing away from him, but I'm so tired of the sympathetic looks from nurses and my parents that his energy fascinates me.

"Time for what?" I ask him, propping myself up onto my elbows.

Don't ask! Julia says. She has understood immediately what sort of man he is. *Why would you encourage him?*

"Time for ev-er-y-thing." (That's exactly how it sounds.) "You're a young man now, a *person*." He's gripping the railing of the bed in his zeal. "If you do this thing, Evan Weary, you will become something that's not meant to be."

His voice and his certainty are mesmerizing. I feel as though he has pressed something sharp into my malfunctioning heart. The Reverend Tadd-not-sure-if-it's-his-first-or-last-name sees that he's gotten to me, and he follows up immediately.

"Do you *want* to turn yourself into a demon? A life-devouring creature?" he asks me, his face getting close enough to mine that his minty breath washes over me. "Is that your goal?"

Do you know the sensation when you've been injured but the pain hasn't reached you yet? I am having that feeling now. I think it was his use of the word *life-devouring*.

I know resistance is called for. "Um . . . I don't know if I even believe in demons—" I begin, but he rides right over me.

"You *don't* want to be one! That's the answer. No good person wants that!"

I can feel Julia's outrage that I'm taking these insults lying down. *Roll over and kick him in the nuts!* she tells me.

But I don't have to, because our mother has finally found her courage, and she grabs the Reverend Tadd by his shoulders.

"You have to leave now," she tells him, her voice quavering

but firm. When he doesn't budge, she puts her hands on her hips and says, "If you don't leave, I will call the nurses—and security! I mean it, Reverend."

He stands up, unrushed, as if he were done anyway and is leaving only because it's his own choice. He brushes off his pants and stares down at me and Julia, calmer now that he's succeeded in calling me a demon—or, I guess, a soon-to-be-demon. The full demonification hasn't happened quite yet, as he has thoughtfully pointed out.

"Reverend!" our mother says, warning him against further pronouncements.

Close-lipped, Reverend Tadd walks to the hospital room door, yet before we're rid of him, he looks back at me and takes another stab. "You don't have to do this selfish thing," he says.

Selfish. It's the word that's always there, in the back of my mind. How did he know?

Sensing that I have become paralyzed before this man, Julia steps in. *Can't you see it's already eating Evan up?* she yells at him. *If Jesus were here, He'd slap you! You—you—creep!*

But Reverend Tadd, of course, has not heard her, and he's already left the room.

"I'm so sorry, Evan," our mother says. "I said he could say a prayer here, that's all." She's leaning against the closed door and has dissolved into tears, which, actually, has been her most common state over the past few months.

What's Mom crying about? Julia asks, still half yelling. *She's the one who let him in here. Oh, Evan . . . are you crying too?*

. . .

I wake up and know that my parents have tricked me, or rather, that they had the nurses drug me. I'm in my own hospital bed, even though I don't remember moving back. Sunlight is pouring in my window. It's morning. The Day.

"Julia," I say as my eyes open.

The room is full, but empty of her. Nurses are crowding in with prep carts and rubbing alcohol and IVs. They're checking my vitals, slipping tubes into my veins, talking to me with that impersonal friendliness they must learn in nursing school.

I catch sight of my father, so tall that it feels like he's in the way, even though he's standing in the corner to stay clear of the bustle. He smiles benignly at me.

"It's okay, Evan. She's gone on ahead of you."

"Julia!" I say again, louder this time.

The nurse closest to my face makes little noises that are half shushing, half consoling. Well, mostly shushing.

I hear Julia very distantly. *Evan. Evan.* That's all there is, only the ghost of her voice from somewhere far below me in the hospital. *Evan . . .*

. . .

It is . . . I'm not sure how many days later. Maybe four?

They took Julia's heart while I was unconscious, and then, inside my chest cavity, they used her "compatible tissue" to rebuild my own heart, and then they jolted the super-heart into action, and (I heard later) they all clapped when it began pumping blood. Pictures were taken. A day later they did the kidneys, the liver, and everything else that required renovation.

I have a line of metal staples down the middle of my chest. They look pretty badass, like Dr. Frankenstein was given free rein to close me up. There are stitches and staples in lots of other places too. Supposedly, modern medicine is excellent at minimizing scars, but my nurses assure me that mine will still be amazing after they heal. I'll look like a scattered train track for the rest of my life. It feels like the train on that broken track hit me, then backed up to finish the job. Except . . . even with all the pain, I actually feel better. My heart is beating strongly and regularly, my body seems lighter. How crazy is that?

"Here I am," I say.

The hospital room is empty except for me, so I can get away with talking to myself without drawing frowns from the nurses. I lay a hand across the mess of staples down my breastbone. "And here you are," I tell Julia. "Keeping me alive."

She doesn't answer. It's rainy today, and the only response I get is the patter of raindrops on the hospital window. Even if you're one of those people who love the rain, I think you'll agree that the things it says are, at best, extremely boring. At worst, they're only raindrops, which are no substitute for your dead twin sister.

"Dead," I say, trying out the word that I haven't let myself think. I've shied away from it since the operations. Now that I've said it aloud, though, I have to ask her what I've been afraid to ask.

"Julia, were you dead when they took out your heart? Or did I steal it from you while you were still alive?"

She doesn't answer. Of course, she doesn't need to. Everyone—the doctor, my parents, the nurses—danced around this question. But I always knew the truth.

. . .

I am growing again.

It's been twelve days since the last surgery and there's enough oxygen in my blood, and my digestive system actually gets nutrition out of the food I eat, and and and and, you know, all the things the doctor optimistically suggested would happen, are happening. I've grown an eighth of an inch and gained three pounds. That eighth of an inch, by the way, makes me as tall as Julia was, though I'll keep growing, they assure me. I might even get as tall as my father.

"Fortune has been smiling on us all this time, Evan," my father is saying. Did I mention he was in here with me? He is. He's helping me get into my clothes. I'm strong enough to dress myself, but I'm letting him feel useful.

My mother's here too, though she's outside the room, to give me privacy while I get dressed, and probably also because she feels guilty about letting Reverend Tadd crap all over the last few minutes I had with my sister.

They're releasing me from the hospital today. Over the past several years, Julia and I have spent a combined total of over five hundred days here. During those five hundred days, I've imagined this final day many times. In my favorite version, we walk out the front doors, and shortly afterward, the hospital is leveled by an earthquake, and then ripped apart by a tornado, and then set on fire by roving bands of zombies. After that, if "fortune keeps smiling on us," packs of wild dogs will urinate all over the rubble as a warning never to rebuild.

"It's nice to see you smiling, Evan," my dad says, when my head emerges from the sweater he's pulling into place over my Frankenstein torso.

I decide to let him in on the daydream. "I was thinking that after we walk out of the hospital's front doors—"

"You know we're going to wheel you out in a wheelchair, right? No walking just yet. But soon!" he tells me cheerfully.

"Oh, right," I say. He is so literal.

Every doctor and nurse on this floor is lining the hallway as I'm wheeled toward the elevator by my parents. Even some of the more mobile patients are standing in their doorways to watch us, the medical pioneers. My father waves and smiles at all of them. My mother is soundlessly mouthing *thank you,* as though she were always one hundred percent behind this whole cannibalize-your-sister's-organs scenario.

I'm dying to hear what Julia would say about this sad parade to the elevator. Would she tell me to feign a stroke? Or clutch my heart?

"That's right, smile," my father says quietly. "Let them see how grateful you are."

Am I grateful? I haven't heard her voice for two weeks.

In the main lobby, and the world outside is visible through

the huge glass doors. My mother's gone off to pull the car around, and when we see her driving into the pickup area, my dad says, "Here we go," and pushes me out through the doors.

"Oh!" I cry out, because the strangest thing happens the moment I cross the threshold: the super-heart stops. There's a heartbeat, and then there is nothing, stretching out from one instant to the next and the next and the next. I cannot breathe, I cannot move. My super-heart has walked off the job without giving notice.

My father's smile falters, and then, in a panic, he shakes me. "Evan? Evan! Is it your heart?"

There's a *thunk!* in my chest as the heart starts up again. Then, *thump-thump, thump-thump,* it's going—as if nothing at all went wrong. If anything, I feel a new surge of vitality.

"Evan?" he says again, frantically.

I wave him away. "My heart . . . is fine," I tell him.

"Are you sure?" He looks back through the doors, ready to flag someone down.

I nod, give him an emphatic thumbs-up. My mother has pulled the car up right in front of us, so I push myself to my feet, and before he can even catch up to me, I've opened the back door of the minivan and climbed inside. In moments, we're all in the car and my mother is driving away.

I watch the hospital growing smaller as we get to the end of the street. When at last I can see only a sliver of the hospital's upper floor above neighboring buildings and it's about to disappear from sight entirely, I think, *Cue the earthquake!*

Julia should laugh at that, but she doesn't. I'm sitting in the back of the minivan alone, looking past my parents at the road ahead. Traffic and life are out there, ready to take me in.

It's not until we are stopped at a long traffic light that I hear it. Very quietly, a voice asks, *Do you want to kill all the other patients?* The voice sounds not so much upset as curious, and it's as soft as the murmur of an insect or a mouse.

I'm so startled, so unsure of what I've heard, that I can only bring myself to whisper an answer. "I don't mind if they're all evacuated first," I breathe. "But the building has to go."

There's silence in response and I sit there, holding my breath. I've imagined the voice; it's nothing but my hopeful ears playing tricks on me. The quiet stretches on as we travel through the city. My ears strain for anything besides the noise of the traffic, and they are disappointed.

But when we've gone a very long way and the hospital is nothing more than an anonymous mass far behind us, I hear this:

I agree. The hospital building has to go. The voice is growing as it speaks. It's not a mouse's voice anymore, it's a kitten's. *So . . . ,* it says, growing into a child's voice, *what were the results of the operation?*

"Just the usual," I whisper, for fear of scaring her away. "You know, new heart, liver, pancreas, blah, blah, blah."

No new brain? she asks. Her voice has become her real voice.

I shake my head.

So they screwed up the one thing you actually needed?

I nod. And smile.

Did you hear about that kid who was taken into the operating room, but then he had a change of heart?

"He didn't know if he was going to liver die," I whisper.

Aorta laugh at that.

"Like me—I'm in stitches."

I don't mean to cry, but tears spring to my eyes and a bunch of them are pushed out by a sudden burst of laughter that is incredibly painful to all of my recently sutured parts, which doesn't make it any less magical.

"You were so quiet," I whisper.

That was on account of being dead, she tells me. *By the way, I heard you call it "your heart." That was a little cold.*

"I didn't mean it," I say, squirting out another set of unstoppable tears. "I meant *our* heart."

I've said this last part loudly, and my father and mother both turn back to look at me.

"Our heart!" I say again to her.

"That's right, Evan. Our heart," my father says.

Is he serious? Julia asks. *Are they going to take credit for everything forever?*

"Probably," I answer.

Julia sighs. Eventually she says, *I guess it doesn't matter what they think. What do we care?*

There.

She has said it: *we.*

And I am happy.

I invite you to look beyond the current capabilities of tissue and bone repair. Those will soon become unremarkable. In a very short time, we will be able to create novel structural elements, forms that don't naturally occur in the human body—forms that we haven't yet imagined. I find myself a pioneer, daunted by the infinite size of the frontier.

—Dr. Emily Brownstone-Naik, at the British Medical Association symposium on genetic engineering, London, 2029

A few more years from now . . .

PART TWO

ST. LUDMILLA

1. GO GET 'EM TIGER

How can I tell you what happened in the right way? If I explain it wrong, you'll probably hate me. But if I can tell it right, maybe you'll understand.

I knew he saw me inside Go Get 'Em Tiger, which serves coffee so good I actually tingle all along the border of . . . parts of me. I knew Gabriel saw me inside, even though his eyes slid past me, as though he were just looking, just browsing, just checking out the bags of coffee beans and logo mugs for sale on the shelves along the walls and not seeing Milla sitting right there, staring at him over the top of my newspaper. Before you ask, I'll answer: Yes. I'm a sixteen-year-old girl who gets the newspaper, by special order, delivered twice a week, because I do the crossword puzzle, because it focuses me, and when I focus, I relax, and when I relax . . . well, things work right—like my lymph system and most of my hormones. The doctors all agreed that I needed to find calming techniques, and this is one. Plus, holding a newspaper is deliciously retro; it makes me feel like a girl from the year 2015, to whom nothing catastrophic has ever happened.

But back to Gabriel. He ignored me. It was so crowded, he had plausible deniability, and I had . . . I had the echoes of thirty people laughing at me the week before as I shoved my lunch into the trash can and ran out of the school courtyard. Not crying. If I could have cried, that would have been awesome.

But why had the laughing bothered me so much? There was a story in the newspaper I was holding about a teenager beaten into unconsciousness in the stands of his high school football stadium in Ohio. He'd had one of those partial spinal replacements where he could walk, but not a hundred percent properly. His assailants had been watching his gait when he got to his seat. They'd waited out the whole game, and then they'd attacked him at the end and spray-painted the word *WRONG* across his chest. They were drunk teenagers, but still, it was an example of the way some people were offended by anyone who'd been severely damaged and then put back together. "Fanatics Behaving Badly" was practically a regular newspaper column. In my case, you couldn't tell what had happened to me. I walked normally, I spoke normally. You wouldn't know, unless somebody told you. And I'd only had to put up with laughter.

Gabriel left Go Get 'Em Tiger and I watched through the window as he stood on the sidewalk outside, rooting around in the brown paper pastry bag he'd gotten with his cappuccino.

He's kind of tall, and I could keep an eye on him easily among the crowds of passersby. He had those headphones that hide behind your ear, and he idly tapped his right ear to turn them on—just a guy eating a scone and listening to music.

He didn't spare a glance back to see if I was watching him. And he also wasn't trying to get away quickly. Maybe he *hadn't* seen me after all. But that was worse in a way, wasn't it? That would make me just wallpaper or something, not even enough of a presence to ignore. Anger made my heart beat faster. It was necessary to go after him.

Gabriel took another bite of scone and I drained my mug, already feeling the tingle of the caffeine along the meshline and furious that he'd ruined my coffee time by being there. (Okay, I've said it. *Meshline.* There's a meshline zigzagging through my body. It's why I'm here now instead of in a grave or cremated or whatever. Fair warning, zealots: you can turn away right now if my existence offends you.)

When I was out on the sidewalk, I caught sight of him at the crosswalk. Well . . . no. I want to be honest. The truth is that I searched the crowds wildly until I spotted him again, and then I fought my way over.

What was I thinking at that moment? I've asked myself this question a hundred times. And the answer is this: I wanted to radiate my fury, my humiliation, at him. That's all. I'm pretty sure that was all I wanted.

The light there takes forever, and a bunch of people were waiting at the crosswalk. Next to me was a girl with a subdermal bracelet implant, and for a moment I was distracted by the patterns it was projecting up through her skin. Flickering lights danced around her wrist, looking too cheerful with her heavy black makeup and the safety pins through her eyebrows. She obviously didn't mind tinkering with herself, and no one nearby seemed to mind either. But some of them probably did.

It was hard to breathe. I wanted to cry.

The sound of Gabriel slurping his coffee brought me back. He was right at the curb and I was directly behind him. He turned his head, so I could see his face in profile. It was so odd. He was still really good looking, all blond, with dark brown eyes and thick lashes and that square jaw. But his looks had morphed into something I associated with pain, and staring at him wasn't the same as it had been a week ago.

I thought, *Can't he feel me standing here boring holes into his back with my eyes?*

Obviously he couldn't.

The traffic from the north was coming at us—four lanes at full speed, half of the vehicles without drivers, including a huge, automated City of LA bus that filled up an entire lane. The noise of the cars was punctuated by the constant whine of the air-drones that fly north and south above La Brea Avenue all day, along the route to the airport. I could have whispered Gabriel's name and he wouldn't have heard me. I didn't, though. I gave him no warning, other than my silent, hostile presence.

I stepped forward so I was right behind him, reached out my hands . . .

Shit. You're going to hate me.

I have to start earlier.

2. CHURCH BELL

I go to an Episcopal school that only has about three hundred students. Everyone knows everyone, even if everyone isn't friends with everyone, if that makes sense. I'm pretty smart, maybe a little bit nerdy, but honestly, a lot of kids at my school are smart and a little nerdy. I'm reasonably good looking, but again, there are plenty of good-looking girls at St. Anne's. So I'm average, socially, economically, academically. Is this even relevant to my story? I don't know. It's possible I'm stalling.

So.

A week earlier, a week before what happened outside Go Get 'Em Tiger, my mom dropped me off at school. I'd been leaning against the passenger door, using the minimum possible number of words to respond to her attempts at good-morning-sweetheart-how-are-things conversation. Then, just as we arrived, she asked the question she'd probably been working up the courage to ask all along: "How was your date last night?"

My reaction surprised even me. My dark mood snapped into something worse, something that could not be contained in sullen silence. Without any warning, I yelled, "Can't you let me live my own life for one second, Mom, for chrissakes? I'm not five! Can't I keep a secret if I want?"

I slammed the door behind me, leaving her sitting behind the wheel, shocked but resigned. ("Just let her be angry," my father was always saying.) I stomped off into the main building, knowing that fury directed at my mother was ridiculous and unfair. And seriously, how would her asking me about my date imply that I was five years old? There was no logic. Also this: I hadn't meant to yell, I honestly hadn't, but it's weird what I can and can't regulate. Sometimes the volume of my voice is in the "can't" category.

People at school were looking at me, but, you know, obviously, I thought, because I'd just slammed the car door like a five-year-old. It wasn't until my friend Lilly caught my arm, pulled me into that weird little alcove by the trophy case, and whispered, "Did you *really*, Milla? You hardly even *know* him," that I realized I had no secret to keep. Everyone already knew.

I walked to class feeling like an accident victim staring back at the rubberneckers who'd slowed down to watch me bleeding all over the roadside. That last part had literally happened to me, though when it did, I wasn't awake to watch. I don't even think I was alive.

I digress.

Kevin Lopez smirked as he leaned against the wall. Next to him, Kahil Neelam was making a weird hand gesture at me—he was using one hand to snap at the pointer finger of his other hand, like a fish biting a stick.

I was pushing through my homeroom door when I saw Matthew Nowiki—Matthew, who had been my friend since middle school—*doing the robot* and snickering as his gaze swept over me. He disappeared into his own homeroom, but not before snapping his fingers, pointing, and bestowing upon me a dramatic wink.

I had taken a seat at my desk when I realized what Kahil's

hand gesture had meant. The pointer finger had been a penis, and the other hand grabbing it was supposed to be a robot vagina crushing it, over and over.

Humiliation spread between my organs like sticky black tar. Heat bloomed across my face, informing me that I was turning red. The thing is that I don't really blush anymore, because blushing, in my current configuration, is almost impossible. That it was happening now meant *so much* adrenaline was flooding into my blood, it was literally bypassing the entire meshline to set my face aflame. I was blushing and sweating, which attracted everyone's attention.

Just kidding. They were already looking at me anyway.

"I don't even see *where* . . ." I heard behind me in a loud whisper.

"*How* did he even . . . ," someone else asked.

"He has no fear, obviously," a third person said, in a whisper so loud people on the other side of the city probably heard it.

This would have been an excellent time to cry. But I haven't managed to do that in a year. Instead, I sat through my morning classes as the humiliation slowly hardened into something else.

· · ·

At lunch, I went up to Gabriel in the courtyard where we all ate and I threw my soup in his face. It felt wonderful, it felt like vindication, even though the soup was lukewarm clam chowder and didn't make much of an impact. Still, every person in the courtyard was watching me as I screamed, "How could you be such an enormous dick?"

Looking back, I realize this wasn't the worst insult I could have chosen. I'm not sure anyone noticed my phrasing, though, because the words had come out so unbelievably loud that I thought the church bell on top of the chapel had somehow rung at the exact moment I opened my mouth.

It wasn't the church bell. It was my voice. Gabriel stared at me, spellbound.

Jesus H. Christ, this is still making it look as though I came after Gabriel like the unhinged robot girl people were whispering that I was. Correction: no one was actually whispering. At that moment, Kahil Neelam, a few yards away from Gabriel in the courtyard, was yelling, "Does not compute! Does not compute!" again and again and miming smoke coming out of his ears. He was pretending to be me. Get it?

I'm sorry for using Jesus's name to swear. I'm trying to be better about that. I'm pretty sure Jesus would be solidly on my side, so I don't want to piss him off too.

Shit.

I have to explain the night itself.

The drive-in movie and the making out.

I'm blushing even to think about it. (I'm not, though. There's a sensation in my cheeks, but no redness—I checked in the bathroom mirror. Sometimes things work and sometimes they don't. I'm glitchy.)

Anyway.

3. CAST OF THOUSANDS

It was the night before that day in school. We were at Cast of Thousands, the drive-in movie theater in Sherman Oaks with the huge screen that doubles onto your own car's windshield. You look through the movie image on the windshield to the much larger screen in the distance and somehow your eyes combine both into the most oh-my-God-that's-incredible 3D image. The sound was piped directly into the car's stereo system, so it was like our own private movie, and *I was in Gabriel Phillips's car.*

I haven't explained my history with Gabriel because there was no history, except for a long trail of lustful thoughts that were, as far as I knew, all on my side. Still, I should fill you in. He came to our school when he was fourteen. He was kind of gangly and his voice was still kind of high, but the blond hair and dark eyes really got to me. I became weirdly focused on his hands too, which were too big for the rest of him, the hands of a man, I thought, and right away I wanted them to touch me. It was the first time I had ever lain in bed and imagined a specific boy doing specific things to me. Jonas and I had been boyfriend and girlfriend before he moved away (before I'd even met Gabriel) and we'd actually *done* specific things, but I'd never fantasized about Jonas. I'd never had to; he was always with me. The at-a-distance crush on Gabriel was something new.

Other girls liked Gabriel too, in a more general way—he was good-looking and he went to our school, so, yeah, he was naturally on the list of Guys to Like. It wasn't until he was fifteen and had shoulders and biceps and a deep voice, though, that other girls really started to pay attention. They liked him when he was an obvious choice. I'd liked him so much longer. He flirted with girls at school, but the rumor was that he had "other girlfriends" outside our little St. Anne's group.

I thought about him for a year, and then in the hospital, when the lights were off for the night and I was alone with the sounds of machines that were keeping me alive, while the meshline and its various internal components were being created, I thought about him some more. That fantasy Gabriel diverged more and more from the one I had vaguely known at school, until, when I finally returned to St. Anne's, it took me a moment to recognize him. But only a moment. Then the real-world crush was back, as strong as ever.

So here we were, in his car together, the first time I'd even been alone with him. We were in the front seats, with a cardboard tray of tacos between us, and I'm not going to lie to you, the conversation was awkward. In my imagination, conversation hadn't been necessary, if you know what I mean. Fantasy Gabriel had done whatever I wanted. But here we were, stuck with words.

"Is the volume okay?" he asked, fiddling with the knob unnecessarily. It felt like our taco tray was the Pacific Ocean and he was all the way on the other side of it, by Japan, maybe.

"It's fine," I answered.

"Seems like we never really talked before this year. Why is that?" he asked. Before I could answer, he added, "When you came back to school, I realized that—that I wanted to get to know you."

"Yeah, me too," I said, trying not to stare at his sexy hands. "We've been at the same school for almost three years. Why don't we know each other better?"

Honestly, I was spouting almost random words to fill up the space between us; I wasn't looking for an answer to this question. I already had a theory as to why Gabriel had finally noticed me after basically looking through me for years. (Even back when we were fourteen, when he'd still been short and really skinny and I'd had *breasts*, he hadn't been interested.) But when they'd rebuilt my left eye, the orbit had changed shape a little bit; I'm talking about just the ordinary plastic surgery when the surgeon had to put it back together, not fancy stuff like they did with the rest of me. Then, because the left was different, they'd changed the right eye socket to match so it didn't look like the two halves of my face were arguing with each other. When this was done, something in the overall appearance of my eyes and eyebrows had been subtly altered for the better. I don't think it was on purpose, but when I healed, my eyes were a little wider and more perfectly shaped, and I was a little bit prettier.

So . . . Gabriel's new interest was easily explained: I'd been attractive when I got back to school, and he assumed I was just growing into my looks, because as far as anyone at St. Anne's knew, I had only broken my legs and my jaw in the accident. It felt like cheating, getting his interest this way, but why should I be ashamed of finding a silver lining?

We lapsed into silence as, up on the screen—or rather, hovering in the air outside our car, so crisp and hyper-detailed that they were almost more real than reality—a parade of super-heroes in the coming attractions threw 3D stuff at each other, stuff like cars and horses and battleships and, I am not kidding you, even an orca that appeared to spin around right in front of our windshield, spraying water from its toothy smile onto the glass. I laughed involuntarily and made a sort of choking snort—a sound my friend Lilly had kindly pointed out was like a barfing dog. (Laughs are weird sometimes; it's something to do with the partial larynx, or maybe the way the meshline travels through it. I forget exactly.)

"Are you okay?" Gabriel asked, because of, you know, the barfing dog sound.

"Um, yeah—taco went down the wrong way," I lied.

He held my drink out chivalrously, and as I took it, his hand brushed against mine, sending a shiver up my arm.

"Is, uh, is Milla short for something?"

I dread this question, because the answer usually takes too long—but this time it didn't. I said, "I'm named for St. Lud-milla, who lived in the Czech Republic like twelve hundred years ago—"

"Wait," he said, interrupting, "are you talking about St. Ludmilla of Bohemia?"

I was thrown. "Yes."

"I know her."

"What, like personally?" The sarcasm slipped out. It wasn't intentional. I didn't want anything to get in the way of the genuine interest that had appeared in his eyes.

"I know who she is," he said. He was shaking his head in mild disbelief. "St. Ludmilla."

I stared at him a moment. "You are seriously one of the only people who has ever known who she was."

"She brought Christianity to her people," he continued, very pleased with himself. And even better, our conversation no longer felt awkward.

"Well, she tried," I said. "Then her daughter-in-law had her strangled."

"You mostly don't get to be a saint by living happily ever after," he pointed out, with what struck me as a rather sophisticated worldview.

"That's true. Getting murdered helps a lot. Are you Catholic?" We recognized saints in the Episcopal church, but he seemed unusually knowledgeable.

"My mom's sort of Catholic, but the Episcopal school was less expensive and she says it's basically the same. My grandmother thinks I'm going to school with a bunch of dangerous nonbelievers, so she made me memorize the life stories of a hundred saints before I started at St. Anne's."

"And Ludmilla was one of them?" There were thousands and thousands of saints. This was a huge and unlikely coincidence. Had he secretly been researching me? Had he been as in love with me all this time as I'd been with him? When I'd imagined him touching me with those hands, had he been imagining the same thing?

"My grandma's from the Czech Republic, so it was, like,

mostly saints from around there that she wanted me to focus on," he explained. "I liked St. Ludmilla. She was cool."

Ah. I felt a stab of disappointment. *Only a coincidence.* Still, the ice had broken. Gabriel was gazing at me and I fancied there were hidden depths in him that I hadn't suspected.

"You have really pretty eyes," he told me.

I smiled, and mentally I thanked Dr. Watanabe for his facial reconstruction skills.

On the screen were more movie trailers, and on every side of the car were rows of other cars, all the occupants trying hard to block out the rest of the audience and pretend, like I was doing, that they were the only people in the world at that moment.

His comment about my eyes, and the way he kept glancing over at me, sent hormones racing into my bloodstream in poorly regulated batches. He was *into me*, I realized. More than I could have hoped. My body translated this knowledge into an unbearable level of excitement and an equal portion of terror. The adrenaline and make-out hormones were sliding past each other like aggressive rival gang members. All the parts beyond the meshline were beginning to give me that weird tingle/hotness/overload feeling that meant the fake parts didn't know what to do with everything I was throwing at them. I started to freak out. What had I been thinking, coming on this date with him? My body, my voice, any part of me might do something drastically wrong—

"Do you care about the movie, Milla?" Gabriel asked.

The trailers had ended and the theater was dark as the movie began. His voice had gone all whispery. He was leaning toward me so his breath brushed my cheek.

Holy shit, he was *really* into me. Something was going to happen *right now*, unless I stopped it. But Gabriel was giving me his full attention, those dark eyes, his jawline, the curve of his shoulder muscles beneath his shirt, his *hands* . . .

"No, I don't care about the movie," I found myself whispering back.

He turned down the volume, inched closer, and said, "Hey."

Stop him! I yelled at myself. *Get out of here!*

I did neither of these things. Instead I sat rooted to the seat as he gently put his lips on mine.

Gabriel Phillips *was kissing me.* Alone in my hospital room, alone in my bedroom at home, I had seen this moment a thousand different ways. But now it was real: lips, pressure, warmth.

When the kiss was over, my mind replayed it obsessively on an auto-loop. I might have been staring at him in mute shock for a full minute.

He didn't notice. "Do you want to get in the backseat?" he asked, with that combination of excitement and nervousness that I used to see on Jonas's face when we were first boyfriend and girlfriend. "We could, I don't know . . ."

"Okay." My body was telling me to *Run!* but it was also, very much, telling me to stay.

It's not like I've had so many boyfriends (I've had two, if

you count the one from middle school), but I knew what was what with the kissing and whatnot, even if I hadn't done any of it in ages. (Jonas had moved away, and then I'd been in the hospital for almost a solid year. Believe me, no one wanted to kiss you there.) I *liked* making out, and the sexy hormones were winning out over the adrenaline, even as the parts behind the meshline continued to send me uncomfortable warning signals.

In the semidarkness, I climbed between the front seats into the wide backseat, and Gabriel slithered after me, laughing as he pulled his legs through. One of his feet hit the radio and it switched from the movie soundtrack to a talk radio station.

". . . but it's about our definition of what it means to be *human.* What did the Lord in*tend* for us? What was His vision for humanity in this world?" a smooth, slightly Southern male voice was saying, filling the car. Half preacher, half rabble-rouser. "What did He with*hold* from us? He *made* us in His image. We know that. This, this *or*dinary human body is in His image, then." He sounded young, but his voice made me think of liquor and cigars. He emphasized words I would never have expected him to emphasize, as though he paid more attention to the cadence of his sentences than their content. "We can't go *tin*kering around and making fake *hearts* and *liv*ers and growing new stuff Jesus *never* wanted to see—"

"Ah, sorry." Gabriel was obviously embarrassed. He hurriedly reached forward and switched the radio back to the movie track.

When he got to the backseat, he leaned over to kiss me again. It was a shock to see myself move out of reach, but that's exactly what I did. A sense of dread was spreading through me, the real parts and the fake, crossing the meshline like no other emotion usually could. I had stumbled upon something here.

"Was that . . . was that what's-his-name?" I asked, nodding at the radio.

"Reverend Tad Tadd? The one with two first names?" he said with a laugh. "Yeah. My grandma listens to him all the time."

It took a few moments to unpack the various implications of this answer. I grasped at the easiest piece to question and said, "Wait, this is your grandma's car?"

It was a big, old car, which I'd thought was kind of cool when I thought it belonged to Gabriel. I mean, it's retro for a teenager to even have a car, and having a really old car is doubly retro. But now that I looked around the backseat a little more closely, in the movie's low light, I saw old-lady signs that he'd failed to hide before our date: a crocheted blanket spread across the space behind the head rests, a pair of very thick reading glasses in the little rear door pocket, next to a lace handkerchief. These unsexy articles, that voice on the radio—

"Yeah. I mean, I use the car all the time," he said, following my gaze and seeing traces of his grandmother. "It's, like, a family car. My grandma sometimes still drives it—and listens to Tad Tadd, like half the people in LA." He shook his head as if to say, *Grandmas—what are you going to do?* Then, seeing something in my face that told him everything was not okay, he added, "She barely drives it anymore, if that's what's bothering you. It's basically mine."

My eyes were fixed on the front seat, where I envisioned an old woman turning to stare at me in disgust as she listned to Tad Tadd. She wagged a disapproving finger in my direction.

"What's the matter?" Gabriel asked.

"That guy spews hate. Why would your grandmother listen to him? How can he use faith to attack people who have medical problems? And why can't he have a normal last name?" The words were out of my mouth before I could stop myself. The meshline was tingling with adrenaline, an unpleasant version of how it felt when I drank coffee. It was like needing to pee, but feeling that sensation everywhere.

"Have you ever listened to talk radio?" he asked me, laughing a little. "It's full of crazy people. It's *mostly* crazy people. Hey, come on." He reached over and tucked a lock of my hair behind my ear. Despite the dread and adrenaline, I was touched by this. Like he and I were a team. Or we could be.

"Does your grandma agree with him?" Again, the words were out before I could stop them. Why was I arguing about his grandmother's political/religious/racist views on our first date? I shouldn't even *be* here in a backseat where . . . But since I was here, I definitely shouldn't be bringing up this subject. I hadn't brought it up, I reminded myself. The radio had been set to that station. Even if Gabriel's grandmother was the one who'd set it, he must have listened in at least once or twice.

"I don't know," he said. The romantic energy was visibly leaking out of him. "I guess she agrees with him. She's really old and super religious. They were going to grow her a new heart last year, you know, where it's mostly real heart, but some of the parts are, like, robotic or something?"

I did know. I knew because a heart matching that description was currently beating way too fast in my half-real chest. And I cared about that heart very much.

"She refused, because she thinks God wouldn't approve," he went on. And then he shrugged. "She's old. You can't argue with her." He wasn't saying whether or not he agreed with his grandmother, but his tone hinted that he didn't.

It was dark again, because up on the screen, something was happening in a shadowy hallway. Gabriel was close to me, the outline of his face traced by movie light. When he saw my expression soften, he touched my lips with his own. A light kiss, an exploratory kiss, but ready for something much better.

"What do *you* think?" I asked, pulling away. I wanted to kiss him more, but I could not keep my mouth shut on this topic. It was like the mesh was my baby sister and even though I fully intended to keep it hidden, I felt honor-bound to root out any signs of prejudice. Because prejudice was everywhere. You didn't know that until you crossed an invisible line and you yourself were in its crosshairs.

"Why do you care so much about Reverend Tadd?" he asked. "He's just a nutjob on the radio."

This was the precise question I didn't want to answer. I felt myself retreat in fear and I stammered, "I—I just wanted to hear what you think. I'm trying to get to know you." I managed to make the last part sound flirty.

Gabriel shook his head, as if he would humor me because obviously he was so into me. "I don't know." He shrugged again. "I mean, we're religious, all of us at St. Anne's, aren't we? And, like, should we be doing *everything* that God can do? What about these people who are going to other countries to freeze themselves and avoid a natural death? Even kids? They might be frozen forever. Is that what their lives are supposed to be? Does that seem like something we should be doing? I don't know."

"So you agree with Reverend Tad Tadd?" I whispered the question, knowing that if I tried to say it in a normal voice, it would come out too loud.

Here's the thing. I'd heard snippets of Reverend Tadd's broadcasts from time to time and seen him spouting sound bites on TV, but I'd never really thought about him too much. Sure, he was a ridiculous bigot, yet the important word had always been *ridiculous*. Tonight, though . . . tonight his hatred had unexpectedly intruded upon our intimate space, and it was like his voice and his sentiment had somehow become tied up with the pain and with the monstrous weight of death that had pressed down on me for so many months. And now, even if I was scared of where the conversation would lead, I couldn't let him go.

Gabriel said, "I think Reverend Tadd is crazy. He sounds like . . . like . . ." He groped for the words.

"Like he tells everyone else how to be holy and then he goes back to a house full of alcohol and hookers?" I suggested. The words had been enraged inside my head, but they came out sounding more like a joke. Thankfully.

Gabriel gave me a whispery laugh. "Something like that. Maybe not *that* bad. It's just . . . My grandma's from a different generation—"

"But what's the difference between a half-real heart and taking antibiotics, or getting a doctor to set a broken bone?" I asked, still whispering. I was starting to feel ill. And I needed to hear him say the right thing.

"Yeah, that's what's crazy," he agreed. "How are they drawing the line? It's so . . ."

"Arbitrary?" This word came out too loud, but it was only one word, so I don't think he noticed. I bit my lower lip to try to rein in my voice.

"Right, arbitrary. But my grandma is *so sure* certain things are too close to what God is supposed to take care of. Or not take care of. Maybe certain people aren't meant to live—she thinks," he quickly added.

I closed my eyes, took a deep breath, tried to untie the knot in my stomach. I was not lying unconscious, crushed inside a car. I was not watching helplessly as doctors called for more blood. I was here at the drive-in and no one was singling me out. To Gabriel, this was only a theoretical debate and I was one of those religious girls who loved to argue. Maybe he was walking a fine gray borderline between skeptical friend and thoughtless objector, but what he was saying wasn't terrible. No matter what his grandmother thought, Gabriel was trying to be tolerant, which was all I could hope to ask in a world where the Reverend Tadd and others were turning medicine into philosophy.

"I didn't know you were so into politics," he said, teasing me a little.

"I guess this isn't the best topic for a first date." I managed a little laugh.

The adrenaline pumping through me was calming down. And I was calming down. His arm was around my waist, which was keeping the make-out hormones flowing, in spite of everything. My attention came back to his hands, his lips, the backseat. I was here because I wanted to be here.

So we kissed then. I mean we *really* kissed. We started out sitting up, but soon I was lying wedged in the corner of the seat and he was almost on top of me, and it felt so good. Like, *unbelievably* good. The only damage I'd received to my face had been a small jaw fracture and that thing with my eyes, so my mouth and tongue and teeth and everything were totally normal. They wouldn't feel weird to him, which was important because he was totally *in* my mouth with his tongue. Which I liked.

But then I didn't.

As the adrenaline settled, the make-out hormones (some of which were naturally mine, and some of which were, you know, added extras from the meshline) were also cutting out, my body sputtering like an old-school gas engine with dirt in the fuel line. Suddenly it was like watching myself kiss him, like this was another movie, playing inside the car, and I could think that it looked sexy, but I couldn't feel that it *was* sexy. It was more like our mouths were raw chicken breasts we were mashing repeatedly against each other.

I was thinking about this while still kissing him, trying to recapture why I'd wanted to put my tongue into his mouth when that now seemed, essentially, disgusting. Because I was distracted, I didn't notice that he had worked my shirt out of my pants and his hand was sliding beneath it.

"Wait—" I said, struggling to sit up.

"You're so pretty. I want to touch you. . . ."

"Wait—"

But it was too late. His hand had expertly worked its way up my torso and his fingers were under my bra. Yes—that quickly. The tips of his fingers—some of the most sensitive and discerning parts of the human body—had touched the exterior skin-layer of the meshline. His fingers stopped and I watched confusion vying with arousal in his face. His hand slid out of my bra, down my torso, this time sensing more artificial skin, which he had not noticed the first time he'd touched it.

"What's . . . ," he began. That question had already led him up a blind alley he didn't want to be in. He sat back, confused. "Are you—are you *all right*?"

4. CAST OF TWO

I pulled my shirt down, wiggled upright. He had felt that some things were wrong, but he didn't have to know the extent of it.

"It's just, in the accident," I mumbled. "Some things had to be fixed." This sounded weak, possibly because it was an absurd understatement.

"Lilly told us it was just your legs. You broke your legs." The movie played out across his cheek as his shadowed eyes studied me.

"That was . . . mainly what happened," I hedged. It was not right that anyone should pass judgment on me if I told the truth. And yet I did not, I did *not*, want to tell the truth.

"Is it *your* skin under there?" He sounded almost mesmerized. A lump of fear had formed just above my stomach. He reached for my shirt, but I held it down.

"Mostly."

That was a lie. The artificial skin he'd felt, covering more than half my torso, was based on my skin, maybe you could say it was *partly* my skin, but it was combined with the mesh that made a bridge from the parts that were all me to the parts that weren't me anymore. It felt like skin—until you touched my real skin right next to it, which was what had happened when his fingers traced the meshline across my right breast. Then the difference became glaring.

He was already pulling my shirt back up and I didn't stop him this time; panic held me motionless. He would *see*, he would *know*! What should I have done? Slapped him? Escaped from the car and run from the drive-in?

The movie had gotten brighter and in its light, the variance in texture and color of my body was discernible. The meshline traveled up from beneath my bellybutton, curved across my stomach and then cut across my right breast. On one side of the mesh was me, real flesh, one hundred percent Milla. On the other side, things were harder to categorize.

"How far does it go?" he asked, looking at where the line disappeared beneath my waistband, down toward my "lady parts," as my mother referred to them.

I was transfixed by . . . by his searching look, maybe? By the shock and concern in his face?

"You're looking at most of it," I whispered.

Another lie. Not visible from my current position was the line that ran from my right breast across the ribs beneath my right arm and then traced a path down the right side of my back. Nor could he see how the damage extended inward to my heart and one of my lungs, to my other organs, and yes, to my lady parts too.

"Your heart?" he asked, as if I had spoken those thoughts aloud.

I could have said that I was burned and the fake skin was just to cover burns. Why did I owe him any explanations? But . . . the heart in my chest had saved my life. It deserved better than a shamefaced excuse.

"It's like what you said for your grandmother," I whispered.

"It's a real heart, mostly. From my own cells, but there are some other parts that make up for the parts they can't grow yet. Tiny little robotic parts made out of squishy stuff. It's a combination."

He sat back, and I yanked my shirt down. A series of emotions marched across his features. Not all of them made sense.

"This is why you hate Reverend Tadd," he said.

"Yes," I agreed.

"Why haven't you told anyone? Lilly told the whole school it was just your legs. It's—it's—"

"More than my legs," I said. What was I seeing on his face? Fear?

"How much of you is real?" he asked. He was starting to sound agitated. He wiped the back of his hand across his mouth, as if unconsciously scraping off the taint of my counterfeit lips.

"My mouth is real," I whispered. He was repulsed.

But he wasn't.

Tenderly, he asked, "You've been living with all of this, with no one to talk to about it?"

I was undone by the sympathy of this question, and in the face of his concern, the tension in my chest shifted. It was as though the meshline itself began to relax.

"People don't need to know all the bad things, Gabriel," I said quietly. "And how do you even tell people?" I could feel things bubbling up inside me, things I had promised myself I would never say. "How do I even explain that when the car crashed, my mom was thrown free and only broke her arm and her hip? But I was pinned in my seat when the truck came spinning into us? That, like, the whole dashboard went through the right side of my body, crushing it to pulp?" I had begun in a whisper but knew I was about to lose vocal control. Now that I was letting the truth out, it would be no gentle trickle. Wedged in the corner of the backseat, I was going to unload it on Gabriel like a drunk sorority girl spouting the remains of her half-digested tuna sandwich all over the floor. "That the dashboard was what was holding me together all that time while the paramedics and firemen were cutting me out of the car? That I should totally have been dead, first when the truck hit, then before the ambulance got there, then in the ambulance? I should have been dead like ten times, and I probably even was dead for a little while, but we were so close to UCLA, and they began culturing my cells as soon as I arrived, and the doctors are, like, the best in the world at this stuff? So because of a chain of lucky breaks, I'm here, but half of my torso is fake, and my heart is fake, and one of my lungs is fake, and I will never have children because they don't know how to fix that stuff yet." The sorority girl was emptying out the full contents of her stomach right into her party date's lap. And that relief you feel when you throw up? I was beginning to feel that. "And that I can want to make out with you and I can think you're really good-looking, but I can't count on how my body will respond to anything? Kissing, laughing, hiccupping—hiccupping is the worst. I sound like a howler monkey when it happens. That I thought about you while I was in the hospital, and I wondered if anyone would ever want to touch me again? How do I tell people that I'm so grateful to be alive, when I know they'll never be able to look at me with anything but pity, or, or, or judgment from here on out?"

Gabriel was sitting on the seat next to me, the red and blue color from the screen dancing across his face and through his blond hair. I hadn't been yelling, quite, but almost.

"I'm sorry, Milla," he whispered.

"Me too."

We sat in the backseat, looking at each other. I had emptied myself and I felt hollow, but it was a clean sort of hollow, the kind of hollow that is ready to be filled with something new.

Very gently, Gabriel pulled me toward him and wrapped his arms around me. I leaned into him, and I almost cried—I even had the feeling of tears forming behind my eyes.

"You don't have to tell anyone, you know," he murmured into my ear.

I nodded into his chest. "Some people, they get weird about this stuff. My dad says when he was a kid, everyone wanted medical advances—any kind, they were all good. But now people get . . . funny."

"Not very funny," he said ruefully.

"No, not very funny," I agreed.

When my breathing had evened out, I became more aware of our bodies touching, of his arms around me. The meshline had no idea what to do with the changing emotional tides of the last few minutes, but somehow the make-out hormones were taking over again.

"It feels really good to tell you," I told him.

He drew back so he could look down at me. "Did you really think about me when you were hurt?" he asked.

"A little bit." It was a lie, but it was the best I could manage.

"Can I kiss you again?" he asked softly.

I nodded.

He gently touched his lips to mine. And it was different this time. I had been holding myself back before, and now I wasn't.

We were kissing and then, by inches, we were doing more than kissing. My bra was unhooked and hitched up by my neck. His lips were everywhere. You may be familiar with how it goes. At some point I realized that my pants were off and his hand was moving gently but insistently. "Can you feel that?" he asked, his lips by my ear. "Does it feel good?"

"Yes," I whispered urgently. I was actually *feeling*. Everywhere.

"Can you feel it all the way? I'm not touching . . ." I was grateful he didn't finish the sentence: *I'm not touching parts that aren't real, am I?*

"Yeah, I feel it all the way."

That part of me was me. It was above that, the uterus, the ovaries—those had been crushed into oblivion and replaced with, well, nothing.

I was touching him and I knew what I was doing because of, you know, Jonas; I'd had practice. "Wait," he breathed, pushing my hand away from him. "Let me . . . Can we . . . ?"

I looked at him carefully from only inches away. He was

asking to have sex with me, and I was so blissfully wrapped up in hormones that I almost said yes immediately.

"No, I can't," I said, pulling back a little.

"Why not?" he asked gently. He was kissing my neck and Jesus Christ (I'm sorry to use your name again in this vulgar context) it felt heavenly (again, sorry).

"Because I've never done it before," I managed to say, while at the same time my body was screaming *Let him do it!*

"Never?" he whispered.

"My boyfriend and I got close one time, but we didn't. And then he moved away. And I . . . I was in the hospital for a year. And I . . . haven't been ready."

"It's okay."

We were kissing again, and he was lying on top of me. The make-out hormones spiked and the meshline was letting just enough of everything through. . . .

"Oh God, Milla, don't you want—"

"Yes," I breathed, "I do."

My pants came off. My underwear came off. Was I really going to do this?

"Wait," I whispered. "Do you have a condom?"

"A condom? But if you can't . . . ?"

"It's not that. . . ."

I couldn't get pregnant, but I could still get diseases (how many girls had he been with?), and the effect of a disease would be so much worse in my current state—

"Right, of course," he whispered, still kissing me.

He sat up, scrabbled with his backpack on the floor of the car and then with the crinkly condom packet, before coming back to me.

And then we were doing that thing that was supposed to be such a momentous experience in my life as a teenager. I expected pain, but I felt only good sensations.

When it was over, we lay in the backseat together, with my head on his chest and his arm around me.

"That was amazing," he said, catching his breath.

I intertwined my fingers in his hand, marveling that I was touching one of those hands I'd been lusting over for so long. "That's not how I expected it to happen," I murmured. The tides were changing inside me again. I felt as though I were floating in an in-between state.

"What?" he asked.

"You know, my first time," I said. "Kind of a big deal. You imagine how it might be and then—"

"It's not really the same, though, is it?" he whispered. "I mean, it's not really like virginity exactly."

"What?" It took a few moments for me to be sure I'd heard him correctly. When he said nothing else, I sat up enough to look down at him. In the semidarkness, he was nearly hidden in shadows. "What?" I said again.

"Well . . . you were all cut up inside there," he said, lifting himself up onto an elbow.

A flower of misgiving bloomed inside my chest. "What are you saying—"

"The doctors' hands were everywhere," he whispered earnestly, "and the robots. They use robots, right, to fix stuff? All over you and in you and through you."

The flower grew, twisted itself into outrage. Was I understanding him correctly? "What does that—?"

"I'm just saying, I wouldn't have tried if you were really . . . but it's not like you were still actually a—"

"Do you think I fucking lost my virginity to a surgical robot? I was in a car accident, not an orgy!" I had totally lost control of my voice and was, like, SHRIEKING. His sympathy, my admission of what had happened—had it only added up to an easy way for him to sleep with me? "I've never had sex with anyone before. It's kind of a big deal to me!"

I pushed him away and I yanked up my pants, and then I started to open the back door, even with my bra poking out the neck of my shirt.

"Wait, Milla! Stop, please." He'd gotten up and was half kneeling on the floor, trying to pull the door shut. "I'm sorry, okay? I'm sorry!"

"How could you say that?" I screamed. "How could you *think* that?"

"Please, Milla!" he whispered frantically, knowing my voice would carry to other cars now that the door was open. "I didn't mean it. I said the wrong thing!"

The light had come on when I opened the door, and in the brightness, he looked desperate and repentant. I had just remembered that we were parked in the middle of the crowded drive-in, with cars all around us. My voice and the dome light were beacons. People in other cars were turning toward us.

When I tried to picture myself actually getting out of the car and walking away, my anger deflated. I pulled the door closed, extinguishing the light, and then I ducked down until the heads in other cars turned back toward the screen.

Gabriel had his hands out as though I were a wild animal he was trying to soothe. "Of course it's a big deal, Milla," he said. "I don't know why I said that. I don't . . . I'm sorry."

I leaned against the closed door, waiting for my heartbeat and breath to slow.

"You said it because it's what you think, isn't it?" I asked him, when I'd gotten my voice under control. The damned movie was still playing out beyond the windshield and across our bodies. "You think I'm something different, something less." I nodded toward the radio, which had broadcast Reverend Tadd's voice. "You think I'm like . . ."

He was shaking his head. "I didn't want to think that I'd pressured you, that I'd made you do something you didn't want to do, so I said—"

"You didn't pressure me." I had chosen, willingly. Didn't he understand?

"I'm sorry."

Every emotion I'd felt throughout the evening seemed to have been mixed in a blender and poured down my throat. They added up to exhaustion. I leaned against the backseat and looked out through the windshield at the enormous images hovering in the air.

"I'm sorry," he said again.

"Okay, okay," I said. "Can we just stop talking and watch the movie?"

"Yeah, let's do that."

He eased closer to me on the seat. I stared at the movie images without seeing them. When a few minutes had passed without me yelling, he tentatively took my hand, and when I didn't resist, he continued to hold it.

We sat together like that until the end of the movie.

He took me home after that.

At the bottom of my parents' driveway, he pulled over, turned off the car. We kissed again. This time, there was no adrenaline, no make-out hormones. I was wrung out, the real parts and the parts beyond the meshline equally numb. He leaned his forehead against mine.

"Milla?" he whispered.

"Yeah?"

I could feel his hesitation. "You still don't want to tell anyone about . . ." He gestured toward my body in a way that let me know he was referring to the damaged parts. "Right?"

"Honestly it's kind of a relief that it's not a complete secret anymore. I don't know. Eventually I might. Or not. I guess I'll have to see how I feel."

I pulled away from him, and then I paused, my hand on the door handle. Something about his demeanor was odd. He looked almost scared. I wondered if he was worried that I would tell people he'd forced me.

I touched his hand. "I'd never make you look bad, Gabriel," I whispered.

"Right." He nodded, first at me, then toward the view beyond the windshield, as if to a large, invisible audience out there. "Sure," he said.

We glanced at each other, contemplating another kiss. Without a word, we both decided against it. Those moments of intimacy had passed and they already felt a long way away.

5. MIRACLE

So, yeah. That happened.

And then the next day at school, everyone knew. Gabriel must have started telling people immediately, maybe even on his way home that night. He had told them everything—but mostly about the strange new contents of my body.

Kevin Lopez smirking in the hall, Matthew Nowiki doing the robot with extra hip thrusts thrown in, Kahil Neelam making that hand gesture that told the story of my robotic vagina eating Gabriel's penis, over and over, because obviously that's what robot vaginas would be designed to do.

It wasn't like I could yell back, *I don't have a robotic vagina, okay? That part of me is still real!* I don't think that would have helped.

After I threw my soup in Gabriel's face and yelled at him so loudly my voice echoed off the Hollywood Hills, I ran out of the courtyard. Behind me I heard hoots and high fives, and girls giggling, and Kahil going on and on with the robot jokes. My meltdown was the most exciting thing to happen at St. Anne's in at least a year. I like to think someone back there stood up for me. Maybe Lilly came to my defense, though maybe not. She was upset that I hadn't told her about the sex. Or the injuries. She felt left out, and it was true, I'd left her out.

The headmaster, Mr. Kinross, found me by the back fire stairs, sitting in the shadows and not crying. My eyes stung, the meshline was pulsing with my shame, and that was all the relief I could hope for. He took me to his office, where he offered me a large bowl of wrapped toffees. I immediately stuffed two into my mouth and was surprised at how much they helped.

Mr. Kinross was fairly young, in his midforties maybe, Irish with black hair and blue eyes. There was even a hint of an accent still in his voice, kind of retro, because he'd come to the US when he was a teenager. It was as though the board of St. Anne's had found him through a casting call. He was nice.

He let me eat my toffees in silence for a few moments, and then he said, "Ludmilla"—he was one of only a few people who insisted on calling me by my full name—"your parents told me about the extent of your injuries, when you came back to us. It's not my place to discuss them with anyone else, of course, but I do have some idea what you went through. You sitting here is a miracle. I want you to know that we treasure miracles at St. Anne's."

Through the side windows bracketing his door, I watched

students passing by in the hall. A few glanced in at me but turned away quickly when they realized there was a chance I might make eye contact.

"It's like they think I'm a heretic," I said.

It was such an old-fashioned word, but it felt right. Mr. Kinross thoughtfully unwrapped a toffee and put it in his mouth.

"There's nothing so medieval as high school," he muttered.

"I didn't want to tell people because I thought they would feel sorry for me. Or secretly think I was unnatural. I didn't think they would, you know, decide that I was a disgusting joke."

My voice broke and I looked down, trying to blink away the burning in my eyes.

"Something ugly is happening to our world," he said. "If God gave us minds, should we not embrace the fruits of those minds? Surely it is a mercy, and a beautiful calling, to minister to the injured and the ill?" This didn't sound as formal as it might have, because it was said while sucking at a piece of toffee that kept clicking against his teeth. His kind eyes studied me—sad, seething, half-artificial me. "And yet, I see families with an entirely different view. They have taken it upon themselves to decide what God allows—which is surely exactly what they accuse the doctors of doing."

It was a relief to hear an adult—a *religious* adult—say what I was thinking. Even so, I kind of wanted to get out of there, because he'd probably heard about the sex too, and I guessed

I would be in for a lecture about the evils of premarital intercourse if I lingered in his office too long. The prickle of a nonblush was coming over me.

But all Mr. Kinross said was "I will have a chat with the boys." He must have seen the worry in my face, because he quickly added, "I won't let them make it worse for you, Ludmilla. There are some advantages to running a religious school. I can call on the fear of God when it's warranted." He smiled. "Think of your namesake, St. Ludmilla," he said gently, when he saw my lingering doubt. "She faced opposition at every hand and yet she held to her faith."

I muttered, "Did she? Or is she a saint only because she died?" And then I asked him the question that had been haunting me all year. "And was . . . was *I* supposed to die?"

"Ah. Do you think you were meant to be St. Ludmilla of Los Angeles?"

"I could never be a saint," I said, "but I do wonder if I'm supposed to be here at all."

"Perish that thought, Ludmilla," he told me with a gentle certainty that was as soothing to my ears as the toffee was to my stomach. "You are being tried. Do you know that it's often much harder to stay alive? You've chosen the thornier path. I admire you for that."

Even if this sounded like a speech he'd lifted from a 1950s film, it made me feel better.

6. ST. LUDMILLA

Gabriel told Matthew Nowiki that I had been so desperate to prove I was still normal, I'd begged him to have sex with me. Actually *begged*. Like a prostitute offering her "wares" to a policeman to avoid arrest. Gabriel had been very clear with Matthew that my parts "didn't feel right"—the implication being that something *down there* had been irregular, that Gabriel and his manhood had had a lucky escape.

According to Matthew (as relayed to me by Lilly), Gabriel had wanted to take me home early in the evening, but I hadn't let him because I'd wanted to lose my "human virginity." As if I'd been having sex with aliens and werewolves and centipedes for years and was trying to prove that I was still a real girl. "My human virginity." This phrase captivated everyone. In an objective corner of my mind, it even captivated me, and I recognized how well it summed up my differences, my desperation, and how I'd abused Gabriel. That the latter two were entirely fabricated didn't matter. And I was weird. Let's face it. Everyone sensed that something had been off since I'd returned to school.

I didn't go outside for lunch that week, but when I peeked through a second-floor window at the courtyard below, I could see and hear Lilly and my other friends gossiping with everyone else over the details and whether I was still, technically, a normal human. Maybe I would have done exactly the same thing if it had been someone else they were talking about. Even nice people didn't want to commit themselves until a general consensus could be reached: Was I a perversion of nature to be shunned, or was I in the category of the meek and thus worthy of protection and sympathy? What if I was both?

. . .

So I was standing right behind Gabriel on the street corner outside Go Get 'Em Tiger. There was a tingle all up and down the meshline from the coffee, but this sensation was at war with the hot jitters rushing through me. Gabriel was slurping his coffee, and when he turned his head slightly, I saw his square jaw, his dark eyes beneath his blond hair. So handsome, but painful to look at now. *Can't he feel me standing here boring holes into his back with my eyes?*

Four lanes of traffic came at us. In the closest lane was the huge City of LA driverless bus, so wide it almost didn't fit in one lane.

I was overcome with thirst, which wasn't real thirst but a side effect of internal imbalance. *She wanted it so bad, and I gave it to her so hard, but it was weird down there. . . .*

I was so close to Gabriel that none of the other pedestrians could see my hands. They were crowded around, but all looking at the crosswalk light, or at the traffic.

How much of you is real?

I flexed my fingers. There was an irresistible gravity between my palms and his body.

It's not really like virginity exactly.

So help me God, Jesus, and all the saints, I pushed him.

The bus was bearing down on us, the last vehicle through the light, and I shoved him, both hands at his hips, every bit of strength I could muster in the move.

Gabriel had been taking a drink of coffee, off balance on one foot. He flew off the curb. I reached after him, as though trying to grab him back, as though I'd seen him tripping before he even realized it himself and was attempting to save him. Was I really trying to save him? I don't know. What I do know is that Gabriel flailed wildly, the coffee going everywhere, and I accidentally grabbed one of his arms.

That kept him from dying, because I yanked him back toward me on reflex. The top half of Gabriel's body was tugged to safety. The bottom half . . . well, the bus hit him full on. I mean, the bus was programmed to protect human life, including pedestrians, but what the hell was it supposed to do? If it came to an immediate stop, it would endanger everyone inside. So the bus passengers got a moderate jolt, and Gabriel got . . . all the rest. It was the most disgusting thing I'd ever seen, if you don't count those few moments I was still conscious, when I saw the windshield break in front of me and the dashboard dislodge and go through my rib cage, taking out the vital organs in its path. I only saw that for a moment or two; I saw the whole Gabriel incident in full consciousness, from beginning to end.

The bus struck him and the sound was of something both firm and wet colliding with something very hard. Maybe like what you'd hear if you stomped on stalks of celery with heavy boots, or if you dropped a half-melted bag of ice from a second-story window onto concrete. He was shattered from the ribs down. His hand, grasped tenuously in my own, was pulled free, and he was thrown a dozen feet as the bus screeched to an immediate halt.

"Oh my God!" I yelled.

Everyone was yelling some version of that. We rushed in a mass to his limp form lying half in the traffic lane, half on the sidewalk. His eyes were open, and as we all crowded around him, they fluttered closed. Not before he'd seen me, though. There was a moment: his eyes, my eyes, recognition.

More people were looking at me as someone called 911. A siren was already audible only blocks away.

"What happened?" one woman asked me. "You tried to pull him back, I saw you."

"Did he fall, or did he jump?" someone else demanded urgently.

"I—I don't know," I stammered. "I just reached out . . ."

"You saved him."

And just like that, I was not the villain of this moment but the hero.

7. GO GET 'EM AGAIN, TIGER

I think my parents suspected.

It was too much of a coincidence, me happening to be on hand at the time Gabriel was hit by a bus. Yet they asked me very little about that afternoon. I gave them the official version of events and we didn't discuss it further. But as the days passed, I noticed they never mentioned to any of the other parents from school that I had been there, that I had tried to save Gabriel, just as I never mentioned it. The topic was a gray cloud that hovered in the air between us. Days turned into weeks and the cloud dissipated into a thin fog, but it never went away. They had decided, I suppose, that they would rather not know.

Now here I was, months later, with my mother driving me to school in silence. Sometimes we chatted in the car, in the way we had always done, but other times, like this one, there was nothing to say. I leaned against the door, my eyes half closed, and concentrated on my breath, in and out. Since the accident with Gabriel, I had learned to achieve a better state of equilibrium with the meshline. If I kept my body steady, my motions smooth, things felt almost normal—my lymph system, my lungs, my hormones. The doctors had told me I would get there eventually, and I had.

My mother smiled when we pulled up in front of the school. I was her broken girl, put back together now. "Have a good day, Milla."

The moment I got out of the car, I sensed that something was different. For no clear reason, my heart rate increased. I knew he was there even before I turned around.

Gabriel. He was walking through the front door of the school, surrounded by friends who were welcoming him back. His time in the hospital hadn't been kept a secret. Rumors had floated back to school weekly: the rift in his family when his father and mother decided to allow the doctors to use every tool at their disposal to save him; his grandmother's disavowal of his parents and him; the fact that the bus had absolutely demolished his lower intestine, his liver, his pelvis. There was rampant speculation about whether he had a working penis or not. The most up-to-date rumors suggested his man parts were fake, but they still worked—a miracle of squishy biomachinery.

If he saw me, he gave no sign, but it took me an hour to get my body calmed. At lunch, I sat in my normal spot, at the rickety picnic table in the far corner of the courtyard, my back to everyone, alone. Sometimes Lilly and a few others sat with me out of a lingering sense of duty, but mostly they had given up. I'd stopped being friendly.

The newspaper that day carried the story of a hate crime in Boston against a woman who had just returned from the hospital, rebuilt. I scanned the words, then folded them away so only the crossword was showing. I had been chewing my sandwich methodically, staring at the half-finished puzzle, when Gabriel sat down across from me. I couldn't help sweeping my gaze over his midsection, looking for any sign of what might be underneath his uniform pants. His face was the same, his blond hair a little longer, some light stubble on his chin, his dark eyes still beautiful, if I could ignore the uneasy mix of feelings they provoked in me.

I assumed people in the courtyard were staring at us, because I could hear multiple whispered conversations, but I was turned away, and I ignored them all. Gabriel unwrapped his own lunch and started eating across from me. He wasn't avoiding my eyes, nor was he seeking them out. He was simply sitting there, an inescapable presence. I continued to chew, the food cardboard in my mouth.

"Why are you sitting here?" I muttered after a while.

He shrugged. Then, looking at me without malice, he said, "I saw you there." He didn't need to explain. I knew he meant at the scene of the accident. "And before, in the coffee shop."

I forced down a bite of sandwich, made myself take a sip of water. For months I'd been living in a state of hopeless isolation with the knowledge of what I'd done. Hearing Gabriel say those words out loud made me feel wretched, guilty, caught.

But also relieved.

His gaze on me was searching. "Did you do it on purpose?" he asked.

He was giving me a chance to lie. But I had already died once in my life. Keeping this secret any longer would kill me again.

I met his eyes and I whispered, "Yes."

All the parts beyond the meshline felt like jelly, unstable, dissolvable.

"It was . . . it was the most awful, evil thing," I said. "And I did it."

He stared at his burger for a little while. At last, meditatively, he said, "I hated you for months. I lay in the hospital, hating you. But . . . I did it on purpose too. After the movie, telling people. I wanted to . . . I don't know . . ."

"Keep away from the freak?" I prompted, still in a whisper.

"Yeah."

"Make it *your* story, not mine?"

"Yeah," he agreed. "I kept thinking about my grandma finding out. I thought she'd get into the car and she'd just *know*—what we'd done, and what you are."

It didn't offend me to hear him say *what you are*. Because whatever I was, he was too. He'd been scared that people would learn about me, and he would be tainted by association: the guy who got off on machines; the guy who liked weirdos; the guy who had sex with the artificial girl because he couldn't get anyone else. So he'd thrown me to the wolves preemptively. And I'd thrown him to the bus.

"I shouldn't have told people," he said.

"You shouldn't have told people," I agreed. "But I shouldn't . . . It was . . ."

"You, like, martyred me for my beliefs," he murmured, taking a bite of his burger. He licked a gob of ketchup from the corner of his mouth.

"You didn't die," I pointed out. "A martyr has to die."

"Did you want me to die?" he asked. He was looking at me with open curiosity. I imagined him in the hospital, turning over this question in his mind.

I shook my head. Even a moment after I'd pushed him, I'd wanted so badly to take it back. *Undo, Undo!* If there had been such a button, I would have pushed it over and over, taking back the bus, the theater, my accident, everything.

"If I'd died, then I really *would* have been a martyr," he went on, as if the idea pleased him. "Or even a saint. You'd have to light candles to me and memorize my life story, Milla."

"Hagiography," I told him. "That's what you call the life story of a saint."

"Yeah. I think I knew that," he said around another mouthful of burger. "You'd have to memorize my hagiography and ask for my help warding off evil and interceding with God on your behalf and finding your lost keys and stuff."

I smiled at that, and then, setting down my sandwich, I declaimed, "St. Gabriel. A true warrior of faith. Succumbed to temptation and slept with a cyborg, then became one himself."

He laughed.

And there was nothing more to say about what had happened between us.

"Want my fries?" I asked. "I'm not that hungry."

"Yeah." He dumped the fries on his napkin, squeezed ketchup all over them. He ate the fries with an expression I recognized. He knew he liked fries and the taste was good, but they didn't provide him with quite the same feeling he was used to. "Ugh. They're like fry-flavored Styrofoam," he said, his mouth full. "But coffee's different now, isn't it? It's, like, *way* better."

My eyebrow quirked up almost lasciviously. *Coffee.* "It tingles around the edges," I told him, hearing dreaminess in my own voice, "like the coffee is eating the mesh, digesting it so—"

"—so it blends back into everything else," he finished for me, in the same rapt tone. "Like the fake parts are starting to become real again."

Yes. That was exactly what drinking coffee felt like now. It was why I'd been in that coffee shop in the first place.

"Have you had the coffee at Go Get 'Em Tiger since . . . ?" I asked him.

"No. Is it special?"

"It's like what you were describing," I told him, "but ten times more."

"Hm. Maybe we could go there sometime," he suggested casually.

I snorted at that, sounding less like a barfing dog than usual. Laughs, snorts, coughs—they were all getting better. Was he really asking me out?

"Sure, we could get coffee," I told him, "but don't think that I'm going to have sex with a robot."

It's a popular myth that the most deadly animal in history is the human, because murder and war and genocide can be laid at the feet of our species. However, the deadliest animal is of course the mosquito.

Fortunately, both species can now be significantly improved.

—Erik Hannes Eklund, Chair of Bioethics and Species Design, Columbia University, in his opening remarks to first-year medical students, 2041

Let's leap ahead a little more. . . .

PART THREE

THE REVEREND MR. TAD TADD'S LOVE STORY

Elsie Tadd woke up in a room she did not at first recognize, with a dry throat, a throbbing head, and aches and pains all over. It appeared to be nighttime when she first opened her eyes, but when she sat up on the edge of the cot with the faded patchwork quilt, she noticed a hint of sunlight coming in through the window up by the ceiling.

"Church basement," she whispered, identifying her location.

This was the spare room of her father's old church, where he would sometimes sleep if he stayed late to speak with parishioners or to work on a sermon. Elsie knew the room well, though she hadn't seen it in a long time. Besides the little bed, there was an old desk and a couple shelves full of dusty books—mostly rare versions of the Bible. One wall was covered by a rather beautiful mural that had been painted by Elsie's own mother. The painting depicted God, in radiant robes, up near the ceiling, and below him was Jesus, healing the ten lepers who had called out to him on the way to Jerusalem. In the

Bible, the men had said, "Jesus, Master, have pity on us!" but Elsie had always wondered how they'd been sure it was Jesus and whether they might have started out with something like "Excuse me, young fellow with the beard. Are you that Jesus everyone's been talking about?" or maybe they'd called out "Jesus!" really quickly and waited to see if he looked around. When she was younger, Elsie had spent hours in this room, drawing and doing her homework, and she'd imagined painting speech bubbles over the lepers' heads and filling in their words.

"But how am I here?" she whispered, because her presence in the church basement didn't make much sense. Elsie's father had been the minister of the Church of the New Pentecost for all of Elsie's life, until a year and a half ago. Since he'd lost his ministry, no one in their family had set foot in the place. Yet here she was. "Did I dream about Africa?" she murmured.

No. Africa was there, in her mind, though it was like a mirage that lost its shape when you tried to look directly at it. Still, she recalled details—the city of Tshikapa in the Congo, the feel of thick cardboard in her fingers as she held up her protest sign; wet, miserable heat; everyone chanting.

The church was silent around Elsie, but she could hear the distant *whoosh-whoosh* of auto-drones commuting across the city. Her little brother, Teddy, used to run around this room saying "Whoosh, whoosh, whoosh!" while pretending that he could fly.

Teddy. The image of her curly-haired, seven-year-old brother brought other images along with it: Elsie's mother sweating in her blouse and skirt, her green eyes alight with energy, leading the chant. Teddy holding a sign as big as himself that read *I Am GRATEFUL For The Hole In My Heart!*

Elsie swallowed, which reminded her of her sore throat and by association of every other part of her body that hurt. She felt her face. There were no bandages, only several spots that were painful to the touch, including all the skin around her right eye. The eye itself felt uncomfortable and strained, though she could see out of it perfectly well. She pulled up her long skirt to find bandages covering both of her knees, with scabs poking out beneath the edges of the gauze.

Another trickle of recollection came, as if through a haze of painkillers: A fall on a rocky patch of ground. A trampling of feet. Her father on a makeshift stage, singing and lifting his arms. Teddy, singing next to Elsie with all his heart: *I was made this way! Oh, I was made this way!* And the sensation in Elsie's chest, the feeling that came over her whenever she thought about Teddy's birth defect—the hole between the chambers of his heart that made him tired and one day might kill him—the sense that a giant had taken hold of her and was squeezing her ribs.

Maybe there had been painkillers, lots of them.

Elsie let her skirt drop.

"There really was a hospital," she whispered to God in the mural on the wall. She imagined a speech bubble above His head that said, "No argument here."

More images crept out of the shadows. There had been a clinic in a small building of decaying plaster on the edge of a muddy town square, a banner announcing *Malaria Prevention and Treatment for Birth Defects.* A line of Congolese women and children, waiting to be seen. Aid workers watching with irritation as Elsie's father ushered his followers out of trucks to take places in front of the hospital.

More. A little Congolese girl, with beautiful dark brown skin and a sad face, standing stoically while a doctor gave her an injection beneath her belly button. Elsie knowing what the injection was: Castus Germline, the reason her father had dragged them to the Congo. Save the Third World, even if the First World has been lost. Once inside the body of a young girl, Castus Germline would edit diseases out of all her eggs and edit in protections against malaria and other infections, so that her children's and grandchildren's health would be close to perfect. Elsie's father chanting: *Arrogance! Blasphemy! That's not how God created me!* Pointing at the tiny girl and the others waiting in line, enraged that no one in the hospital was listening. Elsie lifting her own protest sign—*Why Do You HATE What You Are?*—so she didn't have to see the girl's face, because that giant had been compressing her chest again.

The giant was squeezing her right now. She rose from the cot, fought off a spell of dizziness, and dashed out of the room into the cold hallway outside. Across the hall stood a little bathroom, which she stepped into in order to examine herself in the mirror over the sink.

Except the mirror was gone. Someone had pulled the whole medicine cabinet from the wall—recently, judging by the freshness of the broken plaster surrounding the large cavity that had been left over the sink. The cabinet was sitting on the floor with the mirror side toward the wall, as if the mirror had been offensive, as if it had been ordered to stand in the corner.

Elsie noticed deep scrapes on her elbows now, and these tugged more memories free: Congolese men pouring into the town square, rocks being thrown, people yelling. An old woman with her head wrapped in a brightly colored scarf, spitting at Elsie's father, throwing clods of dirt. Elsie's mother leaping forward.

"Mama," Elsie whispered. "What happened to us?"

Elsie was afraid she already knew the answer. There had been another hospital, bright lights. People lifting Elsie onto a rolling bed, the endless floating of drugs in her bloodstream . . .

She reached for the medicine cabinet, to turn it around, but a sound from down the hall stopped her. It was her father's voice, deep and soothing, and he was saying, "Elsie, are you awake? Come here to me, girl."

"Daddy?" she asked, sticking her head out of the bathroom. It was slightly frightening to hear him in the stillness of the basement. She'd been hoping for her mother's voice, she realized. Or Teddy's.

"Daddy?" she called again. Elsie was fourteen years old. Calling her father *Daddy* was beginning to sound childish. Yet that was the only way she'd ever been allowed to address him.

He didn't say anything else to her, but her father's voice continued on in a murmur. She followed the sound down the hall and found him in the old storage room, among the props for the Christmas pageant and the Easter decorations, the extra folding tables and chairs, and stacks of out-of-date paper hymnals that had long since been replaced by tablets. The Reverend Mr. Tad Tadd, Elsie's father, was kneeling in one corner of the room, facing a large plaster Jesus that had once hung on the wall in the room where Elsie had woken up, before one of its feet had fallen off. Elsie had thought the Jesus looked more roguish with one foot missing, and perhaps more historically accurate, considering his injuries on the cross; however, most people were not looking for roguishness or perfect realism in their Savior, Elsie's mother had explained, and so the broken Jesus had been relegated to the storage room.

Her father, turned toward the wall, was murmuring to himself, with his personal Bible open in his hands. Elsie could catch only a word here and there. He might have been saying, "We are all the fish. . . . You tried to tell me. . . . Fish of different sorts, the fish . . ." Which made no sense, since her father did not care to eat fish of any kind. And yet he sounded as though he were holding up one end of a quite serious conversation with God.

His hands and arms, like Elsie's, were scratched, but she could see nothing else amiss from where she stood.

Tentatively, she asked, "Daddy, what are we doing here?" She didn't like the idea of interrupting, but her father sometimes spoke to God at such length that it wasn't practical to wait until he was done.

"They never changed the door codes," her father said,

without turning from the plaster Jesus. "I didn't want to bring you home just yet."

"But how did we get here?" Elsie asked.

"Joel helped me. We got you released and brought you here so you could wake up in peace." Joel, a doctor, had been one of her father's parishioners and his best friend, before the Reverend's fall from grace.

"But . . . Tshikapa, the Congo," she said.

"Yes, Africa," her father answered heavily. And then, as if to explain, he added, "Airlift and two hospitals."

Yes. That. The mirage in her head was taking on solid form. The mob, and the rocks.

Elsie had been standing just inside the doorway, but now she got closer. Hoping the words were wrong, she asked, "Mama and Teddy are dead? I didn't dream it?"

One of her father's hands went to his face, and when it came away, Elsie could see that it was wet. He was crying. He turned his head slightly as he said, "You didn't dream it, baby girl."

She wanted to feel shocked, but she didn't. Part of her had known the moment she woke up.

Elsie took a seat on an aged footstool with the stuffing coming out of it. A broken hymnal tablet shared the stool with her. When her leg brushed against it, a four-inch-high three-dimensional Japanese woman sprang up from the tablet's screen, lifted her arms, and began to sing the Japanese version of "Crown Him with Many Crowns." A crack down the center of the tablet caused half of the woman's body to be a smudged rainbow of disconnected colors. Elsie switched off the tablet.

"Are they gone?" her father went on. "In a sense, yes. My beautiful wife and beautiful little boy, but—"

"But they'll live on in heaven at the end of time?" Elsie interjected automatically, because that was the sort of thing her father would say at a moment like this one.

"Yes, they will. But they don't have to wait, because they are living on already."

A rock to the back of her mother's head. Teddy trampled. She had seen those things.

"How?" she whispered.

The Reverend had his forehead leaned against his Bible in an attitude of most fierce prayer, and Elsie wondered if it was possible that he had conjured up a miracle. She imagined a mural of this very moment, herself and her father and God hovering above them in his radiant robes, and she saw the speech bubble above her own head: "Excuse me, Lord God? Have You got something remarkable up those flowing sleeves of Yours?" But the God in the imagined mural looked as curious as Elsie was to hear what her father was going to say.

"If there's one thing I've always said," the Reverend told his daughter, "it's that a man who cannot admit he's wrong is not much of a man."

It was true, she'd heard him say that, but—

"Do you mean *you*, Daddy?" she asked.

"I do."

This surprising admission took several seconds to unfold within Elsie. Her father was criticizing himself?

"What—what were you wrong about, Daddy?" she asked.

In the mural, God gave Elsie a look of disappointment. "You know what he was wrong about, Elsie," His speech bubble admonished her.

Elsie's speech bubble said, "I need to hear him say it."

The Reverend Tadd said, "A revelation, my sweet girl, is like turning on a light or opening a window. Have I told you that?" Elsie still couldn't see his expression, but she imagined that it looked as it often did during the most ecstatic portions of his sermons—one part joy, one part pain. "You're in a dark room and then—poof!—the sun floods in. And what you thought were formless shapes and terrible shadows are not. In God's light, you understand that they're something else entirely.

"Do you want to know what I've been shown?" her father asked. "Should I try to put it into words, even though words won't do it justice?"

"Sure, Daddy." If there was one thing Elsie understood about her father, it was that he knew how to use words that would do his ideas justice. His pride in his verbal skill burned intensely. In the mural in Elsie's mind, she saw that pride like a glowing coal where his heart should be. Her father's skill with words was the only thing that had buoyed him in the face of his lost ministry, his failure with the church board, his public humiliation. And his skill with words was part of that tight grip the giant had around Elsie's chest.

"I've been shown that my expulsion from the Church of the New Pentecost was fair. I was as wrong as a man could be," he told her, the words coming out in a toneless stream. "I went on the radio all those years, I stood at the pulpit before my congregation and told them they were defying the Lord. Changing themselves, growing new hearts and lungs and now even eyeballs!" His voice grew more resonant, as if he were in rehearsal for a public performance.

In the mural in her mind, God said, "He impresseth Me greatly with his beautiful voice! At least he's got that going for him."

She silently agreed with the Lord; she'd always loved her daddy's voice. But would he say the things Elsie could feel caged up inside her own chest?

The Reverend continued, "But what if *I* am the one who defied the holy design? I can still see the look in that boy's eyes, Elsie, years ago, when I told him he was turning himself into a demon!"

He stood up and reached for Elsie's hand without turning toward her. Elsie got to her feet and slipped her hand into his. She thought they were going to pray together, but instead he led her out the door and back into the hall. The Reverend moved swiftly, pulling her along in his wake as he walked up the stairs, through the vestry, and out into the church itself. The lights were off, but late-afternoon sunlight came in through the stained-glass windows, turning dust motes into burning stars. He walked to the very edge of the dais, still holding Elsie's hand, and there he faced the empty pews as if they held a Sunday's worth of worshippers. He raised his arms toward heaven, and because Elsie's hand was clasped in his, her arm was lifted too.

Addressing those empty benches, her father spoke with full sermon resonance: "When I was a young man, we were made to accept the doctrine of evolution. We came to terms with it by telling ourselves that the Creator *could* use evolution as part of His grand design, could He not? We *said* this, but I never believed with my full heart." His voice was the sail of a great ship full of the driving ocean breeze, and the words he emphasized were the snaps of that sail in sharp gusts of wind. Elsie, his parishioners, radio listeners across the country—all became passengers on the Reverend Tad Tadd's ship when he spoke like this.

She looked up at her father as he slowly lowered his arms, and her own lowered along with them. She could see only the right side of her father's face—in fact, she had seen only the right side of his face since finding him in the basement—with his dark hair falling in loose curls around his ear and just a few strands of gray to show that he was forty years old. Only his right eye was visible from where she stood, but that eye, with its piercing black iris, almost glowed in the sunlight.

"*But* let me tell you," the Reverend continued, addressing that empty church, which felt, under the assault of his deep and lovely voice, full of sinners ready for salvation, "evolution is not a side note. It's not something to be accepted begrudgingly. It is the *sun* to our Earth and moon."

There was a pause, during which he let go of Elsie's hand.

"Why?" she asked him timidly. Her full question was

probably longer: *Why is that the important point? Why aren't you talking about the things that matter?*

In the mural, God's speech bubble said, "It's time to ask all of your questions out loud, Elsie."

"He's been telling us since the beginning!" the Reverend boomed out to the empty pews, startling his daughter. He held up his Bible in his left hand, open to the beginning, where the word *Genesis* was written in fancy script at the top of the page. "We know the story of creation so well, but we've been *gliding* over the meaning. We read about *swarms* of birds and fish and whales and cattle and insects. But what God created was the *potential* to become all of those things. He blessed the *essence* of these creatures with the breath of life, with the ability to *become* all the wild and tame things of the world."

Her father shook his Bible at the empty pews and his invisible congregation, that congregation that had been wrested from him eighteen months previously because of his years of constant radio attacks and protests against anyone—sick people, surgeons, desperate parents, World Health Organization volunteers—who dared to get tricky about altering the human body.

"The Hebrew word for *living being,* do you know what it is?" he asked Elsie and the empty pews. Elsie opened her mouth to tell him that she did not know, but he wasn't looking at her, and he didn't wait. "The Hebrew word for *living being* is *Nephesh.*"

"Ah, not *fish* at all, then," Elsie whispered next to him, now understanding some of what the Reverend had been saying back in the storage room when he'd been talking with God.

"God calls us all *Nephesh*—the spiders and the eagles and the starfish *and* the humans. He gave humankind *dominion* over all creatures. But we're all *Nephesh,* living beings of the same stock and origin. He gave us the capacity to evolve, even beyond natural selection. And now, we can evolve de*libe*rately and to*gethe*r!"

Elsie's father turned away from the phantom congregation to look directly at his daughter for the first time since she had found him in the church. The sunlight through stained glass hit him full in the face, and she took a step backward, and then another, as a gasp escaped her mouth.

In the mural in Elsie's mind, God was looking just as startled as Elsie felt, and the speech bubble above his head asked, "What manner of creature is he?"

The right half of her father's face was just as it had always been, weathered, tan skin, dark eye, dark hair falling over his forehead, the beginnings of dark stubble along his jaw, but the left side . . . the left side was not.

"She is beginning to see the possibilities!" the Reverend boomed out to the invisible audience. He knelt in front of Elsie and took both of her hands in his. Quietly, just to her, he said, "Can you see what I've done?"

Elise felt like the Jesus without his foot, distressed and yet able only to stare in mute astonishment. The left half of her father's face was smooth and pale, covered in different skin entirely. Even the stippling along his jaw was gone from the left side, as if no beard would ever grow there again. His left eyebrow was light brown in contrast to the dark hairs of the right, and his left eye . . .

Her father's left eye was a pale green, the green of her mother's eyes. It was even slightly smaller than his right eye, the proper size to fit into her mother's face.

"You've taken Mamma's eye," Elsie whispered. To look at the left side of his face was to look at a twisted version of her mother, trapped in her father's body. "Did you need her eye, Daddy? Was yours missing?"

"No, mine wasn't missing. You and I were lucky, Elsie," he told her. "Twelve killed by that godless mob, yet we survived. But your mother . . . her eyes were undamaged. I couldn't throw them away. And feel—"

He brought one of Elsie's hands up to stroke the skin on the left side of his face. It was soft to the touch and delicate.

"It's her skin too?" Elsie felt as though she were slipping backward, out of her body, away from this man with mismatched eyes.

"Now it's *our* skin," he told her. "And feel here."

He pushed her hand through the hair on the left side of his scalp, which Elsie noticed was a shock of light brown curls, baby soft to the touch. She combed her fingers through that delicate hair as she had done hundreds of times before, when it had been growing out of her little brother's head. Elsie felt as though she were plastered against the far wall of the church, trying to escape from this moment.

"You took Teddy's hair?" The words were hardly audible.

The Reverend nodded solemnly. His eyes—*their* eyes—pierced Elsie with a kind of ravenous ecstasy.

"We are wonders of po*ten*tial, Elsie. They took your mamma's eyes and her skin, and your brother's hair, and they bathed them in the essence of life—my life, her life, all life—"

"Stem cells?" Elsie asked. She knew about the sorts of things doctors could do; it was impossible to avoid such knowledge, even if it went against her father's beliefs.

"Whatever you might call them—stem cells, cultured cells, mixed cells, cells that have been stripped down and reprogrammed, nanobots wrapped in cells. Doctors quibble over details, but it's all the evolved essence of life. They put the eye, the skin, the hair into me, *me* joined with *them,* to live on."

In the mural in Elsie's mind, the speech bubble over God's head was blank. He was looking down at Elsie, mystified. Her father was in a state of rapture, holding his Bible in one hand and touching his new half-face with the other.

"No," Elsie said. As she spoke the word, she stopped trying to escape. She felt a strength in her own body as she faced her father.

In the mural, God's robes had changed from a bluish white into a majestic purple. His speech bubble read, "You have put a name to that feeling in your chest!"

The image of Elsie in the imaginary mural said, "It's not a giant crushing me, Lord. It's *doubt* and *hatred.* They've been squeezing me for a while now."

"Give them a voice," God said, "and they will crush you no more."

In a series of almost comical stages, the Reverend Tadd had shifted from ecstasy to curiosity to annoyance as he focused on his daughter.

"What do you mean, *no*?" he demanded. The Reverend Tadd's black eye and green eye were both fixed upon Elsie.

"You know how we would listen to those other preachers on the radio together sometimes?" she said. Her voice sounded different in her own ears, older than fourteen. "You would hear those other preachers say something wrong, Daddy, and you would tell me, 'See there, Elsie. He had a notion in his mind already, and he found a way to twist the words of the Bible to suit what he was already thinking.' That's what you're—"

"You think I'm *twisting* God's words to suit my own thoughts?"

"I think you're missing the point, Daddy!" she said. She discovered that the words she wanted to say were already there. Perhaps they'd been there for years. "You're missing the *whole* point! You've changed your mind now because someone you love died. But—but—kids in hospitals, that little girl in Tshikapa—they've been dying all along. You made us protest removing diseases, making their lives better. You drove them to attack us. You and Mamma kept that hole in Teddy's heart— you—you told him he needed that hole because that was how extra love got in and out!" They had said that to Teddy, and Teddy had proudly repeated it to others: *I don't mind the hole, it makes me extra sweet.* "But now it's *your* loss that bothers you."

"Do you think I would change the holy book to suit *me*?" the Reverend Tadd asked, with an indignation that appeared to inflate his entire body. "Elsie, I was *wrong*, but now I've seen what God intended all along."

In that mural in Elsie's mind, God's speech bubble said, "That's what every self-centered preacher hath always claimed!" His radiant robes had turned to a deep red.

The Reverend Tadd knelt before his daughter, leaned closer to her with his hybrid face, and took her gently by the shoulders.

"Elsie, we are going to share this triumph. I can't do this without my girl," he whispered. "We will evolve *together*."

Her father got to his feet and walked to the lectern at which he'd stood hundreds of times before, in front of a real congregation. From a hidden shelf, he retrieved something. Elsie watched him with a sense of foreboding as he came back to her.

He was carrying a mirror.

He knelt down and with a flourish he turned the mirror to face her. There were no gasps this time, no backward steps to escape. Elsie had felt her swollen cheek, the aches in her head. She knew, in the moment before she saw her reflection, what it was going to show her. Half of Elsie's face had been changed. Her left eye was the same brown eye that had gazed back at her from mirrors since birth. Her right eye was her mother's green eye, the mate to the one in her father's head.

Across the right side of her face, her skin had been changed, she thought, turned into a combination of her own and her mother's, smooth, soft, but older than Elsie's own skin. And her hair . . . her own light brown mane still fell past her shoulders on the left side, but on the right was an uneven blend of her brother's curly brown locks and her mother's long blond hair. Patches of each were vying for position, so that she resembled a child's hairdressing doll after a particularly enthusiastic slumber party.

"Oh" was all she said.

In the mural in Elsie's mind, God also said, "Oh."

Putting the mirror into Elsie's own hands, her father took her again by the shoulders. His black and green eyes were alight with intensity, but he wasn't angry. He was *certain*. He smiled.

Elsie pushed him away. "You made us both into monsters, Daddy. And you did it for yourself."

"For myself, for you, for them, for everyone. We can keep them alive, Elsie. And I will have a new following, so that everyone will see the sunlight that has flooded into my soul. The whole world will evolve."

In the mirror, Elsie watched herself grimace at the remnants of her mother and her brother, now tangled up and drowning inside Elsie forever.

She didn't want to speak to her father anymore, but she managed one last word, which came out with the ringing force of an oath:

"No."

Dr. Chiyo Nilsson: Senator, with all respect, you're trying to make this a religious issue, but it's not. This movement transcends those labels.

Senator Mia Reed: Your movement was founded by modification evangelists, as the American people well know. These evangelists started this—

Dr. Nilsson: Forgive me for interrupting, but that's simply not true, Senator. Yes, many followers of Mr. Tadd support this cause, but I myself am an atheist who represents the Alliance for Sexual and Gender Diversity and the American Civil Liberties Union. Groups from the Modern Primitives to the Committee of Concerned Scientists to the National Physicians Alliance are united in the belief that all citizens, all people—

Senator Reed: Half those groups accept funding from for-profit clinics that couldn't survive

in a world without modification. Where's the
"belief" in that?

Dr. Nilsson: Senator, people are allowed to
make a living. Potential profit doesn't change
the fundamental, the intrinsic, essential—

Senator Reed: Even the language you use is
the language of zealots. How can we take you
seriously?

Dr. Nilsson: We use language for its intended
purpose—to convey our feelings. We want control
over our own bodies, over our own physical
presence.

Senator Reed: You're arguing for biological
anarchy. The world won't stand for it.

Dr. Nilsson: Senator, we're arguing for
freedom.

—From televised hearings in the US Senate, 2077

A *lot* of time has passed. . . .

PART FOUR

EIGHT WADED

1. THE INTRUDER

Eight waded.
   Hag died wet.
   Headed twig.
   Dig wethead.

These are the words in my head when I wake up. Do you see the pattern? Each of these phrases uses the same letters; each one is an anagram of the real phrase that is posted in my mind today, neon letters across my frontal lobe: *Dead weight.*

I am speaking in metaphor. There are not real neon letters.

Dead weight. Ten letters in an unpleasant order. But rearranged, they are not so bad: *Had wit edge.* Better.

The world is perfectly clear this morning. I emerge from my sleeping habitat wearing the rebreather, and when I blink my eyes to see in the water, I have a view past the kelp forest, past the sunken arc of the old Ferris wheel with its fringe of seaweed, to the encircling net and even to the small island beyond. That is a distance of seventy-five yards from where I'm floating. Seventy-five yards, you may be interested to know, is nearly the limit of how far one can see underwater, even with the eyes I have been given.

My given eyes.

Envy my siege.

Anagrams again. Am I explaining too much? I never know how much I should explain about puzzles. To me they are breath and blood. (Metaphor.) To others I have noticed they are less important.

The dolphins are patrolling the perimeter of the sea paddock, too far away for me to make out anything more than their silhouettes through the kelp, but my ears know them individually by the sounds of rusty door hinges, squeaking balloons, fishing reels unwinding—their signature speech patterns, which travel to me easily through the water.

I will check in with the dolphins later, but the first order of business every morning is to survey the flock of chimeras. They are huddled close to my habitat, as they usually are, because they prefer the shallows, where the finest, tastiest sea grasses grow in the sandy sea bottom and where the sun heats the water. This morning, sunlight kisses the chimeras' mottled backs, winking and flashing because of ripples along the ocean's surface.

Sunlight kisses. This, too, is a figure of speech. Sunlight is merely visible radiation with no awareness of what or how it touches.

As I float toward the chimeras, I stretch my arms, which I

have been instructed to do frequently after reentering the sea each morning, in order to keep up my new skin's elasticity. I am a rubber boy in a world with no bounce.

Hello, Alexios! the chimeras say as I get closer, though their words are only grunts and clicks. Several of them turn in my direction as I approach, their whiskered faces and small, sunken eyes curious for a moment, before turning back to the seaweed.

The chimeras are manatees, by the way. You can think of them as underwater pandas, if you are one of those people who love all sorts of creatures and like to consider them in the most charming terms possible. To me, however, they are sufficient as themselves without such comparisons.

But

> *underwater panda*
> > can become
> > > *unwanted parader*
> > > > and also
> > > > > *deadpan water run.*

That last one feels almost appropriate, though the manatees aren't deadpan—in fact, they are quite expressive. Here comes Bluebear to make this point for me, doing a barrel roll and greeting me with enthusiastic morningtime chirps and grunts.

I switch the translator on my chest to "Manatee"—not because I need its help to understand, but because it is my job to teach the translator what I have already learned. The language of the manatees is rudimentary, easy to grasp once you get used to listening. Bluebear is saying hello and asking me to scratch him. When I check the readout on the translator, it says *hello hello hello touch scratch.* Excellent.

Scratch, scratch, Bluebear says, his whiskery jaw snuffling toward my face and his flippers almost pulling me into an underwater panda hug.

I enter "scratch" into the translator and it grunts the word out into the water. That is the translator's real use to me, as a means of vocalizing to my colleagues. The Blessed Cures Consortium has changed many things about me, but they haven't given me the power of underwater speech. At least, not yet.

While I scratch Bluebear's back, I examine my own arms and skin. I don't like to look, but I am supposed to make this examination at least twice a day—once in the habitat and once in the water—to see if I am healthy. My skin is grayer than the natural skin I was born with, and it is rubbery, as I mentioned, because they made it for me out of dolphin skin cells cultured in a mixture with my own. I note that my fingernails continue to disappear as the new skin takes over, but there is still enough of them left to allow me to scratch Bluebear to his satisfaction. Fingernails are useful for some things, but they are an unnecessary luxury here. What is important is that my fingers retain their nimble human agility, which they do. Really, when was the last time fingernails were essential to humans? Probably before we learned to walk upright, and even then, they were weak claws at best—a kind of dead weight.

There it is again: *dead weight.*

The neon letters across my brain flicker when I am distracted, but they never quite go out.

Metaphor.

Bluebear has turned over so that I may address his stomach. I have named him Bluebear because this name sounds like the word *blubber* with the word *bear* mixed in. I know about blubber and bears, and human evolution and algebra and world events, and so many other things from my learning sessions in the Genetic Radiance clinic when I was younger and from my ongoing lessons here at the Blessed Cures Consortium's clinic, but I have always been told that the key to true learning is being able to connect facts with the real world. These connections are especially important for someone like me—or so I've been repeatedly informed. Naming a manatee Bluebear is an example of me trying. I have named everyone here in the sea paddock, and in each case I have made a connection to the world.

Bluebear's chirp changes. *Play?* he is suggesting. I check the translator, to ensure that it has correctly interpreted this sound. *Fun,* it says. That is close enough for manatee work.

A joke.

I type in "follow" and the translator squawks out the correct sounds. Bluebear brightens and when I swim toward the center of the flock, he follows right behind me. The large calf I have called Splotch, due to the single splotch of moss on his back, gets in line behind Bluebear. Follow-the-leader is a favorite manatee game. Through a blue world of filtered sunlight, they are zeppelins gracefully trailing me.

Metaphor.

After I have circled the whole flock twice, with Bluebear and Splotch as my shadows, I settle to the ocean floor next to a manatee called Mountains. I have named him after the pattern on his back, made of algae and small barnacles, which looks very much like a mountain range. In point of fact, it is a near replica of a section of the Ural Mountains that you can plainly find on a satellite map of the world. I have even managed to move one of the barnacles into a slightly more accurate position.

Mountains sees me, but he does not stop the careful progress of his mouth through the sea grass. I scratch his hide, which causes Bluebear to float between me and Mountains, in order to divert my scratches back to himself.

"Go," I say through the translator.

Bluebear tosses his head and chirps, but he is too friendly to argue, and in a moment, he and Splotch are lumbering to a free patch of seaweed on the other side of the flock.

"See," I tell Mountains, who slowly, at blimp speed, rotates so that his stomach is toward me. I have told him I wish to "see," and he has correctly understood that I wish to see his cuts. They lie on either side of his abdomen, each about nine inches in length, discolored, but healing. The sutures are disappearing as they are meant to do within days.

Mountains patiently regards me with his tiny eyes. It occurs to me that he is studying my Frankenstein limbs while I study him. He has seen many humans in his life, but does he recognize that my head is too large and the wrong shape? Can he distinguish that my legs are not human at all, but separate long, powerful limbs, ending in flippers, almost as though a dolphin had been cut in half? Does the rebreather that covers my back, recycles my air, and lets out a constant stream of pinpoint bubbles appear to him a part of my body? Am I, to him, an unusual human or a different creature entirely?

Frankenstein.

Ten knifes ran.

My name is Alexios, as I think I have mentioned. This is a traditional Greek name, which means *defender,* though you have perhaps guessed that I am not a traditional Greek boy. And yet, are you filled with admiration? Behold in awe Alexios, defender of manatees!

I gently clear off the algae that has begun to grow over Mountain's healing surgical scars. Then I tell him "Good" through the translator. He was taken to the surgery pod a week ago, where the clinicians removed a liver and a heart, which by now must be residing in their intended human recipient in some distant corner of the world. Mountains knows nothing about this human, and he never will. And he doesn't know that he still has a bellyful of other organs waiting to be harvested.

Living organ tank.

Vagrant king lion.

That one pleases me, even though a manatee is nearly as far from a lion as you can get.

Chimera. It means a living thing that contains tissue from two or more distinct organisms. Humans have used pigs and sheep and even rats to grow human organs cheaply and safely. But manatees are so much larger, and their lumbering ways and gentle attitudes so ideal to peacefully cultivating alien tissue, that my employer, the Blessed Cures Consortium, chose them as far more perfect chimeras than lowly pigs. Also, they can hide manatees underwater and leave their competitors guessing.

I pat Mountains before allowing him to move off and wiggle his way back to the seabed between other members of the flock. Half of the manatees in the flock are full of human organs. The other half are the mothers, the ones who carry the chimera embryos and give birth to these living organ farms. The magic is done at the embryo stage, you see. Heart cells, liver cells, pancreas cells, even breast cells are grafted into the manatee embryo, where they grow alongside all the normal manatee parts.

Metaphor again. There is no magic, only science.

Chimera.

Or, switched around:

Ah, crime.

I survey the flock, looking for Handsome, who had surgery the day before Mountains, but—

Enemy! Human!

The water erupts in urgent whistles and squeals and the entire pod of dolphins has materialized around me. Their flukes kick up silt and they are pairing off and doing intertwined barrel rolls, which is their way of saying that they are ready for action. They have spotted an intruder.

I switch the translator to "Dolphin" and have it squeak and click the signature whistle for Loud Mike, the biggest (and loudest) member of the pod. Loud Mike peels away from the others and swims so close that he brushes against my chest, which allows me to grasp his dorsal fin. I type in "all go," and the translator chirps this at them. (There is no point in asking a dolphin "where?" because she can only show you anyway.) A moment later, we are off at full speed. The whole pod—seven dolphins in all—moves as one, because that is the way to approach an enemy. I hug Loud Mike's back and position my body along his so that I am easier to carry.

The water gets deeper as soon as we leave the manatees' grass beds. We whip through the kelp forest, where the leafy tentacles of green-brown, thirty feet tall, float on the current in a slow, dignified dance and silver flashes of fish dart from shadow to shadow. Then we are above the sunken amusement park that once stood on the Greek shore before the earthquake that calved off part of the coastline. The buildings of the amusement park have all but disappeared beneath coral and kelp in the deepest recesses of our paddock, but the Ferris wheel reaches up into the brighter water. The arc of its upper half, bearded with fantastic varieties of red and green algae that scintillate in the sunlight, provides mathematical entertainment for the part of my mind not consumed with the urgent situation: the circumference of the Ferris wheel's "wheel," the area of the "pie slices" formed by its radial struts, the amount of centrifugal force that would be produced at different rotation speeds.

I unhook my stunning weapon from the rebreather when we have gone past the amusement park. Here the sea floor falls steeply away into the deepest blue. And there is the net, that mesh wall from surface to seabed that keeps the chimeras and my dolphin guards corralled in the safety of the vast sea cage. I hold my weapon at the ready as we sweep up to the net. I have practiced this many times, and this is not the first intruder to come here on my watch. The Blessed Cures Consortium is a frequent target of industrial espionage.

He is there on the other side of the net. Full wetsuit with hood and scuba gear. In his hands is a large device that cannot be anything other than a high-resolution camera made to see long distances underwater. He is filming the manatees, of course, but as we approach, he turns to film us. When we are only yards from him, he releases the camera and puts his hands up, as if to say *I come in peace!*

I come in peace

      is more likely to be

           income apiece.

His eyes grow wide in his goggles when he sees what I am, that I wear no goggles of my own, that my legs have been turned into something else, that I am as gray as my dolphin escorts.

I lift my stunner and he holds up his hands more urgently, asking for patience. He gestures to the surface as if to say *Let's discuss this, brother!* Then he touches his heart and points upward again. What does this mean? *I love you, fellow human? I feel a connection with you? My heart aches?*

Unfortunately for him, the Blessed Cures Consortium has a shoot-first-and-ask-your-questions-later (if the intruder survives) policy. I have already pulled the trigger, releasing the dual torpedoes, each the size of my smallest finger. There is recognition in his expression that something has gone terribly wrong. Our intruder dives to one side, but the torpedoes have sighted him and they will find him. In the blink of an eye, the bullets are past the mesh and they pierce his wetsuit and embed themselves in his chest. A few drops of blood escape out into the water, and the smell of it sets off a storm of commentary among the dolphins.

The intruder flails, jitters, and then he convulses as the torpedoes unload tightly focused electrical currents through his torso.

Yes yes yes! Excitement! Happy! the dolphins are chittering all around me. *Win!*

The intruder goes limp. His mouthpiece has fallen out, and bubbles are pouring from his mouth, causing him to float downward.

I unsheathe the special knife at my waist, which is designed to handle the mesh of our perimeter net. Its black blade severs the elastic fibers of the mesh effortlessly, and with three quick slices, I have cut out a panel that drapes toward me, creating a doorway.

"Loud Mike! Quiet Mike! Constantine!" I say through the translator, which pipes out their signature whistles.

These three echo their whistles back to me: *Roger, boss, we're listening!*

"Go take," I tell them.

They are off through the opening I have made. Quiet Mike pulls the camera strap off the man and swims it back to me. Loud Mike and Constantine nose the limp body to the surface, then push it toward the tiny island that lies a short distance from our perimeter.

I myself surface for the first time today, feeling as always that I am a misshapen monster emerging from the deep. (Metaphor?) I allow my large head to peek above the water, where I blink to switch my eyes to air-sight. I am supposed to make sure that the intruder's face is out of the ocean, so he has every chance of surviving. I can see the tip of Loud Mike's nose above the water, poking the limp man repeatedly until half of his body lies above the water line, on the dry sand of the island. It is enough. If the man is alive, he will be able to breathe.

I look to my left, where, on the far side of the sea paddock, the low, long roof of Blessed Cures' ocean clinic rises above the sand, and I let off a flare.

With another blink, I switch back to underwater vision as I dive down. In moments, the whole pod is reunited in the paddock. With a flick of the knife handle, I reverse its function, and I use it to heal the elastic of the net and seal the flap back into place.

Soon the vibration of a small boat motor reaches our ears. Someone is launching from the clinic to pick up the intruder, who will have to answer for his trespassing. Already, this feels very distant. A human problem for the world above. All traces of the man have been wiped from the ocean.

Except for the camera, which I am now holding.

Toy? asks Quiet Mike.

Toy toy toy?! echo the others. They set off in barrel rolls again, but these are playful and not menacing.

Play! someone says.

Play play play! is echoed throughout the pod.

I throw the camera at Shark Girl (named for her tendency to bite and her gender), who catches the strap with her flipper, then lets it fall so she can catch it with her fluke. The others crowd around, looking at the glass lens, the strap. It is passed back and forth between different dolphins, but they soon tire of it. The camera is heavy and sinks quickly—not an ideal dolphin toy. Shark Girl lets it fall when it next comes to her, and she picks up a piece of kelp instead, which she swims away with, the other six in pursuit.

I dive to the bottom and retrieve the camera.

2. THE CLINICS

The world through a camera lens is not the same world one views with the naked eye. There is a moment, when you take a picture, when you see something familiar and discover that it is not familiar at all—it is alien and new, because you have studied it through a new eye.

Camera world.

Coward realm.

A warmer cold.

By the time the clinic signals me, hours later, I have gazed at the whole of the sea paddock through the camera. The signal is a piercing buzz, tuned to my human ears, that pulses through water until I swim back to the jetty and press the Off button.

Even though I hate the noise, I swim back slowly, because I do not like the clinic. I do not like the feeling in my stomach that appears magically when that buzzer sounds.

Metaphor. There is no magic. It is adrenaline.

Just in front of the clinic building, a stone jetty extends into the sea paddock. Beneath the water line, a steel door is built into the jetty, and it is to this I swim. The signal button, large, red, and obvious, is located to one side of the door. I press it, and the alarm goes silent. Simultaneously, the door unlocks, and when I pull up on the handles, there is a sucking sound, and then the rush of water pouring in. The door glides open, as clean and white on the inside as the clinic itself. I glance back to see if any of my underwater colleagues have decided to investigate, now that the buzz has been turned off, but there is no one nearby. The dolphins and manatees instinctively know to stay away from this door.

Beyond it, underwater now that the door is open, is the bottom of the conveyor belt that leads upward at an angle, with handgrips every couple of feet. As soon as I swim in and take hold of the nearest grip, the belt whirs into motion. In a few yards I am above the water line, and my flipper feet and dolphin legs lie heavily against the belt, reminding me of the existence of gravity.

Dead weight! I think.

My gray skin begins to tighten and pucker immediately. But none of these minor discomforts are why I don't like the clinic.

By counting the seams in the tunnel's ceiling, I calculate how many feet above the ocean I am with each second that passes.

Hated clinic.

Iceland itch.

I clean ditch.

Better.

Eventually I remember that I don't need the rebreather here and I let it fall from my mouth. The air of the world, or at least the air of the conveyor tunnel, floods into my lungs. It is fresher, which is nice, but on the other hand, it is laden with the taste and scent of the human world.

The tunnel lets out into the clinic's pool room, which is large and open and white, with a high ceiling and sunlight pouring in everywhere. Lab technicians, also in white, are waiting for me as the conveyor belt spills me out into a kind of rubber net that waits at the very end.

"Alexios! Thank you for coming."

That is Mr. Tavoularis, the man in charge of the clinic.

Two technicians have grabbed me beneath my arms and they are lifting me over several yards of pavement, which I am not able to navigate on my own because my new legs do not walk. (My old legs didn't walk either, but at least they had feet, giving the impression that walking might be possible.)

"Just a quick hop," one of the lab techs is saying in a friendly voice as I'm whisked over the floor, "and here you are, Alexios!"

They lower me into the saltwater pool and then they and several other techs stand at the edge, peering down with intense interest as I swim to the underwater sling chair they have designed just for me, just for meetings like this one.

"What have you got there, Alexios?" Mr. Tavoularis asks me, when I am settled comfortably, only my head above the surface. He has spotted the intruder's camera, which is slung over my shoulder.

I hold it out to them and a lab tech leans over to take it from me.

"Can you speak, Alexios?" Mr. Tavoularis asks. He is conversing with me in English, as everyone does. It is the official language of the clinics in which I have spent my life, and so it is the only tongue I have ever used.

Tongue. Figure of speech.

Mr. Tavoularis is tall, with a very large, dark, well-combed mustache that curls upward on each side, while the hair on his head is cropped close to his scalp. He wears a doctor's lab coat with a fine linen suit beneath.

Tavoularis

     or, as I often think of him when he lectures me,

       saliva tour.

I have not been to the clinic for weeks. This means that I have not used my human voice for weeks. The strange rasp of air in my throat surprises me as I say, "I can speak." My voice is rough and sounds older than I am. But this is typical. It will improve as our conversation progresses. "That's the camera I took from the intruder," I tell him.

"Excellent," Mr. Tavoularis says. "We have revived him, you know. You and the dolphins did a wonderful job of keeping him alive. We will discover who he works for, which will be quite helpful to us. It is always our aim to stay one step ahead of our competitors."

He tells me this as though I will be relieved, but I am not paying much attention. One of the lab techs is a woman with large breasts, and another is a man with a plump stomach. I am thinking that, if positioned correctly, they could both fit into a rectangular box together without wasting much space. I begin to do calculations of their combined weight and how much room would be left over. I never imagine fitting chimeras or dolphins into boxes, but I am always thinking about this with humans, due to their varied shapes.

"So," Mr. Tavoularis says, clearing his throat slightly, which I have learned is his way of saying *I need your full attention now, Alexios*. He rolls open his tablet, preparing to take notes. "Recount for me the incident with the intruder."

This is the procedure every time something unusual happens near the paddock. The Blessed Cures Consortium calls it a *postmortem*, even though that means *after death* in Latin, and the intruder didn't die. Though it does occur to me that Blessed Cures might kill the man when they have finished questioning him. Still, that would make this a "premortem," wouldn't it?

Blessed Cures.

Bleeds Curses.

As I describe what happened with the intruder, Mr. Tavoularis says things like "Oh, I see" and "Do go on," and it is very difficult for me not to associate those bland conversational encouragements with the examinations I used to have in the clinic where I grew up—Genetic Radiance. The Genetic Radiance clinic was also owned by the Blessed Cures Consortium, though its medical specialty was different. *I* was the specialty there. Here at Blessed Cures, I am merely an employee.

Mr. Tavoularis is nodding and making shorthand notation with two of his fingers into his tablet's holographic input, so I suppose I am saying the proper words to describe how I disabled the intruder and so on, and yet I am not hearing myself anymore, and I am hardly seeing Mr. Tavoularis or any of the lab techs who are huddled attentively at the edge of the pool.

I am instead hearing and seeing Caroline, my special doctor at Genetic Radiance. If I am not mistaken, I am reexperiencing one particular conversation with Caroline when I was seven years old.

I am not mistaken. This conversation has been engraved upon my consciousness. Metaphor.

Twenty percent of my attention remains on the Greek scientist with the luxurious mustache.

Ten percent of my attention is being used to fit lab techs, like interlocking puzzle pieces, into boxes.

A different ten percent of my attention is occupied in calculating how it is possible to follow several entirely different trains of thought at the same time.

Sixty percent of my attention has retreated into the past and is watching the memory of Caroline unfold before me:

"Mm, yes, I can see that," Caroline says. "If your friend lost his mother, it certainly could help to ask another woman to act as his mother, to replace her. But please think carefully, Alexios—is there any other answer?"

She is administering a test. She is nearly always administering a test. This one is called HEEP, which stands for Human Emotion, Empathy, and Pathos. It is not heaps of fun. The test before this one was the one I have to take most often, FunIntMin, which stands, obviously, for Functional Intelligence in Minors.

"I could move somewhere else so I didn't have to see him anymore," I say, after some reflection.

"Certainly you—you could. But the question was how you could help your friend with the loss of his mother. How would *you* moving away help your friend?"

I don't have an answer for that. That solution would not help my friend with his loss of his mother, but it would dramatically help the situation, because I would not have to hear about it anymore. Most of the HEEP's questions are like this one, boring and long.

"Do you have another answer, Alexios?" Caroline asks me. Her expression remains friendly, but there is something different about her eyes, something less patient.

"Time travel could answer any of these questions," I tell her. "However, no one has demonstrated it as a practical possibility, though mathematically, there are paradigms under which it's possible."

"Yes, we've discussed this a number of times. But is there an answer *to this question*?"

"Yes," I say.

"What is the answer, Alexios?"

"I don't know. But the answer exists. It's written on the answer sheet, of course."

"All right, then," Caroline says. I can hear the frustration beneath her words, though she is good at hiding it. She checks off that question and reads the next question off the projection that hangs in the air between us: "Your pet cat catches a bird and brings it into the house while it's still alive. You see that the animal is in pain—"

"The cat or the bird?"

"The bird. You see that the animal is in pain. . . ."

She stops.

"Is that it? There wasn't a question," I point out.

Caroline shakes her head. She scrolls through the remaining questions on the HEEP with a look of dissatisfaction. I know there are twenty-one more, and yet she does not continue.

I sense an opportunity and say, "Can we do the IQ test instead?"

"Yes, all right," she answers. The words are almost a whisper, but of course I hear them perfectly well.

The IQ test is so much better, because it is full of puzzles like this one:

What letter comes next in this sequence?

TTTFFS

The answer is naturally S, because the letters can be easily understood to stand for ten, twenty, thirty, and so on.

Here is my favorite type of question:

6236 = 2

7032 = 1

9516 = 2

8968 = 6

5367 = 1

3344 = 0

2005 = 2

6819 = 4

2984 = 3

7100 = ?

The answer to this one is 2, because the question is asking how many circles are in the number to the left. I enjoy this sort of puzzle, which demands that you must change your perspective away from the obvious. The test has hundreds more like this and of different kinds, which are almost as good.

We begin the IQ test, but after only a handful of questions (metaphor, by the way), Caroline is called from the room. She sets the tablet on the tray by my bed and lets me finish on my own.

While I answer the questions, I allow my mind to scramble and unscramble words in the background:

Genetic Radiance.

Ice teen cardigan.

Incinerated cage.

Aptitude tests.

Attitude pests.

I have just answered . . .

Six drinking glasses stand in a row, with the first three full of wine and the next three empty. By moving only one glass, can you arrange them so empty and full glasses alternate?

. . . when I notice that Caroline is in the hallway outside my room, speaking to someone.

"I'm afraid there's no change," Caroline is saying.

"None at all?"

I become slightly interested, because that is the voice of my mother! Her name is Philomena, and she visits the clinic from time to time. Sometimes she even brings a man called Paulos, who is my father, though it has been more than two years since I last saw him.

I continue with the test, because I very much want to beat my fastest time, but I am still listening to the conversation in the hall as I work. Caroline often forgets the strength of my mod for long-distance hearing. I can hear them out there, whispering, as well as I could if they were standing inside my room speaking at a normal volume.

"I thought you felt he was improving," my mother says. "The report from six months ago gave us the impression that, you know . . . there was reason to be optimistic."

There is a pause. After a time, Caroline says apologetically, "I hoped he would improve. Perhaps that report reflected my hope more than it should have. We were all so eager for improvement that small changes appeared much larger than they actually were. In reality, the only change we've been able to document over the long term has been a slight worsening in his empathy scores."

"But his intelligence . . ."

"IQ is still climbing," Caroline tells my mother. "That's a certainty. You have a very intelligent son. But not . . ."

". . . in any way that matters." My mother has finished Caroline's thought, it seems.

There is an uncomfortable feeling in my lungs, as if they are straining to get oxygen out of the air. My stomach is doing something odd as well. It is generating a feeling that is very like falling. I don't care for the words either of them is saying, and yet I cannot stop listening.

"He is very good at puzzles," Caroline says, as if this might be a consolation.

I can hear my mother sigh. Sighs, I have noticed, can mean a variety of things. Sometimes they communicate boredom, or monotony, or sorrow. This sigh strikes me as something more final than any of those feelings. "Thank you for your honesty," my mother says. "You know my husband and I were considering legal action. The promises that were made back in the embryo stage . . ."

"I didn't work for the clinic then, but I was brought on to evaluate the scientific basis for our genetic claims. In the most technical view, Genetic Radiance has delivered on its promises to you."

"In the most 'technical'—?"

"Philomena, IQ was what you listed on your questionnaire as the most important trait," Caroline says, "and in test after test, Alexios has shown us an IQ that is far above average. In a strict legal sense, the clinic has fulfilled its contract."

"But we were never told that—"

"That IQ is only a small piece of the picture? That being smarter does not make you kinder, or more interested in helping others, or even more useful? That these are inherent traits or sometimes learned traits? We broke new ground here, Philomena." Caroline uses my mother's first name to emphasize the friendliness of Genetic Radiance. "All of the patients in Alexios's generation surpassed the limits of scientific understanding. We are reevaluating the whole program."

"I'm—I'm relieved for others who are early enough in the process to make changes," my mother says, "but where does this leave me? I'm stuck with a child who will only use his brilliance to unscramble words and calculate how many humans could be fit into boxes of different sizes and how long messages from each nearby star will take to arrive. It doesn't seem to matter to him that there are no messages from nearby stars, and he will never be asked to fit any humans into boxes."

Caroline doesn't answer. I have stopped doing the puzzles. It is twilight outside, which means that the window in my room has become a mirror. Ordinarily, I cannot see myself in that window-mirror, but Caroline shifted my bed when she came to do the tests, and now I find myself staring across the room at my own reflection.

I am the size of a normal seven-year-old boy, if you are measuring by overall volume. The details of my proportions differ greatly from the average, however. My head is twice the size of a human adult's. The intelligence mods that Genetic Radiance tried out on me—when I was just a few hundred cells in a petri dish—resulted in a vastly increased brain and skull size. Their intention was that my head would be slightly larger than normal—within the upper range of what would appear natural—but that this modestly increased volume would allow me to develop ten times the ordinary number of neurons. They did not achieve ten times, but they were still, for many years, pleased with the extra capacity I'd been given. The problem, which became evident around my third birthday, was that my head was much, much larger than anticipated. The other problem, which Caroline eventually explained to me, was that I didn't seem to be using many of the extra neurons. I was employing a similar number to those existing inside an ordinary-sized brain.

And all of this came at the expense of the rest of my body. In the window, I can see my stunted legs, which dangle beneath my torso like the legs of a doll. I cannot stand on them, let alone walk. My arms are closer to the correct size, though they look huge because they hang down far below my shortened torso. I raise one of my arms, with a fist, toward the ceiling and shake it.

Curses and damnation.

Scan dread mountains.

Am Dad's uncertain son.

Caroline is continuing to speak to my mother in the hall, using soothing tones. "You will have to find a life for him. A job, something he will be able to do. There are options we could help you with. As Alexios grows, his mind can be directed."

My mother doesn't seem to be listening very attentively. She says, "Caroline, we could have conceived a child in the ordinary way. We changed our lives to do this, in order to give Alexios every advantage. In that first consult, we were told to imagine what his life would be like with intelligence far beyond ours. New humans were coming, and our children would be disadvantaged if we didn't do something."

"There was possibly some hype involved," Caroline admits.

"*Some* hype? He's dead weight. My son is dead weight, and will be for the rest of his life."

"Philomena, would you consider moving Alexios out of the United States? There's a program I'd like you to consider, run by a sister clinic in Greece. You're of Greek descent, aren't you? This could be perfect. . . ."

I can still hear them, but I choose not to. Nor do I wish to think about the modifications that came next, to my skin, to my eyes, to my legs, to allow me to live most of my life underwater. Instead, I recall the 60 percent of my attention that has strayed into the past and I lavish it upon Mr. Tavoularis in present time.

3. THE REQUEST

Mr. Tavoularis has finished making notes about the incident with the intruder. He rolls up his tablet, tucks it beneath his arm, and smiles at me.

"You did very well, Alexios," he says. He is leaning over slightly to make himself less imposing as he stares down at me in the pool. "As you know, Blessed Cures has many enemies. There are other consortiums all over the world who would pay dearly to know exactly what we are doing here, in the sea paddock you oversee for us."

Sea and oversee.

See oversea.

Same sounds, different meanings.

"And we are saving lives," I say, because I know that is what Mr. Tavoularis is about to say. He says it every time we speak. I sometimes imagine he says it even when he is alone.

"We are saving lives," he agrees, pleased. "Every chimera in the flock will rescue six to ten human beings who would otherwise die." Perhaps he assumes I do not see the obvious flaw in his logic: *If what we're doing is to save lives, why don't we share it freely with the world?* I do not ask this, though, because I'm not sure it matters.

Mr. Tavoularis says, "Now, Alexios . . ."

I know what's coming next. He will ask me about speaking with dolphins. No conversation with Mr. Tavoularis is complete without this line of questioning. The techs are now sitting cross-legged around the end of the pool. I feel them shift closer in anticipation.

"You're storing more vocabulary in the translator every week—you're documenting dolphin language very well, Alexios. And yet when you describe the encounter with the intruder, it sounds to me as though you don't use the translator anymore. Or rather, you use it to speak but not to understand. Is that right?"

He is under the impression that I relied on the translator when I first came to the sea paddock. The truth is, I never found its translations very accurate or useful until I began to program it myself.

I shrug. This has been my standard answer since I was three years old, whenever I haven't wanted to give someone a real explanation. But Mr. Tavoularis is not having it today. He clears his throat and asks, "Can you explain how this works, Alexios?"

He has asked me the same question, with almost the same wording, too many times to count. That is hyperbole. Truly, there is no such thing as "too many times to count," and I happen to know that he has asked me some version of this question forty-six times. He continues to ask because I have never given him much of an explanation. Dolphin communication is a puzzle, and like all puzzles, it becomes obvious once the pieces fall into place. Yet in this case, the process of allowing the puzzle pieces to fall into place must happen in your own mind, naturally; it is not something you can force. Explaining to Mr. Tavoularis will not make him truly grasp dolphin language. He would have to live with them to do that. Also, I don't know if I want him to grasp it.

"They don't communicate to me any differently than they do to each other," I say evasively.

"Can you elaborate on that?" Mr. Tavoularis asks. He is tenacious today. Looking from his mustache to his eyes, to his close-cropped hair, I see only a determined scientist. Perhaps he is getting pressure from his higher-ups. I will have to give him something.

I sigh and tell him, "They used words like *enemy* and *there*, words we have already identified. And to them I said words like *go* and *fast*. That's how we communicated when the intruder was there."

"Those are not a lot of words to achieve the complicated behavior of removing the camera from the man and then pushing him to shore."

"They have practiced those moves before," I point out.

"Not in exactly this way." His voice is growing stern. I am an unruly employee, or perhaps an unruly pet, in need of discipline. "Now, Alexios, how do they know what you mean, and how do you know what they mean?"

"We just know."

"But *how*?"

I could explain to him what I learned in my first month in the sea, when I was still learning to use my new legs and getting used to my new skin. I could tell him that dolphins are much more aware of each other than humans are, that dolphins speak with an understanding of context that is far deeper than humans', that dolphins have . . . not a hive mind, but perhaps a "group affinity" for which there are few parallels among humans, that dolphins know more than half of what is being said simply by where and how it is being said. I could explain this to him, but I don't want to. And even if I did, he would not really understand. Yet he is looking at me so expectantly, and the techs appear to be holding their collective breath, waiting for me to enlighten them.

Grudgingly, I choose a small piece of the puzzle to reveal, and I say to Mr. Tavoularis, "If a little kid pointed at a toy and said, 'Want,' you would know what he meant, wouldn't you?"

"Yes," Mr. Tavoularis agrees. "Please go on."

"It's like that with dolphins, except they're not pointing at one thing, they're gesturing, you could say, to everything. They know so much about the environment in which they're speaking. They know that they are in a location that's near where something else happened, they know that the water temperature is similar to the temperature during another important moment in their lives, they know that something dangerous or fun happened in a situation that resembles the current situation. And all of the other dolphins understand all of these things in the same way. So many words are not needed."

Mr. Tavoularis stares at me. I can see that he is resisting an urge to stroke his mustache. Possibly someone in his family has told him that this is a habit to be discouraged.

"But how do *you* know these things, Alexios?" he asks me at last.

"I don't know," I say.

Mr. Tavoularis stamps his foot lightly in frustration. The lab techs, who by now are leaning so close that they appear ready to fall into the pool, glance at each other, shocked by his lapse in control.

"I'm not mad," Mr. Tavoularis says quickly.

I think he is mad, because he has turned quite pink, but it doesn't matter. Anger comes and goes. I saw that at Genetic Radiance all the time.

Human emotions.

Oh, minute moans!

"Aren't there other people studying dolphins?" I ask him. "Can't you ask them about dolphin speech?"

"The ones who make their research public still know

almost nothing," Mr. Tavoularis answers, less angry now. At least he has regained his composure. "Anyone else is like us—researching privately in order to keep the value of what they learn in their own hands. You understand the concept of intellectual property, Alexios?"

"Yes," I say. It means knowing something and not letting anyone else know about it unless they pay you.

Mercenary.

Near mercy.

"Please think more about how you might articulate dolphin communication to the rest of us."

I don't answer, because I am doing what he says: I am thinking more about how to articulate dolphin communication to other humans.

"I don't mean right now," Mr. Tavoularis tells me, a trace of frustration in his voice again. "I mean over the next days and weeks. All right?"

I nod once. I have not said yes, but he is free to interpret my response however he pleases. My head is half floating, so nodding bobs my chin and mouth into the water. I am ready to go underwater completely and leave these people here. Some of the lab techs are getting to their feet. But Mr. Tavoularis is not done with me. He clears his throat again. I don't think he knows that he has this mannerism. Maybe one day a family member will find it as irritating as stroking his mustache and will suggest that he stop doing it.

"It's your birthday soon, Alexios."

"Yes, that's true." I don't think about weeks and months

when I'm underwater, but some part of my mind is always calculating them anyway. Today is the 413th day since I came to the paddock. I have heard people make comments like "It seems longer than a year!" and, conversely, "Time has just flown by!" but I never experience the passing of time in either of these ways. It is a steady, immovable thing.

Days in the sea cage: 413.

Days alive in this world: 4009.

"You know how old you are, don't you?"

"I'm turning eleven," I say.

"That's right."

Why Mr. Tavoularis's questions are so inconsistent is a mystery to me. He asks me to explain dolphin language and if I know what intellectual property is, and then he asks me if I can calculate my own age. Does he think living underwater washes away basic memories while leaving higher intellectual functions intact? That would be a hard theory to defend.

An idea occurs to me. "Can I have a present for my birthday?"

This causes Mr. Tavoularis to pause, as if he is surprised that I know about birthday presents. But I have personal experience of them, because Philomena brought me one a few times. "Perhaps," he answers. "What would you like?"

"I took pictures this afternoon with the camera." I nod toward the intruder's camera, which is sitting on the concrete nearby. "Can you make prints for me to keep in my habitat?"

"Well," Mr. Tavoularis says, relieved at the simplicity of the request, I think, "I'll see what can be done."

He gestures to a lab tech, who scoops up the camera and disappears into the clinic beyond the pool room. I do not like to think about the clinic's other rooms. My final skin modifications were done in one of them, and the memories are flashes of pain, the smell of iodine and alcohol, and the stinging, stinging, stinging of the new skin cells taking hold.

"While we take a look at your pictures, Alexios, you will have your lesson. It's long overdue."

"I don't care for my lessons," I say.

"So you are fond of telling me," he answers brusquely. "And yet your education is one of the stipulations of your employment here. As agreed to between Blessed Cures and your parents."

So, there will be no getting out of my lessons today. Perhaps my parents really are sitting in armchairs somewhere, reading reports about me. But I doubt it.

4. THE WORLD

"Frances will be teaching you today," Mr. Tavoularis tells me.

Usually I am given my lessons by Mr. Tavoularis himself, or by an older lab tech called Mark, both of whom are boring. He gestures at a young female lab tech whom I have seen only once before. She is placing a projector on the edge of the pool, but she looks at me when he introduces her.

"Hi, Alexios," she says. "I'm Frances."

"Yes," I say, since Mr. Tavoularis has just told me her name.

Mr. Tavoularis leans close to her to mutter a few final instructions, which I can hear perfectly well ("Make sure he actually answers your questions" and "If he acts like he doesn't understand—he does"), and then we are left alone in the high-ceilinged room with all the sunlight.

Frances seats herself cross-legged by the projector. She has dark hair that has been chopped off along one side and braided into strange curving patterns on the other. She has light brown skin and light brown eyes that stand out very brightly due to the large amount of black makeup she is wearing around them. She looks a lot younger than any of the other lab techs.

"Does Mr. Tavoularis think I need someone young to teach me?" I ask her. I have started to paddle myself slowly around the pool.

She says, "I'm on a work-study permit here. I'm supposed to be learning about special-needs instruction."

"Is that what I am? A special-needs student?" I ask. My eyes and ears are just above the surface as I glide along.

"Um . . . technically yes," she says, chewing thoughtfully at the corner of her thumb. "You live underwater. That's special, even though you're much smarter than most other people, which is, I guess, special in a totally different way."

There is no flattery in her voice. She is merely laying out the facts for me. This is proved when she adds, "Also no one else likes this part of the job, so they stuck me with it."

Blunt honesty.
The lost bunny.
Hotly bent sun.

I stop paddling and position myself upright in the water so I am looking directly at this Frances.

"Oh, do I have your attention now, Your Highness?" she asks. That is a joke, because I am aloof. Like a king, I suppose, though there haven't been kings in a very long time. Frances is not the first person to have noticed this about me. "That's good, because you haven't had a lesson in months, which means this could take forever."

Hyperbole. It is impossible for anything to last forever.

"I'm listening," I say. I am meant to have a lesson for at least half an hour each week, but I have successfully avoided it for a long time. "Can we do math?"

"No. You're better at math than I am, so there would be no point. We're doing history."

I say nothing. History is supposed to connect me to humanity, but the attraction of this goal is limited.

"You've been getting your history in random chunks, probably because Mr. Tavoularis doesn't want to explain everything to you," she says. "He told me to slowly bring you up to date, but considering everything that's happened in the last six months, it makes a lot more sense to start with current events, and then fill in from there."

This statement is not exactly intriguing, but it is, at least, not boring. She has dangled a mystery. Metaphor.

"What's happened in the last six months?" I reluctantly ask her. I notice that I have paddled slightly closer to her side of the pool.

"It's a mess, Your Highness," she says. "The world is splitting into two."

She switches on the projector and at once a full-color, three-dimensional video image springs to life above the water of the pool, looking real enough to touch. It shows me the United States Congress, which is immediately recognizable thanks to the words *United States House of Representatives,* which are written across the bottom of the image.

"You're probably thinking, 'This girl got saddled with me at the last minute and is just throwing this lesson together,' but you're wrong," Frances says, her vivid eyes fixed on the video image. "I put thought into what we should cover—what *I'd* want to know if I were you, Alexios." (I'm certain that the concept of what I, Alexios, would like to know has never occurred to Mr. Tavoularis. I am drawn in.) "Really there are three things to tell you. First, what's happening in the United States."

The image above the pool switches to a female reporter standing outside a white-domed building. Her feet seem to disappear into the pool water.

"Today, the United States passed a fourth human germline improvement bill," the woman says, "vastly expanding the list of approved permanent modifications—those that can be passed on through DNA to future generations—and the list of single-generation modifications that can be legally performed in the US."

Frances freezes the video.

"What has Mr. Tavoularis told you about modification in the US?" she asks me.

"Nothing," I tell her. But instead of lapsing into silence, I find myself saying more. "My first clinic was in the United States, though. I was never allowed outside there, but I know they do mods in the US, and the mods don't always work out the way people expect. They keep trying anyway."

Frances is chewing on her thumb and also looking at my body, which is mostly beneath the surface. "That's actually a pretty good summary. But I'll give you more detail that adds up to . . . well, you know." She gestures around her head in a way that is perhaps meant to encompass the whole world. "The first real mods were supposed to be for health. Rebuilding broken stuff and editing disease out of people."

"Mr. Tavoularis mentioned disease editing once," I say.

"So he's not totally useless. That's a relief." She gathers her thoughts. "There were big disease eradication programs, which means, at this point, most of the world has healthy DNA. Inherited diseases, infectious diseases, even things like tendency to get fat or bad eyesight—all gone, even when my parents were kids," she tells me. "And back then, people got into basic cosmetic mods—like this."

She pulls down the wide collar of her white medical shirt. Beneath, she is wearing a tank top, and across the light brown skin of her upper chest there is moving artwork, a dancing tattoo in white and black. A small egg hatches by her right shoulder, and out comes a tiny bird, which stumbles across her chest and then gains its footing and begins to fly. The bird appears to fly right out of her skin on the left side of her body, before reappearing in egg form on the other side and starting over again. I can tell that Frances is proud of the artwork and pleased to have an opportunity to display it.

"Have you ever seen one of these?" she asks. I shake my head, which is partially submerged, so that I send out ripples. "A moving tattoo is pretty easy to do, but when I was little—way before you were born—bigger cosmetic mods started to be possible. Like adding stuff to your body, stronger muscles, longer bones, different hair, wider eyes."

"Bigger brain?" I suggest.

Frances is looking at me and my big brain, floating in front of her. "Yeah, they tried that. Which brings me to the second thing. Do you know who this man is?"

She runs the video again, and now it shows us an eye-catching image of a man standing behind a golden lectern. The lectern is decorated with up-stretched golden limbs—human arms, the fins of fish, the legs of dogs and horses, the tentacles of an octopus, and so on, all reaching ecstatically toward the man.

We cannot hear the man himself but instead are listening to an announcer, who speaks the way most announcers do—in a tone that never changes whether it is reporting on a successful birth or the destruction of a city. She is saying, "The Seekers of Evolutionary Advancement—known to many as the SEA—announced today that the daily broadcasts by the Reverend Tad Tadd now reach a billion and a half people each week."

Frances mutes the video, leaving the man orating silently in the air above the pool. "You've heard of him, right?"

"Yes," I answer, interested despite myself. "Caroline at Genetic Radiance showed me a few videos. He's an American religious figure. This video is more recent, though. He looks different."

The Reverend Tadd still has wavy black hair on one side of his head and lighter, curlier hair on the other, also one green eye and one black eye, but he has done something new to his skin, so each arm is a different color. His right arm has skin that is so dark brown as to be close to black; his left is a rich reddish brown, like mahogany wood. And his hands—they are an odd shade of light green, as if they've leached the color out of plant leaves.

The Reverend Tadd's vast audience, hovering above the surface of the water, is cheering and clapping, displaying in their ranks much strange and varied coloration, and even odder characteristics like extra fingers and bulky solar collectors built right into their skin.

Frances examines the thumb she has been chewing, and then she narrows her bright eyes at the image of the Reverend Tadd. "Um, the weird thing about him is that he started out religious, and also pretty mean, but so many people were interested in modification that he ended up bringing groups together that you wouldn't expect to get along. Like scientists and flat Earthers and human rights people."

The video changes to footage of a huge march with the same white-domed building in the background. Thousands of people are moving together—men on motorcycles with ink over every inch of their skin, people in long robes holding up crosses, children in wheelchairs, a group of women with decorative scarring all over their faces. Many carry signs that say some version of *Human Freedom Now!* and near the front of this march is a younger version of the Reverend Tadd, holding hands with a woman in a doctor's lab coat and a man in judicial robes.

Frances pauses the video and says, "And this brings us to the third thing, probably the most important thing. You saw Reverend Tadd's audience. Whole-body moving tattoos, extra fingers, tiny motors under the skin. The more doctors can do, the more people want. Now scientists can even make human tissue using cells grown from millet crops."

"What's millet?" This is the sixth question I have asked in this lesson—possibly a record.

"It's a grain, kind of like wheat. Engineered versions can produce cells for modding people. Farmers are planting it all over the prairie states. But where are we supposed to draw the line?" She is not asking me this question. It is a mere rhetorical flourish, and she accompanies it with an aggressive nibble along the side of her thumb.

"Do you know who this is?" she asks as she changes the video feed to the image of a woman who looks about fifty years old.

Before I can answer, the announcer is saying, "I spoke today to Elsie Tadd, the Reverend Tadd's daughter, whose message of Natural Humanity—an opposition movement to her father's beliefs—is reaching hundreds of millions of people around the world."

Frances pauses the image so the woman is frozen above the water. She is in extreme close-up, so her head looks huge.

"At Genetic Radiance, I saw a video of her when she was a young girl," I say.

"She had to listen to her father back then," Frances says. "Not anymore."

I am interested to study this child of the famous Reverend Tadd. Like her father, Elsie Tadd has mismatched eyes and multicolored hair, but apart from these features, she looks like an old-fashioned human. And unlike her father, Elsie Tadd is not trying to make herself look younger than she is. She is aging in the normal way.

When Frances rolls the video again, Elsie Tadd is gesturing at her face. She is saying, "I keep these eyes and this hair as marks of humility. An example of what we're fighting against—frivolous, self-aggrandizing manipulation of our species. We're struggling in the United States, but we're being heard across Eastern Europe and Asia."

Disaffected daughter.

Farsighted feud cadet.

"Some people are literally drawing lines, Alexios."

Startling footage appears above the pool. Soldiers are herding citizens in a great mass before them, using batons and tear gas when they encounter any resistance. The people flee in utter panic, some falling to be trampled by the oncoming mass. I can tell the soldiers are Russian by the insignia on their caps.

"This latest purge aims to rid the Russian Republic of any so-called modification apologists, those who support modifying the human genome beyond the curing of disease," the announcer says. "To remain in Russia, citizens are now required to take an Oath of Principle, committing themselves to 'the simplicity of the human form. . . .'"

The soldiers are pursuing the stampede of terrified citizens toward a distant border fence, when Frances pauses the video. "Do you understand what that means?"

"Russia is kicking out people who like to modify themselves," I say.

"Yes, and scientists who work in that field, and college professors who discuss it in their lectures, and their families."

"When did this happen?"

"This last purge? Just after the new law passed in the US. But the purges have been going on for years, in one form or another."

She plays the video again, and in a moment it switches to a new footage, this of Russian soldiers marching and driving tanks through the streets of several old-looking cities.

The announcer says, "Russian troops are occupying the capitols of Latvia, Estonia, and Lithuania, with the stated purpose of 'restoring order.' The Russian foreign minister has described these democracies as 'teetering on the brink of civil war' amid political, religious, and grassroots disagreement about access to modern medical therapies. Russia has stepped in, the foreign minister says, 'to protect the future of their citizens.' The governments of several European countries and the United States are convening an emergency summit. . . ."

She turns down the volume.

"It's not enough for Russia to make rules for itself," Frances tells me. "They've taken over other countries to make sure their neighbors are following Russian rules as well. Europe is neutral on modification, and even they are separating themselves from Americans and restricting trade and travel." She sounds troubled.

"I studied Rome and the Middle Ages at Genetic Radiance," I tell her. "And World War I and II. History is full of invasions and clashing philosophies. Why are you upset about this particular version?"

I seem to have gotten under Frances's skin with that question. (Metaphor.) She gets to her feet and peers down into the pool at me, her outlined eyes, her dark hair, her ragged fingernails suddenly menacing. For a moment, I have the idea that she wants to jump into the water and shake me, but if so, she restrains herself.

Self-control.

Tell of scorn.

"I'm upset," Frances says, with forced calm, "because this is happening *now.* Mr. Tavoularis doesn't tell you about recent events because he's happy to keep your mind in the sea cage. But this is not ancient history, Alexios."

I expect she has a valid point, though I am having trouble

seeing it. "So Russia doesn't modify people?" I ask. Question number nine.

"They don't want people to stop looking human, but they do mechanical and robotic add-ons for their military. So . . ." She shrugs. "I've never been to Russia to see any of it in person."

A piece of the Frances puzzle falls into place then. "You're American?" I ask. I have finally noticed the way she pronounces certain words.

"I have English citizenship now," she tells me defensively.

I do not want to be interested in Frances's life, but I am. "Why did you leave?"

Frances drums her fingers against her leg, gathering her thoughts. Clearly we have strayed off the lesson's path. (Metaphor.) She has rubbed her left eye and smudged her dark makeup, which makes that eye look even brighter. "My parents said Americans were pretending to respect nature, but really they were exploiting it. So we came to Europe, where you can get mods if you really want them, but things are tamer."

A strange question occurs to me and I am asking it before I realize what I am doing. "Would your parents think that I shouldn't exist? That I'm dead wei—"

"Of course they wouldn't think that, Alexios!" She sounds angry now. "But if you'd been given the choice at the beginning, is this what you would have chosen?"

I do not have an answer for that.

"It's more than all the mods, though," she says. "Since the law changed, people in the US are moving into cities. There's a huge tax if you want to live outside a city wall. They're with-drawing from the countryside to leave it pure—for visiting, they say. But I think it's because when you change your body drastically, you have to be in a city so you're close to help if anything goes wrong—like if your new skin starts to peel off or your extra hand seizes up. Russia is starting to mine the solar system, and Americans are going to be getting their unicorn horns polished and designing children with claws and rainbow auras."

I stare at Frances and she stares back. We are both think-ing, I am sure, that whatever a rainbow aura is, it doesn't sound too bad. But Frances sighs. "It was too much for my parents, so we left."

"Was it too much for you?" I ask her. It is rare that I ask such a personal question, because there is no reason for me to care, and yet I am curious to hear her answer.

Frances shrugs and nibbles at her thumb. "Maybe."

I understand that my official lesson is over and she has told me far more than Mr. Tavoularis ever would have. I could request that she send me back to the paddock, but I don't.

"Tell me about the strangest mods you've ever seen," I say.

Frances has no objection. She seats herself at the pool's edge and speaks to me about a man with a tail and a woman with a third eye, and another woman who had mirrored skin so she was almost invisible in certain lighting. None of those mods looked natural, she explains, but someday they might. I listen to her as I float around the pool on my back, staring up at the whitewashed ceiling and calculating how many lab techs it would take to completely cover it so none of its surface was showing. I am also wondering if I will ever sit in the audience at one of the Reverend Mr. Tadd's sermons. Would they wheel out a special saltwater tank for me? The idea is humorous but irrelevant. The Reverend Tadd, his daughter Elsie, the whole world Frances has been telling me about . . . these things feel as remote as the moon.

Land-based problem.

Old bedpans ramble.

And yet I see now that I am not merely Alexios, boy from the Genetic Radiance clinic who now lives at Blessed Cures. I am, in fact, a product, a piece, of the greater world. Mr. Tavoularis's version of history is as clinical as the clinic he works in. But I am a person in Frances's story.

5. THE PICTURES

My own habitat is underwater, built into the end of the jetty. There is a door in the bottom so I can swim up into the pressurized interior and then pull myself all the way inside with the special sling rigging the lab techs have built for me. From the conveyor belt, I return to the sea paddock and then to my habitat, in time for the afternoon meal. I could have eaten inside the clinic, but I do not like the way the lab techs watch me chew and swallow, as if they are planning to make a medical diagram of the process later.

My habitat is one spherical room, which I navigate from

the rigging. Using rungs on the walls, I can pull the sling wherever I need it to take me, and it slides about on a track in the ceiling. There is not much space to navigate: I have a small desk and colored markers, in case I would like to write something down or, I suppose, draw pictures. I have a video screen for speaking to Mr. Tavoularis and the lab techs and for recording my observations of the flock and the dolphin pod. There is a bathtub for washing myself, a toilet, and a tap of fresh water for drinking. My food is delivered by its own small conveyor belt, direct from the clinic's kitchen, and it arrives through a slot in the back wall. There is no bed, because I and my Frankenstein limbs sleep in the sling. Everything is damp, but it has been made for the damp. My new legs and new skin prefer the damp.

Dinner arrives shortly after I get back, and next to the tray of food is a large envelope full of pictures, printouts from my afternoon with the camera. I look through them as I eat my turkey and mashed potatoes. This is my favorite meal, by the way, especially when it comes with cranberry sauce, which it does today. There are also two glasses of what looks like gray sludge, which doesn't taste as terrible as you might think, because the flavor of apple pie has been added to mask all the other flavors—of medicine, of vitamins, of cell-boosting concoctions that will feed the dolphin parts of me. In all it is a kind of Thanksgiving meal.

I am a chimera.

Aim, aim, reach!

I do not appreciate the food fully today, though, because at least eighty percent of my attention is on the pictures. I made portraits of each of the dolphins and each of the manatees, and I am pleased that every creature is clearly recognizable. These portraits I arrange in a long line around the habitat's curving wall with the sticky putty that the lab techs stock in my habitat, which lets me decorate even though things are wet. After the portraits, I took pictures of the amusement park, and of every type of seaweed that can be found in the paddock. There are twenty-seven varieties, by the way, and I arrange the pictures of them by size and color. When this begins to feel too obvious, I rearrange the seaweeds by percentage of the paddock they occupy, and then I try a few other sorting methods, including the order in which I first noticed them. Eventually I am satisfied and I stick them to the wall below the dolphins.

Five percent of my attention is on my hands as I work. Delicate work like this reminds me that my fingers are thicker than they used to be. They have become that way as they've become gray, because the rubbery skin takes up more room. Yet I am still able to grasp the pictures and hold a pen, and do all manner of hand-related activities. My fingernails, though, are little more than slivers at the top of each finger. Soon they will be gone entirely. I am not bothered by this, but I occasionally wonder if I should be.

Vanishing Alexios.

Exhaling is so vain.

In the pile are a few pictures of the clinic, which I took by sticking my head above water. In one of these pictures, several lab techs can be seen eating lunch together on an outdoor patio.

One of the techs in the picture, I notice, is Frances. I put this picture above the manatees, not because I care to look at the lab techs, but because they are one of the life forms, like seaweed and dolphins, that live in my world. I am being thorough.

A funny feeling comes over me when I get to the bottom of the stack, as though I have eaten something bad. The very last pictures are three of me, Alexios. I had forgotten about those, and now, looking at them, I am baffled as to why I took them. There is no mirror in my habitat, just as there was no mirror in my old room at the Genetic Radiance clinic. I do not care to see myself. And yet, here are these three images. One is a close-up of my head. The other two are of my whole body, floating near the amusement park. To take those, I set the camera on the very highest point of the Ferris wheel and used the camera's timer. Why? Thoroughness again?

I shrink from my image.

And yet I cannot take my eyes off these photographs. They hold me in place, pin me to them.

All figures of speech.

There I am, big, gray head, with bulging eyes to accommodate underwater sight. Short torso, long arms. Legs that, when held together, resemble a dolphin's lower body, but when moving appear to be two long gray paddles. And above them is the only article of clothing I wear, a pair of underwear like a wetsuit, as gray as my body, to give me some human modesty.

There is Alexios. I imagine fitting two of me into a rectangular box and I try to calculate the best positions to use. This is made difficult by the size of my head. If there were three of me, though, and a larger box, I could come up with a satisfactory solution.

Three monsters.

Stern theorems.

Ten storms here.

If I were to put these pictures on the wall, in which row would I place myself? With the seaweed? With the lab techs? With the underwater mammals? Instead, I lay the self-portraits across my desk. The world through a camera lens is a different world. Is Frances a kind of camera lens? I cannot explain how, but merely speaking with her has altered the look of things.

My dinner is finished. I swing across the room to stuff the tray back into its slot. It is time to get back to work.

6. THE OCEAN

Above the sea paddock, the sun is going down. It has crossed from Greece to Italy and is heading west. This is another figure of speech, personification. The sun is an inanimate object, stationary relative to the Earth. We are the ones moving, at 1,037 miles per hour at the equator—though it is more like 800 miles per hour here in Greece (if I knew our exact location, I would have a better number, but as it is, I can only estimate).

Estimations.

Time is a snot!

Nevertheless, there is still plenty of light. The flock of

chimeras has moved closer to land, as they do each day at this time, brought in by the tide, you might say, though it would be metaphor since there is hardly any tide here, toward the warmer water inshore.

It takes only a few moments to locate Snake, who is snuffling through the red seaweed near the center of the flock. Snake is fully grown, but shorter than the average adult manatee. He makes up for this with his huge girth. He is nearly twice as fat as most of his flockmates. More beach ball than blimp. So "Snake." Irony.

The flock grunts and chirps as I glide above them. I am carrying a head of lettuce in one hand, and this captures their attention. Manatees love the taste of lettuce—the seaweed of the land—and yet it has a dramatically polarizing effect on the flock. The ones who've had organs removed are shuffling away—not so fast as to attract my attention, but fast enough that in a few moments they have dispersed into the darkening water. The manatees who have never been to the surgery pod are floating eagerly toward me.

You see, the lettuce is the lure, the enticement, the way I get them into surgery. After a few operations, I have to use something better, like bananas. But this is Snake's first time and he grunts with surprise and ecstasy when I scratch his back—out of the whole flock, I have come to him! I peel off a lettuce leaf and watch it disappear into his mouth. Through the translator, I say, "Follow!" and he does, gobbling up the lettuce that I strew, bread crumbs through the twilight forest. Metaphor.

As we swim, I notice all seven dolphins gathered some distance away, observing. They understand the sequence of events beginning with lettuce and ending with an injured manatee who smells of blood and humans, and like fair-weather sports fans they want to watch but also keep the process at arm's length. That is simile and metaphor, but I don't need to keep telling you, do I?

The surgery pod resembles an old-fashioned submarine without any windows. Like my habitat, it can be entered from below by sea-based visitors. The doctors enter from above, by means of a ramp from the jetty.

Food, food, food, food, Snake says, executing a stately rotation to get closer to the head of lettuce.

"Food," I agree, through the translator.

I have lured manatees here ninety-seven times, and yet this evening I notice particularly how easy the job is. When I press the button above our heads, there is the immediate sound of a steel door sliding open. Snake glances up, his sunken eyes regarding the alien structure above us.

"Food," I say again, tearing off half the lettuce.

As the door comes fully open, I can see two doctors and several lab techs in the pressurized pod above, peering down through the surface of the water. The sling is already dropping, and as Snake eats the last of the lettuce, I secure the straps around his body.

Food, food, food? Snake inquires, looking this way and that for more lettuce. But he has eaten it all.

With a creaking whine, the winch engages. The sling tightens around Snake's body as it hoists him upward.

Play? he asks me, noticing the pressure of the thing. There is no fear in his small eyes, because Snake was born in the paddock and has spent his life here. He has no reason to be afraid.

I do not answer him. He is trying to move his flippers, but his body is already half out of the water. To me, he looks distorted where his body breaks the surface, so that the top half of him is tiny, the bottom half far too big. He is passing from his own world into another, where humans and gravity hold sway. Up there, he isn't Snake. He is only Chimera624, property of the Blessed Cures Consortium. If I were to examine the Consortium's books, would I find myself listed as property too?

Snake is fully inside, and a lab tech leans down and gives me a thumbs-up.

All is well here.

We'll raise hell.

For a moment I have a view of the sling carrying Snake toward the stainless-steel operating table, but the door is sliding shut, and I turn away. A heart and pancreas will be removed, and Snake will not even realize he is missing them. He will leave the surgery pod with only stitches and an unfocused sense of dread.

Several manatees are still floating hopefully nearby, searching for lettuce.

Food, food, food? they ask as I swim among them.

There is no manatee word for *no* as far as I can tell. There is only majestic disregard, so this is how I answer them, by floating solemnly away. I am thinking of the six people I saw in the surgery pod, and calculating how many copies of each I would have to make to fill the pod entirely. The answer varies depending on whether I leave room for Snake. I have a strong feeling that I would rather not leave room. In this imaginary scenario, can I not envision him swimming freely, untouched by human hands?

I float aimlessly for a time, until I have an answer: Fifty-one. That's how many of those doctors and lab techs it would take to entirely fill the surgery pod. Several of them would have to be cut into smaller pieces to fill in the nooks and crannies, but that's often the case.

True twilight has crept through the paddock, bringing shadows and mystery. Is this a figure of speech? The answer is not always as clear as I make it out to be. Caroline, at Genetic Radiance, is the one who explained figurative language to me. "It is the language of imagination," she said. "It lets us describe the ordinary world in unexpected ways."

Tonight, what I see is this: the evolution of language is toward metaphor. Hundreds of years ago, if someone said "I burn with desire!" that would have been metaphor. Now, you can find that imaginative definition nailed down, in prosaic detail, in any dictionary. I know because I have been given access to twelve dictionaries. We have taken the imagination and made it routine.

The brush of fate.

The tempest in her eyes.

The dagger in my heart.

All once figures of speech, and yet all tied down, beaten down, by lexicographers. Over time, our speech has become increasingly figurative. Does that mean that humans, as a race, have allowed imagination and beauty to infiltrate their lives with each passing generation? Or have they destroyed imagination and beauty by capturing and codifying them? In which case—am I the final result? Am I a metaphor, an irony, embodied and made ordinary?

The manatees who ran away when I took Snake are now coming back, grunting *hello* as they work their way toward their favorite twilight sea grass bed. Bluebear swims toward me, but then I perceive unpleasant thoughts crossing his mind: *lettuce, play, follow, stomach, ouch.* He thinks better of it and veers away to settle onto the seabed with the others. He will forget by tomorrow, but for now I am tainted by association with the one source of pain in his protected world.

How do I know what has crossed Bluebear's mind? I told Mr. Tavoularis that "I just do," that I know what they are thinking because I live with them. But it occurs to me: I was given a bigger head and extra neurons that I didn't use when I lived on a bed in the Genetic Radiance clinic. Am I using them now? Have they formed, inside my misshapen skull, alternate pathways of consciousness for this underwater world?

Dolphin brain.

I, blind orphan.

I have drifted into the kelp forest, which is little more than slender, looming shapes on every side of me in the low light, when a chorus of clicks and chirps erupts in the distance. Immediately, the noise grows louder—the dolphin pod is swimming toward me at full speed. I blink twice, to bring

my nighttime vision into play. It is a modification I use spar-
ingly, because it turns the ocean into an unnatural seascape
of bright white and takes away most of my depth perception.
But I am thankful for it now, as I see the seven dolphins,
materializing from the darkness around me, screeching in
agitation.

Enemy, enemy, enemy! Human! Many!

Loud Mike swims close, and the moment I have taken hold
of his dorsal fin, we are off. In my night vision, the ocean is a
blur of highlights. We pass from the kelp forest, by the Ferris
wheel, and then we are approaching the net. The mesh appears as contrasting streaks of bright and dark, and just as the
dolphins warned me, there are three human intruders floating
on the other side.

Enemy, enemy, enemy! Loud Mike tells me.

The dolphins, who can perceive the world almost as well in
the night as in the day, because of their echolocation, are never
quite sure what I'm able to see, and Loud Mike is counting the
intruders for me.

I have unhooked my stunner and am raising it toward
them when the three figures on the other side of the net do
something unexpected. They turn on a light and point it not at
us but at themselves. They flare so brightly in my night vision
that I have to shut my eyes and turn away.

Then a voice travels through the water, speaking English.

"We're here for you," it says.

How can they speak underwater? I double-blink, returning
my eyes to normal vision.

"Will you speak to us?" comes the voice again, piercing and eerie.

In the light of their lamp, I see that the closest man is wearing something around his neck, and it is this apparatus that is speaking to me. By their body language, all three are telling me, *Look, we're not enemies. We are showing ourselves to you!*

My stunner is aimed at them, but my fingers hesitate on the trigger. One of the men holds a camera, which was pointed in the direction of the surgery pod until a moment ago, but which is now pointed at me. The other two men have empty hands.

Empty hands.

Many depths.

"We are here for you," the closest one tells me again through the device.

In response, I raise my weapon.

"Wait! Wait!" he says.

I am not supposed to wait. But for some reason, tonight, I do.

"Where is our friend?" he asks.

I could point upward, telling them that the man who came to the paddock earlier is up in the world of air and land, but I don't know for sure that this is true. The Blessed Cures Consortium might be interrogating their friend right now, or he might be walking free back to whichever consortium he works for, or he might be dead and floating in the sea.

My pod of dolphins chirps questioningly, *Go? Take? Enemy?*

The man with the voice box is holding his hands up in a

placating gesture. His eyes, behind his goggles, are fixed on my weapon, and yet he beckons me closer.

"We can take you," he says. "Give you a better life than what you have here. Give you dignity."

So. They have not come merely to steal the Blessed Cures Consortium's industrial secrets of manatee husbandry and dolphin instruction. They have come to steal me.

"We can help you," the intruder says.

He has floated closer to the net. Through his goggles, his eyes are imploring me.

Loud Mike nudges my shoulder. The other dolphins are chirruping anxiously. This is not what we've practiced.

All three intruders float up to the net, three sets of eyes pinned to me.

I imagine myself as viewed through their eyes. Gray, rubbery, a jellyfish-like head, with the rest of me dangling below. At best, a vassal to the Blessed Cures Consortium; at worst, a slave.

If I were to go with them, where would they take me? To another underwater habitat, owned by some other company for whom I would wrangle dolphins? To a research laboratory, where they could pick apart the modifications made by Genetic Radiance? To a human rights group, who would put me on the video feeds as a victim of scientific arrogance?

Human monstrosity!

Man mounts history!

"Please," the intruder tells me with his eerie, mechanical voice. "Come with us."

I pull the trigger of my stunner. Then I aim methodically at the other two men, pulling the trigger twice more. Six torpedoes launch toward the net.

The intruders, blinded by their own lamp, do not see the missiles heading for them and they disperse only at the last moment, when it is too late. In the time it takes me to reach the net, all three men convulse into limpness, until their arms trail behind them and bubbles trickle from their mouths.

I slice the net with my special knife. The dolphins are ecstatic, chittering all around me as I work. *Yes, yes, yes! Excitement! Win, win, win!* When I have created a large opening, I send out the signature whistle of the entire pod:

"Everyone! Go take!"

All eight of us swim through the net to the unconscious intruders. But as I get close to the limp forms, I understand that I have misread the situation. They are not all incapacitated. The third intruder, the one near the camera, is starting to move.

Look! chirps Loud Mike.

The third man kicks free of the other two, with whom he had become tangled. He turns toward the approaching dolphins, and he raises a dish-shaped device.

And then . . .

. . . the world hiccups.

It is as though something travels through the water toward us, past us. A wave of force tickles through me.

The dolphins shriek in unison, a high series of squeals that I have never heard before but that plainly mean *Pain! So much pain!*

The man fires at us again, and I feel the second wave glide through me. My ears pop, while the dolphins go into a renewed frenzy of screeching. It is a sonic weapon of some kind, attacking their acute sense of hearing. And while they are immobilized, he is swimming toward me, a cylinder in his right hand. I know it—it is an underwater syringe. He is going to take me.

In my surprise, I have let my weapon float away to the end of its tether. The man has closed the distance and grabs my arm. I kick him with a flipper, but he pays this no mind—my legs allow me to swim, but they are not an effective means of attack. He reaches the syringe toward my neck, while behind me I can hear Loud Mike saying, *Ouch, ouch, ouch!*

I am infused with a sensation I have not experienced before. I do not want the dolphins to be hurt. And also, this: I hate this man.

More than that:

I am afire with rage!

I burn with indignation!

I glow with fury!

Launching myself forward, I push the syringe away, grab for his throat. The man struggles. He is weak. I see now that a single torpedo is lodged in his chest. He avoided the electrical shock, but he is still wounded. My hands close around his neck.

I boil with vengeance!

He kicks at me with his artificial flippers, pressing me away. I yank the tether of my stunner, pulling it toward me, wrap my hand around the weapon, and then I shoot him from a distance of two feet. There is no getting away this time.

He spasms and jitters, a marionette beneath invisible hands. When he goes limp, the syringe and his sound weapon sink slowly toward the ocean floor.

What was their plan? To disable the dolphin guards, slip through the net, and capture me? Capture me and the chimeras? Capture all of us, including the dolphins? Re-create the sea paddock somewhere else, under their own control?

I now understand the wisdom of the Blessed Cures Consortium keeping intruders. If no scout ever returns to their competitors, then the next set of intruders will be equally unprepared.

"Go take!" I say to the dolphins.

They have recovered from the shock of the man's weapon, but they will not overlook what he did. They twist their bodies angrily as they sweep up to the three floating men, and they use more force than is strictly necessary to prod and push the intruders toward the island.

When we reach its nighttime shore, I surface, blink my eyes, and then crawl up the sand. Flippers are not made for land, but I can move by scooting backward, inching myself up the beach. From there, I help haul the men above the line of wet sand—safe, if they are still alive, until someone comes for them. Then I sit for a while, feeling the evening breeze.

Come, come, come? the dolphins ask, their heads bobbing above the surface, their bright eyes watching me on the shore.

I hold up one hand, which is an answer they understand: *Wait.*

The tops of my habitat and the surgery pod, the jetty, and

the line of net enclosing our cove are all that are visible of the paddock from up here. Across the water, the clinic is lit with its nighttime security lights, and it is quiet, closed up. Someone will be on duty, but most of the lab techs, and certainly Mr. Tavoularis himself, have gone home for the night. It is pleasant to breathe without the rebreather for a few minutes, sitting on the beach. But already my skin is tightening, beginning to itch.

I send up a flare, and then I scoot back into the water. The dolphins are around me as I sink into the cool embrace of the ocean. I blink my eyes into underwater vision, and as I float away from the island, I look past the net, the loose flaps of which are billowing this way and that in the current, to the paddock enclosure beyond. My habitat. The clinic. The world of land and air. Bluebear and the manatees. It is strange to observe these things from above the water and then to observe them again, immediately, from below.

You should see what is there, no matter how you look, and yet that is not always so. The point from which one views something . . . is everything.

Instead of the paddock, what I am seeing at this moment is a multiple-choice question, written in neon letters across the inner reaches of my skull:

A boy is designed to be extra smart, but the procedure goes wrong. He is then given dolphin skin and legs and sent to spend his life tricking manatees into surgery. Is this boy:

A) human

B) inhuman

C) dead weight

D) something else

I know the answer at the back of the book is either B or C. My mother picked C, and Mr. Tavoularis, if pressed, would probably pick B.

Turning my head in the other direction, I peer into the darkness of the open ocean: predators, prey, known and unknown.

And here I am: lungs, rebreather, flippers, hands. I am meant for both places and for neither.

This is something you learn when you have taken hundreds of tests: The person who wrote the test has selected one answer as truth. If you don't choose that answer, you are marked as having chosen wrong. And yet, as the test taker, you still get to select which answer you believe is correct. It is your option, always, to see the answer differently from anyone else.

Do you see that

dead weight

can become

eight waded?

Because there are eight of us, seven dolphins and whatever I am. We have waded to the island and now we are drifting back into the depths of the sea.

I wonder: How do I wish to live?

The answer is not: As a normal person.

Because that has never been possible.

It could be that the answer is this: Differently.

Do I wish to be the boy in the room in the Genetic Radiance clinic or the boy in the sea cage?

Answer: Maybe I don't wish to be either of those things.

Practical question: Is there a choice in the matter?

Answer: Probably not.

And yet: Is there more to Alexios that what has been living contentedly in the sea paddock?

Answer: Maybe.

Perhaps the best question is this: Would I like to find out?

Play, play, play, play? ask Loud Mike and Shark Girl. They are rolling and twisting, proud to have washed their hands of those painful men. Metaphor. I will stop pointing it out.

The other dolphins are copying them, so they are a mass of elegant, circular motion. *Win! Win! Win!* one of them says.

Loud Mike swoops in front of me, allowing me to grab onto him. I do, feeling something new in the touch of my hands along his fin.

When I have taken a firm hold, I do not say "play." Instead, tilting my body toward the open ocean, I tell them, "Run!"

A moment later, as one, all eight of us are rushing, rushing, rushing into the darkness together.

Into the sea

    becomes

        no hesitate.

So I won't. And here we go.

Youth is wholly experimental.

—Robert Louis Stevenson

We are definitely in the future now. . . .

PART FIVE

CALIFORNIA

1. SNOWSTORM

It happened so quickly that Jake didn't realize they'd been spotted until the men were already surrounding them—this was only moments after he and Kostya had crawled through a jagged opening in the chain-link fence that marked the perimeter of the industrial landing site. Maybe they'd drawn attention because, in the middle of what looked like a snowstorm, they were wearing only the shirtsleeves and baggy pajama bottoms and thin knit caps they'd stolen from the crew quarters on the ship. No, Jake saw as he looked at Kostya, who was dodging the men's grasping arms, it was their skin that had given them away. Kostya's terror at being in Russia again was overwhelming his skin supply. His hands were melting back into themselves under the strain, revealing metal and crystal beneath. As two men got hold of Kostya, things got worse: his metal skull began to appear beneath the hem of his hat, and his brow was now glinting in the streetlights.

Chyort voz'mi! Dammit! Jake swore in his head in Russian as he tried to elude the other three men. American swears didn't feel real anymore. The bosses had been yelling at him for God knew how long, and now nothing sounded strong enough unless it was in Russian.

The men were crying *"Zakhvatit' eti katorzhniki,"* which Jake's mind translated automatically into "Grab these convicts!" and then the men—tall, bearded, massive in their winter coats—succeeded in grabbing Jake as well.

He and Kostya made eye contact: *Now!*

Jake deployed his secondary left arm with the knife clutched in the small hand. He felt the weapon bite into a man's flesh.

"*Chyort voz'mi!* Dammit!" the man hissed, letting go of Jake.

Kostya wrenched himself out of the other men's grasp in the same way. With one more glance at each other, to confirm their commitment, they ran in opposite directions, through the heavily falling snow, faster than anyone should be able to run. This had been their simple plan if they were spotted—surprise and sudden flight.

Jake hadn't expected to need the plan so soon after arriving; they'd waited for night to fall before stealing off the ship and venturing out into whatever Russian city this was, in the hopes of finding deserted streets, but the city, which enclosed the landing site in a tight grip, was alive and rowdy. On the crowded sidewalks, he had to slow down as he pushed past knots of pedestrians hunched against the driving snow.

At the corner, he turned back once. Kostya was well away in

the other direction, hidden among the crowds. The man Jake had cut stood in the distance, clasping his arm as it bled. The snow, marred by footprints, looked green beneath the nighttime security lights by the high metal fence, and the man's blood looked brown. So many colors after the darkness on the ship. The other men who'd tried to capture them were yelling to each other in frightened, delighted, wicked excitement— *Convicts? From where? I've never seen that kind before. I imagined they'd be stronger. But they're like children.*

We *are* children, Jake thought as he ran. The Russian bosses weren't stupid. They didn't want their mine slaves able to attack them. So Jake and Kostya and all the others still back in the camps in the distant void of outer space were as weak as kittens if they tried to resist normal people. Only one of Jake's full-sized arms could exert any force against a human— and that was a lucky accident of improper maintenance by the bosses. The secondary arms they'd used to get away from their attackers were feeble limbs, made for delicate work and useless without a weapon.

Jake's feet sank through the snow—it was fluffy on top, where the fresh layer was settling, slushy beneath where the old snow lay. People followed him with their eyes, because his hands and feet were bare. They were still covered in skin, though, and his secondary arms were folded up against his ribs and hidden beneath his shirt, so as long as Jake kept moving, it would be hard to tell that he was different. And Kostya— hopefully his friend had gotten control of his skin and it was growing back over his metallic hands and forehead.

Jake shoved through a group of men who were singing and drinking and blocking the sidewalk. When an alley opened up on his right, he slowed, hunched over, and then crept into the shadows between buildings.

This alley let out into a longer alley, mostly covered in snow, which ran along the back of a city block. It was very dark here except for the small amount of light that filtered haphazardly between buildings. The darkness didn't matter; Jake's eyes could see in both glaring sunlight and near-total blackness.

Come on, you *chertovski rab*! You damned slave! he snapped at himself. Focus. Find clothing!

A man was sprawled outside a grimy back door, his cheek against the snow, a spray of vomit across the ground in front of him. Drunk. The English word came to Jake for the first time in years, and it conjured up a sunlit afternoon overlooking a beach, his father in a deck chair, a beer in his hand. "Go in the water if you like, Jakey, but I intend to sit here and get drunk."

The drunk man was muttering to himself, but Jake couldn't make out any of the words. The nine months on the ship traveling to the mining station had been spent, mostly, in front of screens that had drummed the Russian language into their heads, but mumbled drunk Russian was still beyond him.

Nine months. Learn your lessons, you *grebanyye raby*! You fucking slaves. *How many months to get back?* one of the others had asked the duty boss, when their Russian was good enough to ask questions. The boss had looked down at the hapless girl in her sleep rack and had barked at her, *Back? You won't be able to count that.* None of them had known what he meant, but it had sounded like a life sentence.

As Jake wrestled the parka off the drunk man, the reek of vomit and beer assaulted his nose. He liked both odors; they were *alive*, and so different from the odors one experienced in the mines. In the little inflated domes with their weak atmosphere, all you could usually smell, if your nose still worked, was the electric burn of rock cutters and the tang of melting platinum.

When he'd wrapped himself in the parka, Jake pulled on the man's hat and boots and gloves, so that his face was the only thing showing. This was all right, because his face looked, for the most part, exactly as a face should, as long as you didn't examine it too closely.

He pressed on through the alley. Above, in the heavy, snow-laden sky, were huge shapes—blimps, he thought, or something like them—patrolling the city with ominous serenity. Could they see him and know what he was? He couldn't spare more than a fleeting thought to wonder.

After a time, he came out onto a wide street that was packed with men and women and even children. It wasn't actually late, he realized. It was winter, and if this city was far to the north, it was possible that it was only the afternoon. And here he was, escaping through rush-hour throngs.

Families everywhere. It was strange to see them after all this time, and yet it was the idea of family and home that drew him on. Jake's own family would be long gone. And if their house was still standing, it was standing on the other side of the world and he'd left it by way of a path so long and strange he didn't really have words to describe it. Maybe all the Russian words had pushed out the American words and left him nothing. He felt a tickle at the edges of his eyes, but there was no fear of tears; the mine slaves did not have the ability to cry.

Focus, you *nekrasivi rab,* you ugly slave, he told himself. If he wanted even a chance of discovering whether there was anything left of his home, he had to keep his mind on the present.

He spotted the girl when she paused on the sidewalk at the end of the block. A bubble of manic glee rose in Jake's throat. *Block. Sidewalk.* How could such old-fashioned, every-day things still be here? How was the world so ordinary when Jake himself had become something else?

The girl caught his attention because she looked young— probably still a teenager. Like Jake. Was he still a teenager? *Sfocusiruy,* Jake, focus.

From what he could see of the girl beneath her fur-lined cap, she was very beautiful, but not in the generic way every-one's face had been beautiful in the asteroid belt. The girl was beautiful because she was flawed. Her skin was rosy from the harsh cold. There were tears in her large, dark eyes from the wind. Her lips were chapped, her skin dry. Beautiful.

Something about the girl's posture suggested that she was in familiar territory, that she was relaxing because she was al-most home. He flexed the joints of his left arm and hand, the only limb that would exert any force at all against a human.

How was it done? Looking into the past was squinting against sunlight. The memories were so bright, they were painful. Girls in bathing suits, boys in swim trunks. He'd put his arm around someone years ago . . . her name was Dahlia. Long, tangled blond hair, skin browned by the sun. He'd put his arm around her and she didn't mind. Dahlia had leaned into him. That was how it was done. He unhooked his secondary left arm from his rib cage, let it unfold beneath his parka. The half-sized metallic fingers were still clutching his weapon, a sharpened piece of the metal he and Kostya had pried out of the cargo bay on the way back to Earth. The girl was climbing the steps to the doors of an old apartment building.

Come on, you *rab*! Jake told himself. Go now!

He willed himself up the stairs at a jog, and all at once he was at the top, right next to the girl as she pulled her hand out of her glove to press it to the palm reader next to the door.

"Privet, kroshka!" he said as he wrapped his ordinary left arm around her as tightly as it would go. *Hi, cutie.* The girl's face, stricken, turned to him, and in a heartbeat, she had sprayed something all over his eyes. When he didn't even flinch and his grip on her shoulder remained firm, the girl looked confused and then terrified. "Take me inside," he told her, continuing in Russian. His secondary left arm had come out of the parka and was jabbing the sharp metal blade into her side, just hard enough for her to understand that he meant what he said.

"Please, don't—" the girl began.

Jake tightened his full-sized arm around her shoulder and leaned in as if to kiss her. To anyone walking by, they were two lovers on the front steps of their apartment building.

"Now," he whispered into her ear.

2. APARTMENT

The girl was called Yulia Boykov, as Jake discovered when he had her strip down to her underclothes. The contents of her pockets were now strewn across the cushions of the tiny sofa in her tiny living room: coin money, ID, tissues, hand warmers, cell phone (or whatever it was called now—it was a communications device that lived in the crook of her collarbone, held there magnetically by something beneath her skin). The canister she'd used to spray his face was also on the sofa. It was mace, Jake realized after he'd stared at the container for a few moments. She'd sprayed him with mace and it had done nothing. His eyes looked like his old human eyes, but they had been reskinned and insulated to withstand vaporized platinum and unshielded sunlight. Mace had no effect, and the shock of this had startled Yulia Boykov enough to give him an advantage.

The girl was standing near the open doorway to her minuscule kitchen. Dark, shapely eyebrows arched above hooded eyes fringed with equally dark lashes. Her long hair was very blond at the ends but very dark at its roots. The mine bosses kept their heads shaved, so Jake had forgotten what long hair was like. It was so odd, to grow strands of protein out of your head in an unending stream. Humans were so *animal*.

The girl made no attempt to cover herself as she stood there in her underwear. She was merely regarding him warily from a good distance away. If she was a human animal, he was something else, a sterile thing that had intruded upon her life.

Jake knew from Kostya that the Russians carried their communications devices on the outside, not the inside. This was a matter of pride. So Yulia Boykov would not be able to call the police now that he'd taken everything from her.

"What are you?" she asked him in Russian. "A convict?"

Jake shook his head. His secondary left arm was still holding its weapon, the small hand peeping out from the flaps of his parka. On the wall next to the kitchen door was a cheap full-length mirror, which gave him a wavy view of himself—his human-looking face, his scalp covered by the hat, his body the normal size and shape beneath the huge parka. But where the parka hung open in front, his skeletal shape and crystallized ribs were visible.

"I'm not a convict," he told her, also in Russian. He wondered how strong his accent was. He and Kostya spoke English to each other, which meant Jake's Russian didn't get much use.

"What are you, then?" she whispered, her eyes fixing on the inhuman parts of him that she could see.

"Do you want to sit? Be more comfortable?" he asked her.

She shook her head. A flash of fear sharpened her expression, as if this offer might be a prelude to something intimate happening between them.

"Are you frightened?" he asked her.

"Why did you make me take my clothes off?" she asked, her eyes sweeping over his body.

"Not for that," he said. "Nothing like that."

But the girl did not relax.

Jake took off the parka, and then, while Yulia Boykov watched in astonishment, he stripped off his pants and shirt. Naked, he revealed the absolute sexlessness of his body. His enhanced legs, with their unbreakable latticework of bones, connected into the smooth, crystalline/metallic rib carapace of his upper body, protecting a mesh of cloudy tissues behind it. There was nothing visible between his legs. Some waste functions were still performed in that area, but sex was no longer a possibility.

"You're not a boy?" she asked, still wary. "You sound like a boy."

"I think I still am a boy," he said. "But you can see that I won't be forcing myself on you."

In that long mirror, he watched the elastic, nearly human face he wore rearrange itself subtly. He had all his expressions still. Underneath everything, he was himself.

Yulia visibly relaxed. She didn't sit, but Jake did, lowering himself onto the sofa. There were no fine nerve endings along the metal surface of his legs and buttocks, but he felt himself sink into the cushion and knew that this was the softest object he had rested on in years.

He unhooked his secondary right arm, and with it he accessed a panel along the bottom of his rib cage. The inputs there were specially designed for the tiny fingers of his smaller limbs. Keeping his eyes fixed on Yulia, he adjusted the settings, and in moments the tingle of suffusion began. As the girl watched in terrified fascination, all the nooks and crannies and empty spaces around Jake's body filled up with gauzy fluid.

Looking at himself in the mirror over Yulia's shoulder, he was observing a robot becoming human. His hands and feet and head had already looked normal, but the fluid gradually covered the bones of his legs, the ribs of his torso, his arms. It was not fluid in any ordinary sense, but a substance somewhere between melted cheese and soft leather in consistency. Though it was white when it began to suffuse, as it reached its final shape, as he became a human before Yulia's eyes, it took on the tone of skin, the same color as his face. In the mirror, at a distance, he was real (if you could overlook the lack of boy parts); he had muscles, skin, even fingernails. He pushed off his hat as the skinning fluid finished the parts of his scalp he had been keeping under cover, and turned his head this way and that to see it in the mirror. It had been a long time since he'd fully suffused.

"Convicts can't do that," Yulia said quietly.

"What do they do?" Jake asked her.

He'd seen a few convicts, he thought, on his way through the streets. There had been garbage men along one of the small lanes he'd run through, men who had been built into skeletal garbage-collecting machines, their core human forms just visible inside the shell of mechanical arms. They had been rolling along, diligently collecting bins.

"They do one thing only, until their sentence is over. They put out fires, collect garbage, mend the sewage system, whatever they have been modified to do." She was looking at Jake's secondary arms, which didn't grow skin and which stood out against the rest of him. "What are you made to do?" she asked him.

"Mine the asteroids," he said. He knew those Russian words because they were some of the first he'd ever been taught.

Yulia received this piece of information with surprise. "Why?"

Jake saw himself smile in the mirror. He rifled through the objects on the sofa and picked up her comm device and then her ID. *"Platina,"* he said, which was the Russian word for platinum. He could see the ribbons of platinum running through her official identification, and though he couldn't see the innards of her phone, he knew it had a belly full of the metal. "You use it for everything. It comes from asteroids."

"I thought it came from the Earth."

"Years ago. But not now."

"You could be a convict sent to the asteroids," she reasoned. She hesitated, then added, "But I've never heard of such a thing, and you don't sound Russian. You sound English."

He wondered if she was trying to make conversation to keep him from hurting her. Jake watched his perfect doll body in the mirror, saw his mouth turn downward in a grimace. It was painful to say the words, because they tugged at another lifetime: "I'm from California."

Yulia laughed involuntarily before rushing to stop herself.

Her eyes flicked to the knife in his stunted metal secondary arm.

"Why do you laugh?" he asked.

"No one is from California anymore." She had switched to English, which sounded kind of Russian when she spoke it, the "Cal" in California coming out more like "Kel."

"What do you mean?" he asked, switching to English as well. "Is—is California gone?" Had something terrible happened that none of the slaves had heard about? Or that Kostya hadn't wanted to tell him? The thought was crushing.

Yulia gave her head a sharp shake. "No. Gone from us only. Enemies. We don't talk anymore with America." Her expression became thoughtful. "You are really from there?"

"For how long?" Jake asked. "How long since you've been enemies?"

Yulia shrugged: *Too long to count.*

She had slid down the wall into a sitting position. She was still watchful, her eyes flicking to his knife every few moments, and yet Jake sensed that curiosity was taking hold.

She cocked her head to one side and asked him, "What is California like?"

3. SANTA BARBARA

Sandy beaches and blue water. Chilly night air. Barefoot walks, tides. Cold morning water and surf wax and warm midday sun. A wide stretch of green lawn rolling out beneath his bedroom window, all the way to the cliff above the ocean. His father in a polo shirt and shorts, hitting tennis balls across the lawn for their trio of dogs. His mother in a wide-brimmed hat, keeping the sun off her subtly modified face until all the scars had healed, ordering dinner for delivery as she watched Jake run to the beach.

That was what California was like.

Jake had loved all these things, sort of. They'd been the background of his childhood. In the foreground, the most important element, the star, had been Jake himself. Brown hair, bleached blond from the sun, and tan, tan skin.

When Yulia Boykov asked him what California was like, though, the first thing that came to mind was the bet. A spring night. Hormones and ego.

"Dahlia's not going to do that with me on the beach," Jake whispered. "That's completely unfair. You're already *with* Allie! I made out with Dahlia *once*. You have a huge advantage."

Cody pulled Jake farther from the group of teens sprawled around the bonfire. The sun was setting, casting orange and red drama all over the sky. The sand was still warm but wouldn't be for too much longer. Jake pulled on his hoodie as Cody leaned closer. "It doesn't have to be Dahlia, and you're going to have to get more than one girl anyway—because I'm definitely getting more than one," Cody told him. "Maybe it'll be easier for me with Allie, but I have more to lose when she finds out about the other girls. It evens out."

"She's definitely going to find out," Jake said, shooting a glance back at the group of girls on the far side of the fire.

Their tan legs were stretched toward the flames; their long hair was getting wild in the shifting evening breeze. Allie was obviously looking over at them while pretending she wasn't. Maybe she already sensed Cody's plans.

Cody pulled an absurdly large bottle from the pocket of his sweatshirt. Jake grabbed hold of it long enough to see *pineapple-flavored vodka* on the label, before Cody snatched it back and waggled it in the air between them.

"This stuff is soooo strong, but it's sweet. You basically don't notice the alcohol. The girls will *not* be paying attention to anything after a few drinks."

"Do we have enough of it?"

Cody laughed. "This is like half a gallon. We're good."

"Hmm." Jake considered the final details, asked, "What if we do it more than one time with the same girl? Does that count?"

"No. That could be, like, a bonus score if we're tied. But otherwise no." Cody was good with the details, kind of a savant with these things.

"And what do we get if we win?" Jake asked. He could already feel himself gearing up for the challenge, and his mind was moving ahead, to the spoils of victory. "Loser buys all the alcohol until school ends in June?" he suggested.

"Including prom?"

Jake mulled this over. "No, we can have another bet for that—that's like three months from now."

Cody looked pleased. "Deal."

They both glanced back at everyone around the fire, at the

girls who were starting to roast marshmallows and had maybe forgotten all about Jake and Cody for the moment. They shook hands surreptitiously.

"Show them who's in charge," they whispered to each other.

Their mantra.

. . .

When Jake returned to the bonfire, he sat next to Dahlia at first. Her cardigan was loose over her bathing suit top; the swell of her breasts was plainly visible. Jake smiled at her as he chatted with everyone else and she sipped at a plastic cup of the awful vodka, her pretty blue eyes touched by the firelight.

"Are you gonna kiss me?" Dahlia whispered when they'd been sitting with each other for a while. The sky had gone deep purple by then, with stripes of darkness along the horizon where distant clouds hovered. She had passed her cup to be refilled and inched closer to Jake.

"When I get you alone," he whispered back.

"Always exactly the right answer," she murmured. The smile she gave him was unexpected. Instead of drunk-girl flirtation, she smiled as if she didn't have much confidence in Jake but didn't mind that he was a liar. She let her hand trail down his chest, a clear invitation.

"I'll be back with more drinks," he said, standing up abruptly. Dahlia was going to be a piece of cake. He could save her for last.

• • •

"Finally," a girl called Aubrey said, when Jake had taken the long way around the bonfire to the cooler full of soda and beer.

They were outside the immediate glow of the fire, where Jake was pretty sure no one could see them, but there was still enough light for Jake to note the color in Aubrey's cheeks. She was into her second plastic cup of vodka. They'd been casting each other meaningful looks over Dahlia's shoulder for several minutes.

"Finish that," he said, taking her hand.

Aubrey drained the last of the vodka and threw down her cup. In a moment, they were walking along the wet sand, close to the breaking waves.

"I've been thinking about you all night," Jake told her.

"You've been all over what's-her-name." He could hear the pout in her voice. Aubrey and Dahlia went to different schools, and their groups of friends didn't overlap much—though Jake was one hundred percent sure that Aubrey knew Dahlia's name perfectly well. Still, they weren't friends, which would mean less blowback later.

Jake laughed lightly. "Only because I wanted to be all over *you*." The words sounded so ridiculous, but Cody had been super correct about the pineapple vodka. Aubrey practically rippled with pleasure. She laced her fingers through Jake's and pulled him away from the group and toward the looming shore cliffs, as though he'd said the most romantic thing ever and she wanted to reward him. In the darker darkness of the cliff's shadow, she did.

Afterward, they returned to the bonfire separately. He watched Aubrey slip back into the group of girls so casually, as if nothing had happened. By then there was only a faint line of indigo along the horizon to mark where the sea met the sky. Overhead, the stars had come out, looking three-dimensional in the deep blue heavens. Jake took deep breaths of the fresh air, feeling his own invincibility.

Then came a twinge of worry when he saw Cody heading away from the fire, with the silhouette of a girl capering along behind him. He'd lost track of his opponent. Was he with his girlfriend, Allie, still? No, Jake saw as he got closer to the main group, Allie was by the fire without Cody, which might mean that Cody was in the lead now.

Jake surveyed his possibilities. There was Dahlia, drinking from the same cup as another girl, both gripping the cup with their teeth, while two boys held the girls' hands behind their backs. He still wanted to save Dahlia for last. So who, then? There were a few girls he didn't really know. He could probably make it happen with one of them, but that would be a lot of work. . . .

A wicked and beautiful thought came to him as his gaze fell back onto Allie. Rearranging his expression into a look of concern, Jake beckoned her. Allie came away from the fire, swaying with tipsiness and peering around at the dark beach— she had begun to notice Cody's absence. When they were far enough away for privacy, Jake told her that he'd seen Cody running off with someone else.

Allie was so crestfallen, Jake almost laughed. She was just drunk enough that her expressions reminded him of a cartoon character, comically dramatic. She was *crushed*. She was *outraged*.

"Who was it?" she demanded. Her hands had balled into fists as though she planned to go storming off into the dark to beat the shit out of the girl. And Cody too.

Jake turned his laugh into a cough as he said, "I'm not sure. Do you want to go find them together?"

She was so grateful, he almost laughed again. With a gentle tug on her hand, he started off with her into the darkness— going in exactly the wrong direction to intercept Cody. Soon they were far away from the fire, and the alcohol was hitting Allie harder. She tottered on the sand and he caught her. In moments, he had maneuvered her against the sandy stone of the cliff and he kissed her.

"Stop!" Allie told him, scandalized. She pushed him away. "What are you doing?"

"You're so fucking pretty," he said. "How could Cody cheat on you?"

"He's an asshole!"

Jake put his lips to her neck. "You should show him he's not the only one who can do this. . . ."

"Stop it!" she said again.

"Okay." He pulled away.

They stared at each other for a moment, and then Allie leaned in close and kissed him. A few minutes later, when they were doing a lot more than kissing, she was telling him not to stop.

. . .

By the time he got to Dahlia, Jake felt no sense of urgency. He could enjoy himself. They walked a long way down the beach, holding hands, and when he felt her shivering, he wrapped her in his arms. The breeze off the ocean had gotten colder, but there was still a hint of the warm afternoon in the air and in the sand.

"I don't really do this," she told him as they started to kiss.

"You know how much I like you," he said. "*So* much."

"Oh, really? '*So* much'?"

"Sooo much."

"You are so full of shit."

He kissed her more. "I'm not."

He was guiding her away from the ocean, into a secluded spot where an arm of rock extended from the cliffs. Dahlia was stumbling slightly and she tasted like pineapples and alcohol and marshmallows. She walked backward in his arms until she bumped up against the bottom of the cliffs. "Ooof—you like lots of girls, Jake. You're kind of a whore."

Jake, on this evening, was in the middle of one of the most promiscuous activities imaginable, and yet her words caused him a surge of irritation.

"I am not."

Dahlia laughed. "You're not? Really? What am I, your backup plan for the night?"

Now he was more than irritated, he was angry. How dare she see the exact truth of the situation? "Of course not! I flirt. It's—it's fun. But I've been thinking about you all night." She was still holding on to him, so he plowed past his anger, used it for his performance. "I kept thinking of ways to lure you away from the fire, Dahlia. And look, here we are."

He kissed her again, and as he did, she wrapped a leg around him, was supple against his body.

"Slut," she whispered in his ear.

It sounded sultry, it sounded honest. The irritation was still rolling around in his stomach, but she was so warm up against him, and it was a new sensation to be called out by a girl. He *was* a whore, she *was* his backup plan.

"I don't really do this," she said again, but she wasn't pushing him away. "I'm drunk. That stuff keeps making you drunk way after you drink it."

"You taste good."

There was more kissing and it was different than it had been with the other two girls. Maybe Dahlia didn't know the full extent of him, but she didn't think he was someone romantic or serious or faithful either.

"You're the worst person to do this with," she said as he expertly unbuttoned her cutoff shorts and slid them down her legs. "Probably full of diseases."

If only she had known. If only he had known.

"I'm the best person to do this with," he whispered, "because I know what I'm doing."

And then it was happening with girl number three of the evening, but it wasn't how he expected it to be—it was practically like he was making love to her, their feet in the sand, her body against the base of the cliff, the wind moving across the outcropping above them, the stars and moon creeping across the sky.

"Slut," she said, almost lovingly.

Jake thought: I'm definitely going to win the bet. And then he thought: This girl is amazing.

4. SIBERIA

"That's it? Ocean, sand, girls?" Yulia Boykov asked. "Like an old movie?"

He hadn't gone into all the details. Yulia was sitting cross-legged, her back against the wall by the open doorway to the kitchenette. Jake had slid down to the floor also, in front of the sofa. He didn't need to sit—sitting was no more comfortable than standing or walking, and yet there was something nostalgic about being on the floor. It had felt natural once. He twirled the knife in his secondary left arm, as the lingering images of that night, those girls—*Dahlia*—slipped away.

All those senses. All of those things to *feel*. The reconstructed neurons in his "skin" could sense the rough carpet underneath his legs, the nap of the sofa cushions, the temperature of the air. It was feeling, in a way. But the real sensations were in his torso, where the rest of his body was tucked away behind the crystal and metal. He was tingling in there as he thought about the warmth of Dahlia's skin, her lips smiling against his cheek.

"What about Mr. Tadd?" Yulia asked, drawing Jake back to the shabby apartment.

"Who?"

"Mr. Tadd. He is God to people in America, no? Like pope or something. Or rock star."

"Who?" Jake asked again. His first reaction was that he'd never heard that name before, but then he felt it tickling at a deeply buried memory.

"Mr. Tadd," Yulia said, growing agitated that he had no idea what she was talking about. She waved her arms around her head as if they were octopus tentacles, then made circles with her thumbs and forefingers and stuck them to her temples as if forming two new eyes on the sides of her head. "'Change yourself! Be bird, be fish! God loves you, stupid humans!'" She ended with another energetic octopus arm wave and a huge grimace. This brought on a fit of laughter as she collapsed against the wall, which forced a reluctant smile from Jake. Who in the world was she imitating? "Mr. Tadd," she tried again. "He is big reason why Russia must cut off America from rest of the world. Why Americans love so much to change themselves and stop caring about other things."

A vision of the kitchen in Jake's parents' house on the bluffs of Santa Barbara came to his mind. The television on the counter, an interview of a man with thick, lovely black hair, wearing a minister's collar and talking about human modification or new medical techniques or something like that. The man was waving his arms in a tame version of what Yulia had just done, and his matinee-idol hair had fallen over his eyes in his anger about the topic. Jake had only noticed the TV because his mother had been standing by the sink with a glass of wine in her hand, laying cheese out on a cutting board. *This guy is over-the-top cuckoo,* she'd said. *See how much he's sweating? Who is he to tell people not to improve themselves? Look—the interviewer can't believe he has to ask this guy questions.* Jake had hardly paid attention, and yet . . . had the screen said *The Reverend Mr. Tad Tadd*? The memory was starting to feel like a figment of hope rather than something that had actually happened. Surely no one could be called Tad Tadd.

Yulia had given up trying to explain who Mr. Tadd was and now asked, in Russian, as though she had found the obvious hole in Jake's story, "How did you get from California to the asteroids?"

"Very slowly," he answered.

For fifteen minutes, the proximity sensor in the corner of his left eye, designed to keep miners in contact with each other, had been vibrating, letting him know that Kostya was in range. But now the vibrations were growing stronger. Kostya had gotten clear of the crowds and was coming for Jake. Should he go outside and wait? He would do that only at the last moment, he decided.

"What will you do with me?" the girl asked in English when

she saw his focus shift. She had relaxed enough to broach this topic, but she sounded nervous. "What are you thinking?"

"I'm waiting for my friend to find me. . . . I only needed a place off the street. And maybe"—he looked down at his mostly naked body—"some better clothes. If you have a little money, that would help too."

"You are going, then?"

"Soon."

"You don't do anything with me? I'm just place to stay?"

Jake nodded, and Yulia looked troubled rather than re-lieved. She glanced at her things, still scattered about on the sofa.

"What?" Jake asked.

"Nothing."

But a few minutes later, when he had followed her to the little alcove next to her bed that served as her closet, and she had rummaged up some old jeans and a long-sleeved T-shirt that might fit him—both upgrades from what he'd been wearing—Yulia frowned.

"You really from California?"

"Yeah, I really am."

He pulled on the clothing, which felt unnatural. The min-ing slaves sometimes wore shield gear when they worked, but the jeans and shirt clung to his body, hugged it, showed it off. A tumble of memories swamped him: learning to button his own pants when he was a child, pulling on his soccer uniform, getting into a clean, crisp shirt after a shower.

"We study California in school," she told him. "Land where everything allowed."

Jake almost laughed. "Yes, it was kind of like that."

She was still frowning. The girl had lost her fear, but she was grappling with something else. "What's the matter?" Jake asked.

Yulia swallowed, did not meet his eyes. "Police are coming."

"What?"

"My mace," she explained in Russian. "When I spray it, it sends an alert to the closest station. I thought they would be here sooner, but *government*, you know! Slow as a two-legged dog unless money is involved. But they will be here soon."

This news hit Jake like a blow to his soft, human heart. Of course this girl wasn't as friendly as she'd seemed! Of course she was just listening to him to buy herself time. Look what the Russians did to their own convicts! They turned them into living garbage collectors and sewer crawlers. Why would she help him?

"You turned me in?" he said, grabbing his boots and jacket. He couldn't keep the shameful note of terror out of his voice. "I wasn't going to hurt you."

"It wasn't my choice! The signal is automatic when I use the mace."

She was debating something privately and tugging at the blond ends of her hair while Jake pulled on his clothing. Suddenly Yulia came to a decision, said, "Here!" and threw him his hat and gloves. She began slipping into her own clothes, which were still piled on the floor. Jake ignored her; he was going to run.

He reached for the door when the apartment buzzer went off.

"Exactly when I change my mind they get here," Yulia said in disgust. She looked out the one window, which faced the street at the front of the building. Green and red lights flashed below. *"Chyort voz'mi!"*

She turned back to Jake, who stood frozen by the door. In two steps she was at the intercom panel, her finger hovering above the button.

Jake imagined the Russian police as a stream of mining bosses, syringes of opioids in their hands, ready to put him under and take him apart. Was this girl helping him or not? He reached for the door again, but Yulia laid a hand on his arm.

"Wait." She pressed the intercom. *"Da?"* she said in a relaxed voice, as though entirely oblivious to any reason the police might be dropping by.

Jake's Russian was good enough to understand that the voice on the other end of the line was asking if she was okay after her distress call. She said yes, she was. It had all been a mistake. They wanted to come up and check. Jake tried to recall the layout of the building. Could he charge past them, jump from a window?

"Yes, of course," Yulia was saying into the intercom. "Fourth floor." She pressed the button to let the police in downstairs. Then to Jake she said, "Come!"

Taking his sleeve in her hand, she maneuvered Jake out the door and a moment later they were running down the hallway. She led Jake to dark stairs at the opposite end of the hall from the way they'd come in. They went down two floors, and then paused and hung back when they saw police officers walking up the main flight of stairs on the other side of the building. Then Yulia pulled him down and down, to an old metal door at the bottom of the stairwell. They came out into a cluttered alley. Jake's proximity sensor had reached full alert, and by following its direction, he was drawn across the alley to a row of sorrowful fir trees lining an empty lot. In the shadow of the trees was Kostya. He was wrapped in stolen clothing, his body suffused, so he looked like a normal human teenager—almost. They grabbed each other's shoulders in a version of an embrace, and Jake discovered himself so relieved and grateful to be reunited with his friend that he couldn't speak at first.

"It worked," Kostya told him, of their simple plan to separate and avoid pursuit. "They didn't follow us. Once I got clothes, I was only one more Russian walking in the snow, toward you." He tapped the corner of his eye, where his own proximity sensor had guided him.

Yulia, who had followed Jake into the shadows, cast a look at the swirling police lights coming from the other side of the apartment building, before deciding the three of them were safely out of the way. She studied Kostya and Jake with interest.

"This is Yulia," Jake told Kostya, when he'd found his voice. "The police came, but she helped me get away."

"Pleased to meet you," Kostya said gallantly in Russian, though he looked Yulia up and down warily. "I am Kostya."

"You are Russian?" she asked with some surprise, after hearing his voice.

"Da," he answered.

She was on the point of asking him something else, when the strains of a police radio reached them from within her building. This would have been a natural moment for her to leave, but the girl showed no sign of going. In fact, she cleared her throat and asked, "What is your plan?"

"We go east," Kostya told her.

"Into Siberia," Jake said.

"Siberia? You are standing in Siberia," she told them, gesturing at the city around them.

"We're in Udachny," Kostya explained. "About halfway across Siberia." That had been Kostya's job, when they split up—to find out where they were. "So we must keep going east."

He and Jake shared a look, reaffirming their commitment. They would go as far east as they could. They would keep going until there was nowhere else to go—either because someone had stopped them or because they had reached their destination.

Jake nodded toward the police lights. "Will they keep looking for you?"

Yulia shrugged, tucked loose strands of hair into her winter hat. "Not for long, but maybe. We should get out of the way. You want a train?" Yulia asked. Dumbly, they both nodded. "You have money?"

They checked their pockets, came up with a handful of coins—Russians still used them for everything. Kostya had explained this and a few other details to Jake, though he had had difficulty telling Jake much. Even speaking of his motherland was upsetting for Kostya.

"Not enough," Yulia said when she had looked through their coins. "That will get you ten blocks." She studied Kostya. There was a seam across his bare neck, where you could see his pliable face meet his reskinned throat. Yulia unwound her own scarf and tied it carefully around Kostya, hiding the seam.

"You will tell me how you got to asteroid?" she asked Jake in English.

He and Kostya glanced at each other, wondering what lay behind her interest in them and her willingness to help. And yet her assistance might mean the difference between success and failure.

"Okay," Jake agreed.

Yulia Boykov nodded, hooked her arms through theirs, and led them away.

5. LAST DITCH

"It's a funny aspect of this disease—not actually funny, of course, but *odd* would be a better word, I suppose—that if you're young and fit, that very hardiness, in a general way, can mask most of the symptoms for months or even years." The doctor spoke in concentric circles, tiptoeing closer to the truth, then farther away, then closer again. "If you play sports, like you do with soccer, Jake, the pains in your feet and knees, and wherever else they might be showing up, don't attract the right kind of attention, because you're beating up your body all the time. The good, healthy pain is hiding the bad."

Translation: *You were sick for ages, kid, and no one noticed. Now you're screwed.*

Jake nodded as he stared into his lap. "Yeah, that is really funny."

He thought about the vague aches he'd been feeling and ignoring for months. If he hadn't gone in for an exam when his sprained ankle refused to heal, the disease would still be hidden.

The doctor had projected a series of three-dimensional X-rays of Jake's body over the center of his desk and now he pointed out, in painstaking detail, where the cancer had most likely started and then every place to which it had spread in the months it had been creeping through him, unsuspected. This became a tour of Jake's vital organs: bones, lungs, heart, brain.

"I need most of those, don't I?" Jake joked weakly as the doctor touched one location after another on the rotating images. The cancer was highlighted in glowing silver on each of them. Was there anywhere the cancer *wasn't*?

His parents sat in two old-fashioned wooden chairs, stoically. They asked the doctor a series of questions that Jake understood were solely for his benefit—they had already had all of these discussions with the doctor privately. This was a masterful example of slowly breaking terrible news to someone by giving one piece of bad news after another until the sum total became clear. *You actually passed the "screwed" stage months ago. Now you're on the way out, kid.*

His mother had tears in her eyes, but it was obvious that she had already cried a great deal before this meeting, perhaps alone in her bedroom, while Jake was surfing. His father looked like he'd been hit by a bus but was somehow still keeping himself upright. Jake wondered what he looked like. He should be upset, he knew. But it was hard to feel anything just yet. His hands, tan from soccer and the beach, gripped the armrests of his chair so hard that his knuckles were turning white.

. . .

"But why aren't you doing chemo or something?" Dahlia asked about a week later.

She was pacing Jake's bedroom floor as he lay sprawled on his bed, staring out the window and trying not to think of anything. There was a bottle of painkillers on his bedside table, but he didn't need them much. Not yet.

"Jake," she said, placing herself between him and the window so he had to see her.

"What?"

"Why aren't you going to the best hospital in the country for chemo or an experimental treatment or whatever? I *know* they can cure cancer now. They're using stem cells and special drugs and your own immune system. My mom listens to NPR all the time."

"We did twenty-two consultations," he said. "Like three a day." Since the window was blocked by Dahlia, he stared up at the ceiling, feeling the weight of all of his limbs on the soft bed, the touch of his clothing against his skin, the pressure of his lungs pushing air in and out. All temporary . . .

"And . . . ?" Dahlia prompted.

"And they can cure some kinds of cancer, and other kinds are still . . . winning at being cancer. They're, like, totally excellent at being cancer. And I *could* do chemo, but the chances of it working are less than one percent. Are you good at math? Because one percent is, like, the smallest percent. So I would spend the next four months barfing up everything, turning gray, losing all my hair, looking like a skeleton, and I'd have to lose both my legs first, because that's where it's the worst. So I would be a barfing, gray, skeleton stump." He smiled, because it was ridiculous, though it was also true. His body, which felt so solid on the bed, so alive, was being eaten out from underneath him.

"But." That was all Dahlia said. Jake could sympathize. That was all there was to say: *But.*

She sat on the edge of the bed, where the sunlight from the window streamed through her hair in a flare of fire. He ran his fingers through that sunlit hair, which caused Dahlia to move away. She'd found out about the other two girls he'd been with that night on the beach, and then she'd found out about a lot of other girls. She'd affectionately called him a whore when they were alone in the quiet beneath the cliff, but when she'd been proven right, she hadn't been happy about it. She hadn't let him touch her since then, even though she'd somehow become the only girl he wanted to touch. Dahlia was here only because she felt sorry that Jake was dying.

He wondered how many girls would feel the same way. If he could get them to come over here, to his house, before he became actually feeble, he might win the pre-prom bet he'd made with Cody—number of girls and also number of times. He could go out the all-time winner.

"What are you smiling at?" she asked.

"I was thinking . . . what if you took off your clothes?"

"That's not going to happen," she said with a laugh.

He gave her his best flirty smile and asked, "Why not?"

Dahlia regarded him warily. "Don't be gross."

"Okay, you don't have to take off your clothes. But what if you took off *my* clothes?"

"Are you actually using this situation to get girls?" She was incredulous and offended, but also—just a little bit—impressed.

"Not girls," he said. "Just girl. You." He gently took her hand. "It would make me feel alive. And it's not, you know, contagious. And it's . . . it's you."

He smiled up at her. Joking. But not joking. He wanted Dahlia to kiss him. He wanted to touch her without her pulling away. And he didn't want anyone else. He could see the residual anger just under the surface in her eyes. She remembered that he had used her and lied to her. She understood that he was using her now. But . . . Dahlia *understood* him. That was the thing about Dahlia.

She stood up from the bed and walked to the door. He thought she was going to leave. Instead he heard her turn the lock, and a moment later she had come back to the bed.

. . .

His parents were hovering in the hall outside Jake's bedroom door when Dahlia left. She slipped past them with a quiet, "Bye, Mr. and Mrs. Emmitt," and they pretended to have no idea what she and Jake had just been up to. Or maybe it simply didn't matter to them anymore—girlfriends, house rules, caution, all such things were becoming insignificant.

Jake stood in his doorway, sensing his whole body's weight through his feet. How much longer would he be able to feel that? His parents stared at him without saying anything for what felt like a very awkward interval of time. At last, his father forced himself to speak.

"Jakey, we want to take you to Estonia."

. . .

The rest of that conversation happened after the three of them had read aloud a single definition from the dictionary that stood on the living room shelf, next to the fireplace:

Cryonics: the practice of deep-freezing the bodies of people who have just died, in the hope that scientific advances may allow them to be revived in the future.

The words *have just died* were the catch. If you wanted to cheat death by being frozen in order to be unfrozen at some point in the distant future when the world was full of rainbows and lollipops and every sort of cancer had been vanquished by medically inclined fairy godmothers, you had to actually die first.

But that doesn't make any sense! you say. Surely you should freeze yourself long before the cancer kills you. You should freeze yourself when your disease is still under some kind of control. It would be much easier to fight the cancer in that imaginary future if it hadn't already destroyed you. This seems obvious. And yet, by law, it was not. Even though doctors in Singapore had successfully revived a young man who had voluntarily frozen himself for a year, and doctors in Poland had revived an elderly woman in the last stages of heart disease who had wanted to be preserved so that she and her husband could die together at a later date—despite these and dozens of other cases, the United States did not let anyone go into cryofreeze who was not already dead.

And so, Estonia. Different laws entirely. Estonia, which had made it easy for people to come in for procedures that were a little out of the ordinary. Or a little dangerous. Or even, occasionally, a little bit fatal.

The three of them were sitting in the kitchen, where a bay

window looked out on the whitecaps in the distance as the wind kicked up over the Pacific Ocean.

"There are three facilities that do this procedure, Jakey," his father was saying.

"Dad, please. I'm not six years old. Jake."

"Don't snap at your father, Jake," his mother said. "We're trying to hold ourselves together."

"It's okay," his father said, with a placating hand on his wife's arm. His father, tan, a little weathered around the eyes, in a sweater that cost as much as an entry-level car. His mother, elegant and too young in the face for her actual age. They would get through this trying time together, Jake thought, and figure out how to live without him.

His father started again. "Jake, there's a facility in Singapore, one in Dubai, and one in Estonia." They looked at a map, where Estonia showed itself to be a small country right up against the northwestern edge of Russia. His mother opened a brochure over the kitchen counter, and together they scrolled through holographs of each step in the admissions process. Some of these were real videos of other patients. There was a highlights reel of patients speaking to the camera, giving their names, their diseases, and how long they thought they would be "asleep." The videos of the later stages—of people waking up after having been frozen—were animations, not real footage because, of course, they hadn't actually done any of the awakenings yet. But that magical future, according to the brochure, was just around the corner.

Jake's parents were explaining the logic of choosing Estonia, but he wasn't listening. He was watching the real videos of patients falling asleep, right before they were frozen. They looked okay. Eager, even. When you were facing certain death on one hand, any possibility of life came as a relief.

"But you might not be alive anymore when I wake up," Jake said. He said it because it seemed the polite thing to say. His parents wanted to know that he cared about them and would miss them. Yet Jake already understood that the chances of waking up at all were incredibly slim, and if he did wake, they would be gone, everyone he knew would probably be gone. That was the choice: agony and death now or a quick good-bye and an unforeseeable future.

Some time later, as Jake was staring out the kitchen window, he became aware that his father had stopped speaking. He found them both looking at him, waiting to hear what he would say.

The decision was easier than he had anticipated.

"Yeah, let's do it," he said.

The question was when. But again, this was easier to decide than Jake had thought it would be. His body was still strong and tan and it looked perfect, even if it was rotting under the skin. He could wait until near the end, or he could go right now—those were the two ends of the spectrum. After a long walk and a good dinner, he and his parents chose to do it now.

A week after that sunlit afternoon, Jake and his father were on a plane to Estonia. Jake had said good-bye to no one. His impending sleep, or temporary death, or whatever you wanted to call it, didn't seem true as long as he told none of his friends. He would let his parents do that later. Or never. It was up to them. What did he care? He'd be dead or living without them in some other time.

6. RAILS

Stop staring, you *proklyatyy rab,* you cursed slave! Jake told himself. It's not like you've never seen trains before. Act natural.

But he hadn't ever seen trains like these. Sure, Jake had been on a spaceship twice. He had walked in the world of blinding sun and terrifying shadow of the asteroid mines, hurtling through dead space at twenty-five miles a second. But he had seen nothing else of the rest of the world since he was reanimated.

The train station was run-down, grimy where floors met walls and in the creases of the stairs, graffitied anywhere paint would stick. The walkways were mottled with old chewing gum and dark tobacco stains. And yet it was magnificent. As they entered the station on the main floor, the platforms were a hanging latticework above them beneath a great glass dome. At ground level were the old trains, the sort Jake recognized, though even these were sleeker, quieter, almost floating on their tracks as they pulled to a stop or began gliding away. Above were trains that could hardly lay claim to that name. They were hovering capsules in translucent pneumatic tubes, like the ancient office-building mail systems in the old movies his mother and father liked to watch. The capsules shuttled past in every direction, an elegant dance through the air. And there were slots all around the outer walls for air vehicles to land. ("For auto-drones," Kostya whispered to him.) A few empty drones were parked here and there, shining metal insects with folded wings—grounded because of the snowstorm, Jake guessed.

Despite the snow, Jake caught a glimpse through the canopy of a dark blimp floating by.

"They clean the air in cities, and they're piloted by convicts," Kostya whispered. "They are not surveillance, so stop staring!" He nudged Jake with an elbow.

Kostya showed no amazement at their surroundings. He had never been frozen. This world they were in, it was Kostya's world, and he had a hard time remembering that Jake was from another time.

"Going east, we will take the donkey cart," Yulia said in Russian, directing them toward the older trains on the main floor. The station was busy, though not overly crowded. The interior was brightly lit, providing a stark contrast with the snowy night outside. Jake pulled his hat down lower as he saw passersby watching him. Was the artificial texture of his face noticeable? Or was he attracting attention because he'd been gaping? He bent closer to Kostya as they walked.

Now that Jake was looking for them, he saw convicts everywhere. Along the dark streets on the way to the station there had been more garbage collectors and some others Yulia had called electricians who had been crawling around an opening in the street, their bodies mounted to rolling pallets that could be fed down into the works beneath the pavement, their arms and fingers incorporated into complicated tool rigs. Here in the station, there was another electrician maneuvering beneath one of the upper platforms where he (or she) worked silently with the lighting system.

"Don't stare," Kostya whispered again. "I told you about convicts."

But he'd hardly mentioned them to Jake. Kostya had told him so little about Russia, and Jake had asked even less, because the topic had been painful for his friend. They'd spent most of their time together trying to make each other laugh.

Yulia bought tickets at a kiosk, using all the coins they'd given her and more from her own pockets, so the purchase wouldn't be associated with her own credit, Jake assumed. This provided Jake and Kostya with a private moment.

"Why is she with us?" Jake whispered. "She's so confusing! Is she going to turn us in?"

Kostya shook his head. "She could have done that already. Several times."

"Then why? I—I basically attacked her. Why would she help us?"

"Don't laugh, but I think . . . I think because you're American," Kostya whispered. "Americans for us—it's like meeting someone who lives at the bottom of the ocean or on the moon. Of course you want to know more, you want to talk more—"

"Platform twelve," Yulia said brightly as she returned with

the tickets. Her cheer faded a moment later when she saw a trio of police officers striding through the main station area. Yulia stared pointedly at the ground as they walked toward the platform. "Are they looking at us?"

"No, be calm," Kostya said. "They are only patrolling." But he had adopted the same posture, staring at his feet, shuffling along, and Jake followed suit.

When they reached platform twelve, Jake thought he saw the officers pause to scan the crowds. Yulia tugged him along until they were past the overhanging station roof and were standing in the snow and wind, where no other travelers wanted to be. She glanced back and sighed.

"Police are gone," she told them.

She was shivering in the snowy air, hunching down low in her coat's collar. Jake and Kostya, who didn't feel the slightest chill, who had withstood a world of cold and hot far more severe than anything Earth had to offer, crowded in next to the Russian girl to keep her warm.

"You don't have to stay with us," Jake said. "You can give us the tickets and go home."

Yulia laughed. "You think you can get on this train by yourselves and make it all the way east?" she asked them in Russian. "You'll take off your coats and hats inside, or you will attract attention for keeping them on so long. It takes all day to get to the end of the line. You look human, but not human enough for so many hours with people staring at you." She switched back to English and whispered, "They will see you are not right."

"The police?"

"Anyone!" She continued in Russian, apparently deciding it was the safer choice in this public place: "And we turn in convicts. That's how we get more of them." She nodded at a high platform visible from where they stood. On the underside of the platform, two electrician convicts were digging about in the wiring beneath ceiling tiles.

"It's true," Kostya agreed reluctantly. "We will be obvious without help."

"You're . . . you're coming onto the train with us, then?" Jake asked.

"I have school on Friday afternoon. I must be back by then."

"What day is it now?" Jake asked.

"Wednesday. So good timing. And maybe you will be inspiration for my end-of-term paper."

Jake and Kostya shared a look, and Kostya mouthed, *American*. How strange had things become in America, then, for her to find him so interesting?

"Estonia is part of Russia now," she said, cutting into his thoughts, "so your parents chose wrong place. Bad luck."

"You've told me only pieces of the story," Kostya said. That was true. They had avoided the topic, until recently. "I want to hear it too."

. . .

Yulia, still shivering in her heavy coat, prodded Jake: "Your parents choose Estonia. Then Russia choose Estonia. And many other countries also—even so far west as Germany." She looked to Kostya for confirmation and he nodded.

"Did they invade those countries?" Jake asked. "Was there a war?"

"Kind of," said Kostya.

"You know what Cold War is? Between Soviets and America?" Yulia asked him, whispering, since she'd asked in English, in consideration of his limited vocabulary.

"Yeah, I think so." He hadn't dozed through all of his history classes in high school; occasionally he'd paid a little bit of attention.

"This was Genome War. Kind of a philosophical war. What is okay to do to people and what is not." She gestured to Jake's body, which was completely covered, but which she had seen naked a short while ago.

"This is okay in Russia," Jake said quietly, gesturing down at himself and then at Kostya. "But not in America?"

Yulia shook her head. "I don't know anymore what they do in America. But not this. They change DNA, change their bodies. Biologically. Anything you want. At least, this is what we hear. Russians stay pure but make machines like them." She shot a glance at the convicts above. "And you."

"Not so many people died in this war," Kostya said, "but alliances changed, and politics. Even who we can communicate with changed."

"When you got to Estonia, they freeze you?" Yulia asked.

Far down the tracks, visible now through the swirling snow, were the headlights of their train. It glided toward them, a gleaming silver mass, as bright as the heavy snowflakes when the station lights fell upon it.

The platform was filling up, even out here where they were exposed to the elements. Yulia angled herself so she was blocking the view any passerby might have of her two strange companions. With their faces hidden, they were just three young people huddling close for warmth.

When Jake didn't answer Yulia's question, she asked, "It hurts, being frozen?"

"No, not really," he said.

7. SLEEP

Going to sleep wasn't painless, but it wasn't too bad. All in all Jake decided the vids in the brochure had been pretty honest.

Estonia was a country clinging to its medieval identity, despite the smattering of modern buildings in the city where he and his father landed. It was wintertime and the sloped roofs and church spires were heavy with snow. Like gingerbread houses, Jake thought. Peaceful. This was, in a way, the beginning of a fairy tale.

It was only as the plane touched down that it occurred to him that this would be the last plane flight he ever took—or the last, at least, in this particular lifetime.

His mother had stayed home because she didn't want to make it harder on him, having her around in tears. Jake had been privately relieved. His father kept up a steady stream of commentary as the car took them to the intake center. "Do you see the castle across the river? Did you notice they've gone completely driverless here? I read that it was mandated in the city centers in most of Eastern Europe. Look, another castle—no, it's a church."

"Dad," Jake muttered, his forehead against the window. "I really don't give a shit. I'm not moving here. I'm just here to replace my blood with antifreeze and go to sleep."

"Sorry. I didn't want it to feel like we were driving, you know, off a cliff or something."

"No, I'm the only one going off a cliff."

The intake center was a modern sweep of glass overlooking a frozen lake. Jake and his father asked to tour the warehousing facility before Jake began his procedure. The warehouse, an enormous, squat, brown building, stood a short distance away in the snowy woods. They were advised to keep their coats on as they toured the cavernous space, which was kept at approximately zero degrees Fahrenheit. The racks of metal canisters, inside each of which was a frozen human body—or a space waiting to be occupied by a frozen human body—reached all the way to the ceiling, in every direction. Their tour guide, a charming, middle-aged woman in a lab coat, stopped now and then to point out a particularly interesting specimen.

"This is a great-grandfather from Germany," she told them, placing a hand on a nearby canister and reading the occupant's details off the display. "He will be reanimated when life-extension protocols are able to give him at least twenty more years of life. And here, this is one of our youngest clients. She's an eight-year-old girl with an inoperable brain tumor. On our brain cancer list, of course. We have a projected timeline of when every sort of cancer should be cured. We can only make educated guesses, naturally, but there are so many reasons to be hopeful after the advances of the past decade. Oh, and here, this girl is fifteen years old, only a bit younger than you. Neurological disease."

Jake touched one of the metal canisters on the lowest shelf. *I won't even know I'm in there,* he thought. *I will wake up as if no time has passed. Like magic.*

An hour later, Jake was on an operating table, with a heated blanket over his naked body. The tubes of his IV snaked away to the hissing machine at his left. Through the window of the operating theater, his father was visible, watching him with a hopeful expression—no, not hopeful. *Desperate.* Of course, they were all desperate. No one came here who wasn't. As he looked through the glass at his father, Jake felt his throat closing up. He was going to cry. He did not want to die crying. He did not want to die at all. . . .

"Are you ready?" the anesthesiologist asked gently.

The tears were just behind Jake's eyes, making them sting. He nodded his head. "I'm ready."

A moment later, the anesthetic had begun. He felt it first as a strange taste at the back of his throat and an itch along the artery of his left arm. Then he was easing downward, away from the operating room, away from the doctor. He thought of all the girls he had slept with, all the alcohol he had drunk, all the days spent on the beach, all the early mornings in the water, the late nights by bonfires, the lazy Saturday mornings in bed. All these were receding from him. They were becoming meaningless, a life lived by someone else. He should have been nicer to those girls. Dahlia. He had liked her. He should have shown it.

He was asleep now, he supposed. There was no pain, yet other sensations still existed. Something cold and antiseptic and impersonal flowed through his veins. It was, he knew, the cryoprotectant that would keep his cells from forming ice crystals. Human antifreeze. When it reached his mouth, he found, with his last perception of taste, that the cryoprotectant had the flavor of novocaine and wet dog. And then he was in blackness with no further sense of anything. He slept not the sleep of the dead, but the sleep of the waiting.

8. TRAIN

"Shit," Yulia said, but whether in response to the story or to something else, was not immediately clear.

She elbowed Jake and he followed her gaze. An old man was pointing at Kostya. When he caught Jake looking, his eyes flicked away, and then the man grabbed the sleeve of another old man and together they shuffled off into the crowd.

"Shit," Yulia said again, nodding at Kostya.

Kostya's coat collar was turned down, and his scarf had worked its way up his neck. The seam between his reskinned skull and the artificial flesh of his neck was, in the bright lights, plain for anyone to see.

Yulia quickly removed Kostya's scarf and tied it around her own neck, and then she turned up his collar until it touched his chin. For good measure she switched her hat for his.

Commuters were swarming about the platform as their train at last glided to a halt. The Russian language swelled around them from the mouths of everyone in the crowd. Was it Jake's imagination that he heard the word *katorzhnik,* "convict," floating toward him?

"Shit," he whispered.

With a second glance, they observed the old men approaching the knot of policemen who were lounging near the station end of the platform.

"Old bastards!" Yulia hissed.

She moved them farther down the platform, retrieving their tickets from her pocket as the doors all along the train slid open. Yulia pushed Jake and Kostya ahead of her onto the nearest carriage amid the crush of other passengers. Outside, the old man was pointing a shaking finger at the train, saying, *"Katorzhnik, katorzhnik!"* with four policemen in tow.

"Kostya," Jake whispered, nudging him discreetly. A pair of old-fashioned reading glasses was sticking out of the pocket of an elderly woman's jacket.

With a quick motion, Kostya took the glasses and slipped them onto his own face. He had no ears to hold them, but the arms lodged snugly beneath his hat. Yulia pushed him into a seat and shoved a small paper book into his hands. She and Jake took seats across the aisle.

The police had entered the car with the old man.

"Young fellow in a pink scarf," the man was saying as he squinted at the passengers.

Jake risked a look at Kostya. With the glasses and the book, he appeared to be nothing more than a cold student eager for the train doors to close. The old man and the officers walked right past Kostya and continued on into the next car without a backward glance.

In minutes, the train began to move.

Yulia leaned close to Jake and asked, "You really thought you would wake up?"

Jake shrugged.

9. WAKE

A week, a year, a decade, or a lifetime later—however long it was, Jake experienced only the passing of a single moment— Jake was waking to screams and echoes and bright lights. Human cries were mixed up with a hideous cacophony of other noises—the shriek of bone saws, the whine of drills, the sough of vacuums, the hiss of electrical sparks. The smells came in waves, creating a brew of coppery blood, burning meat, metal, smoke, solder, vomit.

There was pressure. *Pressure.* He could feel his legs and arms, because of the pressure being exerted upon them. Except it was not only pressure; it was becoming something else.

Jake opened his eyes as he recognized the sensation: *Pain! Holy fucking shit, there is so much pain!*

He screamed, and he was screaming into a blurry world, because his eyes were still half asleep. A moment later, his pupils recalled how to focus, and his surroundings jumped into view. He was strapped to a bed, a bed like the one he'd been in when he fell asleep, but this was not the same place. He had gone to sleep in the sterile intake center, and he had woken up in a slasher movie. Men were standing over him in spattered lab coats, wearing full face shields. And they were piercing him with needles and cutting him to pieces.

He screamed again.

"Rak vylechen— Chyort voz'mi!" the man by Jake's head snapped impatiently. *"Ty smotrish smes'? Ili ty spish'?"* Jake spoke no Russian then, but later, when he knew the language, he would recall with perfect clarity that the man had said: *Cancer is cured— Dammit! Are you watching the mixture? Or are you asleep?*

Jake tried to struggle, but he was cinched firmly in place. Another needle stab in his shoulder, and then the icy sensation as the syringe emptied into him. Blessedly, the pain lessened, but he could still *see* everything. They were hacking apart his legs, stripping away the feet, the skin, as if he were a pig in a slaughterhouse. Two men were wrestling with an enormous machine that towered over them, attaching tubes to Jake's remaining bones. One tube was hooked onto the brilliant white of Jake's newly cut thigh bone, which quickly aged, darkened, thickened, and began to bend as the machine roared. They were coating his bones with metal.

This was the warehouse, he dimly realized. He was in the

warehouse he and his father had toured; he was in the room where his metal canister had been laid to rest. Towering space, lost in darkness above him; huge, glaring lights bathing him in whiteness; puffs of steam around the men's visors, because the air was almost as cold as it had been when Jake visited that first time. In every direction were groups of men like the one huddled around Jake, tearing people apart, remaking their bones. A very old man lay on a nearby table, his mouth open to say something to the men busily dissecting him. No words came. He could only stare at what was left of himself.

They were beginning on Jake's arms. When his right hand was sawed off, Jake screamed again, just before he fainted.

. . .

A week full of momentary flashes:

Jake was standing on new legs, skeletal legs that contained his remnant limbs somewhere inside their metal framework of bones. A medic stood in front of him, a flashlight in one of her hands and a computer tool wrapped around the other.

"Right leg," she ordered, in her rudimentary English. "Left leg. Right leg."

Jake could move the new legs. It had taken him a few minutes to get the hang of it, but no more than that. His own nerves had been tied into them in some way. There was no room for horror or confusion in this place. Things simply *were*. He obediently lifted one leg and then the other.

"Arms," she ordered.

He was blinded by the woman's flashlight and by the strong lights above.

"Narrow eyes," she ordered. "Will adjust."

He tried what she said, squinting at the bright lights. Immediately his eyes did something they had never done before—they changed the way he saw the light, muted it, while allowing him to see into dark areas of the room as well. They had changed his eyes, which perhaps explained why his entire head felt as though it were on fire.

He peered at the distant shadows on the other side of the warehouse, able to make out every detail. The metal capsules in which they had all been frozen were stacked, empty now, along the back wall. The towering racks that had once held the capsules were being taken apart and removed by a loading bay. The endless expanse of the warehouse floor was covered in blood and chunks of flesh and other, less identifiable fluids and objects. Jake could still smell some of the odors in the air, but his olfactory sense had been altered, turned down. His hearing, on the other hand, was acute. A cleaning crew was slowly creeping across the floor with hoses, washing everything into drains, and the sluice of water carried clearly to his ears.

"Arms!" the woman reminded him.

He flexed his arms one after another.

After a long series of simple motions, the medic nodded. "Enough," she told him. The tool wrapped around her left hand snaked forward, hooked into a receptacle beneath his crystal-metallic ribs. Behind those ribs were the scraps of his old body. A wash of bliss as an opioid was unloaded into his new circulatory system. Then the whir of tiny drills and dozens of small tools that pricked and sliced and twisted, the sensations they created muted by the drugs, but still discernible, as she made subtle adjustments to his new body.

. . .

Jake in a group of ten, following the motions of another medic who stood facing them. The young man squatted, jumped up, rotated in place. His motions were copied by the ten new . . . what were they? People? Machines? Every part of Jake hurt, with a fiery ache radiating inward from the new metal and outward from his brain and heart.

The medic called out the Russian word for each action, and the ten people-machines repeated it aloud. Their voices were still their voices, each one individual. Jake was supposed to keep his eyes on the leader, but when he risked a look at the others, he saw what he himself must look like: human in form, but remade from dark, crystalline metal, ribs, leg bones, arm bones, collarbones, all prominent. Inside the metallic rib cage was what remained of each person's human organs, held together by the pink, pulpy vestiges of a torso.

And the faces . . . the faces were somehow both identical and unique. They were like masks, because the part that appeared to be skin only covered the front of the head, back to about where the ears should be (but no longer were). And still . . . each face was distinct. They all looked young, or perhaps *ageless* was a better word, smooth, clear-eyed, yet the features of each face were different. They were, Jake hoped, the personal features that had been on their real faces before they'd been modified, but since there were no mirrors in the warehouse, it was impossible to study himself to know for sure.

"Leap and lunge left and touch the floor and leap again," the young man ordered in Russian, translating by his actions.

Jake followed along with everyone else, his new body mastering every motion with ease.

. . .

A severe woman in a lab coat gestured at Jake and said in Russian, "Hit him!"

Jake was standing in front of a male medic and the woman was ordering him to strike him.

"Yes, hit him!" the woman repeated sharply, in English this time, when Jake showed reluctance.

Days and days had passed since he'd woken up, as far as Jake could tell, though he was knocked unconscious so regularly it was difficult to sense the passing of time.

"Do it now," the woman said firmly.

Jake's victim appeared entirely untroubled by the order, so Jake struck the man with his right arm. Except he could not properly finish the action. The blow became nothing more than a caress when he made contact. There was no time for confusion, just as there was no time for any emotion.

"Now left arm!" the woman ordered.

Jake tried again with his left arm, which was, he noticed, just as agile as his right. His right-handedness, like so many other pieces of him, had been stripped away. Still, he could not strike the man with his left arm either.

His victim was watching Jake placidly, and the woman nodded in approval. Jake understood: they were slaves now, and as slaves, they were designed so that they could not hit their masters.

. . .

Hundreds of new, half-mechanical people, everyone who'd been woken up from cryo-sleep, charging around the warehouse like a herd of alien creatures spooking before a predator. Jake could run now, really run. Their trainers stood in the middle of the space, while the slaves ran in a vast circle around them, faster and faster, their new legs responding to their own commands, carrying them at speeds humans could not achieve. A monstrous stampede.

A small section of the warehouse's exterior wall was made of glass, and because it was nighttime outside, this glass had become a mirror in the bright interior lights. A mirror! Over the course of several laps, as Jake discovered that his lungs could easily supply air to his new body, even at high speeds, he maneuvered himself into the outer ring of the herd. When he had reached the edge, he glimpsed himself in that mirrored glass as he darted by. His modified eye captured the image easily. His face . . . his face was still an echo of his real face. There was solace in that. He was not a clone of no identity. He looked like Jake.

. . .

On the last day in the warehouse, the medics activated a new mechanism in each slave's body. Then Jake and the others were instructed in how to adjust the settings of the panel along the bottom of their rib cages.

Jake felt a tingle throughout his body, a sensation that was somehow simultaneously hot and cold. Within moments, the metallic framework of his new body began to fill up with a strange, thick liquid. It was happening to everyone, and the warehouse was full of startled gasps. In less than a minute, artificial skin had grown out to conceal all of their crystal and metal parts. Jake watched in wonder as his leg bones and arm bones disappeared beneath this covering.

None of the reconstructed people could cry actual tears anymore, and yet half the slaves openly wept, by gesture and by sobs, at the sight of their bodies becoming covered by what looked like human flesh. When you had been remade, any sign of your old self was precious. Jake was crying with the rest. There was nothing left, really, except his remembered humanity, and this artificial skin was a reminder, a gift.

10. BETWEEN CARS

Yulia had found them a set of fold-down seats in the luggage area between train cars. It was much colder here, where outside air leaked in around the train doors, so that there was nothing suspicious about the three of them remaining buttoned up in their winter clothing.

She had fallen into a reverie as Jake spoke of the warehouse. When he stopped his narration, she continued to stare at him, her lips parted in distress.

She roused herself to say, "That, that was . . ." But she trailed off without finishing the sentence, and really, thought Jake, what could she say? A new emotion had crept into her face: pity.

"Tickets!"

The three of them jumped in unison. Jake nearly forgot himself, but remembered at the last moment that he must not give a clear view of his face and so kept his head down as he turned toward the young man in the conductor's uniform who had appeared so suddenly between the cars. Kostya was not as careful and looked directly at the man before lowering his gaze.

"I have the tickets," Yulia said in Russian, sharply, which succeeded in drawing the conductor's attention away from Kostya.

She handed over their tickets, one by one, so the man could scan them. "You know, we already scanned them when we got on the train," she told him.

"I still have a job to do," the conductor replied.

Something in his voice was friendlier than Jake expected it to be. Glancing upward beneath his hat, Jake noted that the conductor was only a few years older than Yulia, with the sort of hungry look Jake knew from high school. He was a man who didn't spend all of his time thinking about girls, only ninety-nine percent of it. The remaining one percent had to suffice for everything else, like making a living and remembering to put his clothes on.

"Are you on holiday?" the conductor asked, his gaze wandering off Yulia and onto Kostya.

"Family situation!" Yulia answered. She sounded upset, which immediately drew the man's attention back to her.

Somehow, in the last ten seconds, she had undone the upper buttons on her shirt, beneath the open front of her parka, so that her cleavage was visible. The conductor's eyes latched onto her chest as he fumbled through the rest of the ticket-scanning.

"I can seat you somewhere warmer," he offered to her breasts. Yulia, Jake suspected, was doing something with her arms under her coat in order to press them upward and make them even more noticeable. "I can find a place for you—well, for *all* of you," he added magnanimously, without actually looking at either Jake or Kostya this time, though he did briefly shift his gaze up to Yulia's face. "One less stress for your trip."

"Maybe later," Yulia told him, casually running a hand down her neck.

"So . . . good-bye, then," the young man said.

He hesitated, as if Yulia might have forgotten that she was going to offer to sleep with him and he wanted to give her a chance to remember. Meeting only stony silence in her gaze, he moved off through the sliding door into the next car.

"Is that how Russians flirt?" Jake asked her, when the door had shut safely behind the man, leaving them quite alone in the luggage area. "Without ever smiling?"

"We don't smile unless something is funny," Kostya explained. "I've told you this."

"That *was* funny," Jake said. He mimicked Yulia's posture when she'd pushed up her breasts.

"Americans." Yulia shook her head as she buttoned her shirt. "Making everything a joke—"

The conductor had stopped to peer back through the door, and Yulia grabbed Kostya by the collar of his parka and pulled him into a long kiss. The ticket-taker watched this for a painful moment, before finally turning away.

"He's gone," Jake told them a moment later.

Kostya looked at Yulia in something like shock as she pulled herself away from his lips. Jake, who could read his friend's artificial face so well, had never seen this expression before—shame and surprise mixed. Kostya stared helplessly down at his hands when Yulia released him.

"Sorry. It was the quickest way to get rid of him." When she noticed the depth of Kostya's discomfort, she asked, in English, "Is so terrible, to be kissed? Your lips feel almost like real lips."

Kostya shook his head, too flustered to say anything. Yulia

covered the awkwardness by adjusting Kostya's collar to better keep his face and neck hidden. Then she did the same for Jake, who was amazed again at all the details when he saw her up close: her skin, her pores, the hairs of her eyebrows, her lips, all just a bit less than perfect, and therefore beautiful.

"What?" Yulia asked, noticing his searching look.

"So real," Jake said.

11. LONG HAUL

It took nine months to reach the asteroid belt. Nine months with hundreds of slaves crammed in the cargo bay of the mining freighter. They slept in racks, they were fed by tubes, they were cycled through the waste facility to empty out their bowels, such as they were. They were taught to use their secondary arms for fine work, such as assaying ore using tiny, precise tools, and to use their ordinary arms for the grunt work. The majority of the time aboard, however, was spent under the punishing glow of a learning screen. An anonymous woman on that screen pounded the Russian language into them for hours on end.

Jake grew used to the sight of his new hands, suffused with their fake human flesh, in the white light of the learning screen.

Da. Nyet. Da, ser. Ya budu. Nemedlenno. Moya ruka slomana. Chto-to sluchilos' s moim datchikom geograficheskogo polozheniya. Ya nuzhdayus' osnovnogo sredstva k sushchestvovaniyu. Yes. No.

Yes, sir. I will. Right away. My arm is broken. Something is wrong with my geolocation sensor. I am in need of basic sustenance.

And of course: *Platina, platina, platina!* Platinum. Platinum is your god now. Platinum is your holy grail, your heart's desire. You will draw it from the asteroids, a precious lifeblood to feed the hungry Russian markets back home.

On the freighter they met the bosses. *Boss*—the word was the same in English and Russian, but the Russian plural was *bossy (BO-se),* and this word, which was a friendly sort of insult in English, was entirely insufficient when used to describe their new overlords.

The *bossy* were nothing like the medics back in the warehouse. Those men and women had been aloof but scientifically interested in the slaves. The *bossy* were not scientific. They were stubble-jawed men, with a few women mixed in, who had chosen, out of misanthropy or a misplaced sense of adventure or to steer clear of debt collectors or as a plea bargain to avoid jail time, to work off-world in a remote, brutal, inhuman place. Their natures matched their work environment, either by inborn tendency or because of long years being molded by their occupation. This was, they learned, the first time the *bossy* had had slaves, and they were making the most of the experience.

The *bossy* lived on the upper decks of the freighter. Occasionally they wouldn't see a single one of them for an entire day, but usually there were a handful of bosses with the slaves, ordering them into their racks, or knocking them out to make some adjustment to their inner workings, or messing with the sustenance feed to restrict the calories of anyone they found irritating, or disobedient, or an amusing victim. Several of the *bossy* smoked foul-smelling black cigars (ordinary to Jake but very old-fashioned, according to many of the more recently born slaves), and all of them drank huge amounts of alcohol. Jake had thought, after all those nights on the beach with friends, that he knew something about getting drunk. He'd been nothing but an amateur.

Two months into the journey, a boss hooked Jake to the opioid feed, except it wasn't the opioid feed. A jittery hormone flooded his veins: adrenaline. The boss removed the feed, thrust a knife into Jake's hand, and shoved him into the center of a circle of *bossy* wearing predatory looks. Another slave was shoved into the circle across from him. Neither of them was suffused, so their bodies were metallic skeletons, their fake flesh hidden behind their bones. The other slave was a girl. Jake didn't know her name, but he'd begun to recognize everyone by now.

"*Boy! Ubyts!* Fight! Kill!" the guards were chanting. Jake was shoved closer to his opponent.

Neither victim did anything at first. They looked at each other, ramped up on adrenaline, bouncing from foot to foot, gripping their knives, but with no animosity, only regret. Jake wondered: Had she been young or old when she went to sleep? Had she been American like him or from somewhere else? Had she ever walked on wet sand on a balmy California evening, watching the sun die into the Pacific?

The *bossy* grew enraged when no fight happened. The shoves on their backs got more forceful, and the threats escalated.

"No food for a month! Two months!" they goaded. When this did not force a fight, Vadim, one of the most aggressive bosses, hit Jake's shoulder and said, "I will remove your whole arm, slave—even the real bits that are left on the inside. Then I will take your eyes. Do you understand?"

The girl was getting similar threats on her side. Jitters rolling through him and fear taking hold, Jake stabbed his opponent, watched as the blade slipped between her ribs. He felt resistance as his weapon struck real flesh beneath. He was truly stabbing her. The girl dropped backward, a look of such surprise on her beautiful, fake face that Jake cried out, even though she made no noise at all.

The *bossy* cheered and slapped Jake's back as the girl was dragged away. Someone stuck a cigar in Jake's mouth.

"My little killer," Vadim whispered in Jake's ear. "Show the girl who is boss." And then Jake was forgotten as the *bossy* went off to the upper decks, exchanging money, the noise of their movable party fading as they left the slaves in darkness.

Jake couldn't shed tears, but in his sleep rack, he shook with sobs, overwhelmed by remorse. That was when he met Kostya.

"Anja is okay," a voice said from the rack right next to his. "You don't have to cry."

The voice was male, with a Russian accent, but it was speaking English, and the sound of his native tongue hit Jake like cool water. He had begun to wonder if anything he remembered before the moment of reanimation was true or merely the hopeful dreams of a half-machine. And yet here was English, and he understood it.

He turned to see a face peering at him in the dim light. Jake had been studying artificial faces for a long time now; he could nearly imagine what the original boy had looked like.

"I think I got her heart," Jake whispered.

The boy shook his head. "She will be all right. We watched them take her. They can fix her. It's not even so hard. We're difficult to kill."

"Are you sure?"

"Very sure."

The relief was so great, Jake could hardly breathe for some moments. At last he gasped out, "It was just a game?"

"Just a game," the boy agreed.

"Oh, God." A fresh wave of remorse overtook him, and for a long while he was crying again.

"What is it?" the other boy asked.

When Jake could finally speak, his voice was hoarse. "*I* used to say that, in the same way. 'Show her who's boss.' *I* said it, and I did it."

His companion silently extended a hand to Jake's shoulder. When Jake had begun to recover, the boy said gravely, "I think they would forgive you, whoever they were."

"Do you?"

The boy nodded seriously.

Jake didn't know why this stranger's pardon affected him

so deeply. *"Spasibo,"* he said. Thank you. He lifted a hand to wipe his eyes, but of course there were no tears. He had left all of those back on Earth.

After a few more minutes had passed and Jake's breathing had returned to normal, he asked, referring to the girl he'd stabbed, "Her name is Anja?"

"Yes, she's German."

"You know her?"

The boy shook his head. "I've learned everyone's name. Words, names—I'm good with them."

"What's my name?" Jake asked.

"You're Jake. English?"

"American."

"Really?" The boy thought about this, apparently fascinated.

"Are you Russian?" Jake asked.

The boy paused. His upper lip twitched—in disgust? Disappointment? "Yes," he admitted. "Is my accent so strong?"

"No. Your English is really good. It's nice to hear English."

This mollified him. "Even my father said that," the boy muttered. "And for me, I'm happy to speak anything but my mother tongue." He wiped a smudge from Jake's forehead. He was suffused, his body almost human, his hands soft. "Most of us aren't native Russian, so the bosses are not too careful about what they say. I've been listening to them. They might hurt us, but not more than they can fix. We belong to the mining company, so they can't permanently damage us. They would get in trouble for that."

He introduced himself. He was called Kostya.

"Were you frozen too?" Jake asked him.

"No. Cryo-freeze—that's the word, yes?—it's against the law in Russia. Also forcing people to go to the asteroids is against Russian law. But you aren't citizens. You are kind of . . . spoils of war. The frozen people in conquered countries became possessions of Russian government. They can experiment on you."

"And you? Aren't you a citizen? How can they do this to you?"

"I'm not a citizen anymore," Kostya told him, in a tone that didn't encourage further questions.

A roving boss hit the edge of Jake's rack with a metal baton, startling both of them. They had let their voices get too loud.

"Quiet!" the woman yelled. "No reason to speak! Platinum is what you should be thinking about!"

She yanked Jake out of his rack and deposited him into another one, farther away, where there would be no chance of continuing their conversation.

. . .

The female slaves, though almost identical to the males, had the suggestion of breasts built into their metal chests. The *bossy* made a sport of grabbing these pseudo-breasts and laughing uproariously when the girl-slaves recoiled. On the nine months of the trip out, Jake became very glad that there was nothing between any of the slaves' legs. If they'd been left intact, who knew what the guards might be doing to them?

"Why do you think they make the girls look like girls? It draws attention," Jake whispered to Kostya one day. "They could have made all our bodies alike."

They were in neighboring racks, which had become their custom. To avoid being separated, they spoke so quietly that humans without augmented hearing could hardly catch the words.

Kostya took some time to answer Jake's question. At first Jake had thought his friend was a naturally slow speaker, but now he understood that Kostya, when he paused, was wading through a tangled skein of unpleasant memories, searching for the one he needed. After a few moments, Kostya said, "I was in the first batch of slaves. Before they woke up all of you foreigners. There were maybe twenty of us Russians. The pioneers." He smiled wryly at this word, which smacked of government propaganda. "They didn't give us faces at first. We were just . . ." He ran a hand over his face, as though removing all of his features.

"Blank?" Jake asked. The thought made him cringe.

"Not blank. But metal with eyes and mouth—bare eyes like ping-pong balls, teeth showing. Not human." Kostya shuddered. In unconscious sympathy, Jake shuddered as well.

After a stretch of quietness, Kostya continued, "It wasn't possible. . . . When we looked like that, we thought there was nothing left of us. We only wanted to be gone." He closed his eyes. "We tried to kill ourselves."

Jake could not stop two words from escaping him: "You too?"

"Yes. That's when we began to understand how hard we were to kill. You can stab yourself, you can drop from a great height, you can swallow poison—but mostly you will not die. They simply fixed us up. But after this time they gave us faces. They gave the girls breasts. They gave us our fake skin. Not real faces, not real breasts, not real skin. But still, they are important."

12. ROCKS

Nine months to the asteroid belt. The length of a human pregnancy. When they arrived, they were born into their new world, for which their new bodies were perfectly suited.

The new world was like this:

Broken fragments of rock tearing through black space. Some as big as countries, others as small as pebbles. Some clung to each other, almost coinciding as they orbited the distant sun, so that they appeared to be a string of siblings close enough to touch. These fragment worlds lived in extremes, the glare of unfiltered sunlight on one side, the inky dark of cold space on the other.

The inhabitants were the metallic mine slaves, with their smooth, beautiful faces and extra arms, moving across the rugged surfaces, drawing out the platinum locked in frozen rock.

Slave camps were established on three asteroids that traveled in a group. They were Phaenna5, Phaenna6, and Phaenna7. The slaves were divided among the three, as were the *bossy*. Jake and Kostya, by luck only, ended up in the same group, assigned to Phaenna7, the smallest asteroid.

Mining for platinum was like this:

Inflatable bubble tents were staked into the surface of Phaenna7 over an access point to a platinum lode. An enormous solar collector, miles across, was unfurled, a great flower facing the sun. The solar heat was captured by this flower, concentrated, and then it was funneled down into the workings of the mine, where Jake and the other slaves used it to liquefy the platinum ore, which could be siphoned into holding tanks. Phaenna7's gravity was so low that drops of liquid metal that escaped the siphon would leap up into the thin air inside the tent, forming a molten haze.

The tents were shielded, protecting the slaves from the worst of the ambient radiation, and airtight, providing a weak atmosphere to breathe. They let through just enough light to hint at the great darkness looming beyond the walls.

The slaves did not suffuse during their work hours, so the work tents were full of human faces on metallic bodies, scuttling like ants over the equipment and the rocky surface. The odor of burning rock and melting platinum was constant.

Platinum droplets and rock vapor adhered to the slaves' bodies and worked their way into every crevice between their sturdy bones. These contaminants were hot, and when the particles reached the softer stuff behind Jake's skeleton, they set off an ache that coursed through every part of him. Stiffness followed as the molten metal cooled and constricted motion.

Over many days, this residue would accumulate until it

began to interfere with the movement of the slaves' limbs. To combat this, they would be drugged and the contaminants would be scrubbed from their bodies by a machine that vaporized the surface layer of their bones to collect the valuable platinum molecules—nothing would be wasted. In his floating haze during this weekly ritual, Jake imagined the process as an extreme version of getting his teeth cleaned. Pain from the scraping, pain from the heat, but he was so high he could not complain.

The *bossy* were there to supervise, in full space suits so that their fragile lungs could breathe real Earth air.

· · ·

"Jake, are you awake?" Kostya asked.

There was a hand on Jake's shoulder, shaking him, but he was floating on opioids, swimming through dreams of sunshine.

"Jake, you are missing the soap opera."

The hand shook him again. Jake followed its pressure back into consciousness, where he discovered himself in his sleep rack, next to Kostya. Their racks were stacked in the *zhiloy* tent, the residential tent, which maintained an Earth-like atmosphere and a stronger gravity. They were given four hours in the *zhiloy* every few days to reoxygenate what remained of their human bodies.

The tent was divided in half: on one side were slave racks; on the other were the living quarters of the five *bossy* in charge of Phaenna7. A clear panel divided the two sections—clear so the *bossy* could keep an eye on their workers. But visibility went both ways.

"Lev and Makar are going to fight," Kostya said with quiet eagerness. He added, "I don't want you to miss it."

Jake turned his head. The *bossy* in question were just on the other side of the partition. Lev, who was small for a boss, with permanently narrowed eyes in a weasel-like face and a body so wiry it made you wonder if he ever ate anything at all, was poking his fingers aggressively into the chest of Makar, a brute of six and a half feet, with perpetual stubble along his jaw, regardless of how often he shaved.

"Did Lev find out about Makar and Zlata?" Jake asked. They had seen no hard evidence but were nevertheless convinced that Phaenna7 was host to a budding *bossy* love triangle.

"Probably. Or he suspects. Oh!"

Makar had swiped Lev's fingers dramatically away from his chest. This was their television, an ongoing saga of the barely human humans called the *bossy*. The barely human slaves called Kostya and Jake tuned in whenever they could.

Jake rolled onto his side for a better view. Zlata, the woman in question, was at the far side of the boss tent, drinking with other *bossy* and pretending, very unconvincingly, that she hadn't noticed the brewing trouble between Lev and Makar.

"She gets all the good ones," Jake said.

"Because of her willowy figure. Look at the minx, parading her womanly parts for all to see."

Zlata had stood up from the table, revealing her ample bosom, thick biceps, and shaved head. They had once seen her arm-wrestle Makar and she'd given him a run for his money.

"She's for sure the most beautiful woman on this asteroid," Kostya pointed out. "*And* the least beautiful."

Both statements were true since Zlata was the only woman on Phaenna7.

They observed with interest as Zlata crossed the tent to step between the two men, causing the argument to erupt into a three-way shouting match. Their voices were muted by the intervening wall, so Kostya filled in the dialogue as he imagined it:

"I don't like men who are taller than I am, Makar," he said, in a fair imitation of Zlata's voice. "Or hairier. I am vain about my own facial hair. Hey, get your big chicken hands off her"—that was Kostya's version of Lev, presumably, who was now shoving Makar—"or I will grow out my own beard and shame you both. Beard competition?"—this was Kostya as Makar, a booming voice slurring his words—"I crush both of you with my chicken hands! You will be as insects, splattered across the floor— Ow!" This last was Lev again, because Makar had shoved him to the ground.

Jake was laughing helplessly as Zlata turned her back on both men—"Boys, this is not acceptable!" Kostya said in Zlata's voice—and Lev walked off in a huff. There was nowhere for him to go, so he ended up sitting on the floor, facing the blank wall. "I'm happy over here," Kostya whispered, as Lev. "This is where I meant to be all along."

Still laughing, Jake asked, "Why *chicken* hands?"

"Chicken hands are skinny, with claws." He pointed at Makar's hands, which were of an opposite description; they looked like nothing so much as baseball mitts.

"Makar's hands are huge."

Kostya, who was fond of irony, waved away this objection. "They are the size of a chicken, then. *Chicken* is a funny word."

It did sound funny now that Jake thought about it. "You know chickens don't have hands?" he pointed out. "Only feet."

"Is a detail."

. . .

Details. Not all of the details were awful.

There were moments, when Jake stood unshielded on rock, sunlight burning one side of him, cold freezing the other, holding his breath in the raw nothingness, that he felt freer than he ever had before. His old body would have died in seconds. Now, he could withstand the radiation and vacuum and extraordinary shifts in temperature for whole minutes, with no permanent damage. He could look out, with no faceplate, no atmosphere, nothing between him and the expanse of the galaxy. From Phaenna7, there were colors in the heavens. The Milky Way was a bright wash of infinity. Nebulae and the galaxy Andromeda hung in blackness in perfect clarity. Cosmic and solar rays bombarded him; the cold was another kind of assault. The injury was constant, but Jake had become greater than the pain, as his mechanical feet clung to a rock hurtling through open space. He was something new.

But then, new or not, he would remember that he had become merely a thing, an object, a machine. Working at the molten metal and rock, being tinkered with in an opioid haze, recuperating in a metal sleep rack. He could see the infinite universe, but he was looking with the eyes of a slave.

13. WC

They had found an out-of-order bathroom on the train, and that was where they made themselves comfortable for the long ride. Yulia sat crosswise on the closed toilet, her upper body slouched against the wall. Jake and Kostya had wedged themselves into the floor space, so that Jake was blocking the door if anyone tried to get in—which had happened several times already.

Yulia's heavy eyes flicked to Jake. "They gave you best and worst," she said. "Best view, worst job."

"And many other 'worsts,'" Kostya said. He was looking out the window of the WC. It was daytime, a weak, short day, and the landscape of snow was growing increasingly barren with every hour they traveled. The cities and large towns had slipped by long ago. Now the desolation was broken only by the station buildings of tiny train depots, old electrical towers, and the rare farmstead, entirely frozen in midwinter. And on they went, east and east and east.

Yulia didn't have her phone, but every so often one of her hands would reach up to her collarbone to touch the place where it usually sat. When her fingers found nothing there, she shifted, checked her pockets, as though she couldn't get comfortable without it.

"You want to know what time it is?" Jake asked.

She stopped fidgeting and shook her head. "No, doesn't matter. Just habit. We travel all day."

Someone tried to shove the door open.

"Toilet's not working!" barked Yulia. "Can't you see the sign?"

"Then why are you in there?" a voice outside demanded.

"Fuck off, that's why!" she snapped.

They heard footsteps stomping off. The three of them fell back into a state akin to suspended animation as they watched the snow-covered land roll by.

"I can imagine how the government justified taking you, Jake," Yulia said in Russian, sometime later. "But, Kostya— how could a Russian citizen come to be taken?"

Kostya did not take his eyes from the view or give them any sign that he had heard Yulia's question, and yet she did not repeat it. She understood, being Russian like Kostya was, that he was taking his time. When he spoke, his voice was flat.

He said, "My father gave me to them."

14. FREIGHT

For Jake and Kostya, asteroid mining slaves, the chance to escape came not as a carefully considered plan but as a sudden revelation. The slaves were surviving well after a year on the asteroids, but the *bossy* were getting ill. It was no flu or virus taking down the old-fashioned humans, but rather a gradual wasting away. Recycled air, low gravity, and engineered food rations had taken their toll.

As the *bossy* weakened, the slaves gained a modicum of freedom. Jake had begun to walk outside whenever their overseers took a break from work, and Kostya began to linger just within earshot of the bosses in order to eavesdrop. This was how he heard about the resupply freighter, only hours before it arrived.

The freighter was not properly expected by any of the *bossy*—their comms and record keeping had fallen into disarray—and as the ship approached, the asteroid camps went through hours of disruption and confusion. That day, when Kostya and Jake exited the mining tent at the end of their shift, the hot particles of platinum still radiating against their human parts, Kostya touched Jake's arm and whispered, "Stay close. We're leaving."

On Phaenna7, the weak *bossy* gathered their things and herded the slaves onto the shuttle. They were going to rendezvous with the freighter at Phaenna6, the largest of the three asteroids. But before the freighter arrived, they had decided to rotate the slaves from one asteroid to another, which, apparently, the *bossy* were supposed to have been doing the whole time. If Kostya and Jake had tried to plot out the proper actions, they would have failed. But in the chaos, two of the *proklyatyye raby*—two of the cursed slaves, identical to all the others—slipped away and were not missed.

As the freighter's engines ignited for the return journey, they were hidden in the cargo bay, where giant blocks of platinum, sucked from rock and reformed, were stacked from floor to ceiling. Their own half-mechanical bodies were heavier than ordinary humans, but they were a mere rounding error when hiding among mountains of dense metal.

For food, they had what they were able to grab in those final moments on Phaenna6—a case of nutrient vials. The entire freighter was pressurized, so there was air to breathe. But for insulation, they had only the tarps and ropes that had been holding down a pile of rock samples at one end of the bay. These were enough for their near-indestructible bodies. They made a bed for themselves atop a stack of platinum cubes. For the long, cold months of the journey home, they huddled together in this nest in the darkness. They kept themselves suffused, because the fake skin helped maintain warmth and also allowed them to remember that they were separate from the unforgiving metal all around them. Mostly they were quiet, almost hibernating, and using only a tiny portion of a food vial each day.

"I sometimes think we're dead," Jake said at an unknown moment in what seemed an infinite stretch of moments colored only by the hum of the engines and, rarely, a noise from the upper levels of the freighter. The ex-*bossy* were up there, huddled in their bunks, perhaps, waiting out the journey.

"For sure we're dead," Kostya replied unexpectedly. "They stripped everything from us before we left Earth."

This was almost completely true, Jake reflected. And yet they were here, in this freakish state of existence.

Sometime—days or many weeks—later, Kostya said something so softly Jake almost missed the words. He said, "I think he knew before he found us." His voice gave the impression of being far away, even though his mouth was only inches from Jake's ear hole. Though there had been no conversation for a long time, Jake knew immediately that Kostya was speaking of his father. It was a topic his friend had avoided in all their months together, and it was the one topic, when touched upon, that made his voice disappear.

"When I was little," Kostya continued, "I thought *pidor* was only another bad name you called someone when you were angry. My father would yell it at people who got in his way, or who annoyed him. '*Pidor!*' Like saying *asshole,* I thought. He used the word only for men, but he didn't usually swear at women anyway, so I didn't notice so much that it was a word for men." His words came to Jake like a conversation overheard from a neighboring room, a distant drone.

"I was twelve years old when I learned that *pidor* means something different," he said. "There was a boy on the street when we were walking home at night, my father and I. This boy was maybe eighteen, and he was standing at the corner of a building, dressed like a girl. Almost, you could think he *was* a girl, because he was pretty, but a second look would tell you that you were mistaken.

"This boy, for some crazy reason, he decides to talk to my father. Can you imagine? He said, 'Hey, handsome, give me a few minutes and you'll walk away smiling.' I mean, even a twelve-year-old couldn't mistake what that means, right? It made me—what's the word?—*shiver* with a kind of terrible excitement. My father had a different reaction. He punched the boy without even a pause. He turned, punched, walked away. One, two, three. It took no time at all. The boy had been standing, and then he was on the ground, blood pouring from his nose. Over his shoulder my father said, "*Otvratitel'noye pidor izvrashchenets*. 'Disgusting faggot perverts.' So I realized *pidor* was a special word for boys like him."

Jake heard Kostya swallow in the darkness, a very human sound. "Looking at that boy on the ground, I understood that I had been going through my life happily for twelve years, but that was going to end," Kostya said. His voice was so remote that it seemed he had separated from the freighter and was slowly drifting away through open space. "I was a little kid, so I didn't think about sexy stuff too much. I had curiosity sometimes, like any kid, but that was all. Except, whenever I thought about the future, about kissing and love and taking my clothes off with someone—whenever these thoughts would pop into my head, I saw myself with another boy. Not a particular boy, just a boy. I liked boys, I thought. Maybe I *loved* boys. It had never come into my mind that there was something . . . incorrect about it. But. *Pidor*. Punch in the face. Pervert.

"My father said to me as we walked home, 'Government is getting rid of them, but not fast enough.' A feeling comes into my stomach, like I am falling. Because what if I am one of 'them'?"

Silence and engine noise for a long while, but Jake imagined he could see Kostya among the stars.

"I did not let myself think about other boys after that," his friend continued. "This was easy when I was twelve. Not so easy when I was fourteen and fifteen. I had a neighbor, Vasily, he's three years older than me. God, forgive me, he plays hockey, he's tall, he's got arms like . . ." Kostya shuddered with the thought of him. "It was hard not to look, not to *imagine* . . . but he was untouchable. A man, almost. Girls would follow him after school. Then one day he's at my house, because we live next door to each other, and we were often in each other's houses. I'm in the bathroom washing my face, and then he is in the bathroom with me. I think he has made a mistake, walked in by accident when the room is occupied. But there's no mistake, and then he is kissing me, we are taking each other's clothes off. Even if I had thought about that boy with the bloody nose at that moment, I could not have stopped. It would be like stopping a flood. Or an eclipse. How can you?

"For a month, he was at my house or I was at his house, anytime our parents were out. We kept our secret but I did not let myself think about *why* we kept it; I did not let myself think about my father and the government getting rid of 'them.' "

He paused, and the hum of the freighter's engines filled their ears, along with the distant clink of motion on the floors above. Jake could feel Kostya moving. He was, Jake thought, putting his hands to his head, as if warding off a blow.

"He found us one afternoon," Kostya whispered. "My father came home from work early, throws open the bathroom door, thinking to find it empty, but instead he finds us. You cannot believe how fast he moved. There was one second when he paused, looking at us. We are almost naked, so there is no explanation except the truth. Then he throws his fist at Vasily's head. I'm alive because Vasily was closer to bathroom door when my father walked in.

"There is a sound like a melon cracking open. One punch. Vasily fell like a dead man. He *was* a dead man. When he hit the floor, blood came out in a river. My father called an ambulance and they took him to hospital, but he was dead when he arrived. One blow, brain bleeding, Vasily dead. *Pidor.*

"He slapped me, but he didn't yell. He said nothing. Truth is, he didn't speak to me again. Also he didn't look at me, only looked *through* me, you know? At the wall behind my head, at the floor beneath my legs. And then he drove me to the detention center and handed me over to them."

"What?" Jake had not meant to ask the question so loudly. The sound of his own voice startled him.

"My father surrendered my Russian citizenship and gave me to the man who ran the detention center. The Undesirables Prison, we call it." Kostya's voice was coming back. Jake imagined him swimming through space and climbing into the cargo bay. "It's a place for people with political beliefs that are not allowed, people who believe in genetic modification, people who are non-Russian in nature, like me."

"Non-Russian?"

"If you are not reaching for the ideal, if you don't fit in with our Oath of Principle or our motto—'Live as humans are meant to live!'—you can be classified as non-Russian. What Vasily and I did is not part of the ideal.

"After a few weeks, they sent me and some others to Estonia. You know the rest. We were the first batch, you were the second. The end."

"The end," Jake echoed. "My father gave me away by accident. Yours did it on purpose."

"What a *pidor* he was," Kostya whispered. He was not crying, because he couldn't cry, but Jake could feel his friend's body shaking.

He curled himself against Kostya so they were lying on their sides, fitted together perfectly, matching half-humans with soft, artificial skin. Then Jake put an arm around Kostya's chest and slid his hand up until it rested over his friend's heart.

Unexpectedly, Kostya's story had called up Dahlia, brought her clearly into Jake's thoughts. Maybe he had loved her, in his selfish way. He *could have* loved her, for sure. And he had done nothing about it. He had taken and taken, and what had he ever given back?

"If you hadn't been with me all of these months," Jake

said, "I would have died. I mean, I'd still be alive, probably, because they made us so hard to kill, but it would suck."

Kostya nodded. "For me too." He took in a trembling breath and said, "Going back to Russia . . . it's a kind of dying."

"We won't stay. We'll go to California." Jake didn't know how that would be possible, but they were *gornodobyvayushchiye raby,* mining slaves. If he could walk across an asteroid unshielded, he could find their way to the West Coast of the United States.

"California," Kostya whispered. He made it sound like the name of a magical kingdom. The word hung in the air, blending into the hum of the engines, as if it were powering the freighter and impelling them back home.

"I always thought gay guys were the best," Jake reflected. "They would fall for each other and leave more girls for everyone else."

This drew from Kostya a sound that was both sob and laugh. An improvement, Jake thought. He took his friend's hand in his and brought it to his lips. He could feel with those lips, sort of, as he pressed a kiss onto Kostya's artificial fingers.

15. END OF THE LINE

"It's fucking horrible," Yulia muttered in Russian when Kostya had finished his history.

"No," Kostya said. "Those words are nothing."

"Fucking, shitting, cunting, bastardy! That's what it is," Yulia snapped.

"Better," said Kostya.

Darkness was falling outside, while the snow continued to come down, thick and rich, flakes as large as a man's hand being whisked away behind them as the train plowed onward. This train would take them all the way to Russia's eastern coast, the end of the world. They had been traveling for most of the day and Yulia had told them they were getting close to the final station.

Without warning, Yulia began to cry. Heavy tears ran down her cheeks.

Kostya's eyes snapped to the girl and some sort of understanding dawned in him. "Yulia!" he said sharply. "What did you do?"

Yulia stood up abruptly and wiped her eyes. She looked angry as she said, "How could I know your lives? I couldn't know!"

She reached for the bathroom door, but Jake was on his feet before she could get hold of the handle. He blocked her exit and shoved her away from the door with his left arm. He looked from her to Kostya, confused.

"The whole time I'm thinking, 'She's too nice, this can't be real, but maybe we've found someone good . . . ,'" Kostya said to Yulia in Russian. "What did you do?"

"How do you—what are you—?" Jake asked.

Kostya was also on his feet now, and he poked a finger into

Yulia's chest. "She's not crying because of the sad story, Jake. She's crying because she's done something worse."

Yulia looked between the two boys, whose secondary arms, with weapons, were showing beneath their open parkas. Jake had seen nothing in the girl's tears, but now Yulia put away all pretense. "What do you think I will do?" she said savagely in English.

"When did you turn us in?" Kostya asked. "Did you signal the ticket taker at the beginning? Another passenger? Or did you wait until you went out to get food?" She had gone almost an hour earlier, and come back quickly with bread and cheese and a report that the train was already emptying out.

Jake looked from his friend to the girl who had saved them and then back again. "*Did* you turn us in?" he asked her.

"Yes. When I got food," Yulia admitted. And then, her voice dripping with disdain, she said, "Look at baby American. Will he cry that I'm not his friend? They are exactly like we learn in school."

"But . . . why not do it back in the city?" Jake asked. "You came with us so you could torture the *grebanyye raby*? Let us think we were escaping all this time?"

Yulia shook her head and had the decency to look a little bit ashamed of herself. "I wanted to hear your story. I never met American before. Like meeting a spaceman—you are American *and* spaceman. Maybe I would write paper about you, about social justice. But—"

"But you realized there might be a reward for turning in slaves," Kostya said.

She shook her head. "No. Maybe. Not reward. But when he speaks about all the platinum and all the cost and work . . . I realize how important you were. Valuable government property."

"Property, exactly," spat Kostya.

"I have three behavior demerits at my university," she told him in Russian, almost pleading for understanding. "Two political rallies, one time sympathizing with a genetic modifier. I thought—maybe they'll clean off my record if I bring you back." She shrugged as if to say *What could I do?*

"When?" Jake asked. "When are they coming to get us?"

"Maybe they're on the train already," she answered. "Or they will be waiting in Anadyr." It was the name of the train's last stop. And surely, now that darkness was falling, they were almost there. "Train is almost empty," she went on, in English. "Maybe they wait for you to get off, take you from platform. Easy."

"Easy," Jake agreed, envisioning their freedom evaporating minutes from now.

He took hold of the door handle and opened the door just enough to see out—thinking he would check the hallway and then head for the very end of the train. But four policemen were standing in the corridor directly outside the bathroom. Waiting. It flitted through Jake's mind that the officers had been listening outside the door, or maybe they'd come on at the last station and had been checking every car, but it didn't matter now; they were here to take Jake and Kostya in.

At the sight of Jake, the closest man rushed the door, knocking it and Jake inward toward Yulia and Kostya. This man was gripping an electric stunner as he pushed Yulia aside to reach for Jake.

Worse than seeing the officers was seeing the look of resignation settling into Kostya's eyes, as if he had always known that his journey home would end this way.

"Window!" Jake yelled.

His secondary left arm swiveled up with the makeshift knife and cut the man across his wrist, once, twice, and then again, until the officer retreated, blocking the doorway as he did so that the others, for a moment, could not get in.

"Window, Kostya!" Jake yelled again.

He seized his friend and together they stamped at the window. The glass spiderwebbed into a thousand cracks. The injured policeman was removed into the corridor and another man lunged into the bathroom. Before he could lay his hands upon the escaped slaves, Jake and Kostya kicked the window again. This time it was launched out into the darkening blizzard. The tiny bathroom was whipped by wind and flakes of snow. The new policeman extended his stunner for Jake's shoulder, but somehow Yulia was in the way—not once but twice preventing the man from reaching her companions.

Jake took Kostya's hand and they leaped through the window together, out into the storm.

· · ·

They hit the embankment in a tumble of fresh snow and bounced down and down, into the heavy drifts piled up at the bottom of the slope, where wind had been gathering the downfall for hours. The disorientation was total and there were panicked moments as they extricated themselves from the downy hills and found solid ground. The train, sliding away at a hundred miles an hour, was already receding in the distance. Even with the snow to cushion the fall, they would have been dead if they'd made the jump in their former bodies. Yet Jake felt not even a bruise.

In the failing light and thick snowfall, he narrowed his eyes to scan the countryside. Empty. Dark. Far ahead, almost impossible to see, was the faint glow of a town. If that was Anadyr, it was fifteen miles or more away.

He and Kostya were still suffused, still clothed. Kostya was straightening his hat and retrieving his gloves from the pockets of his coat. In the twilight, he looked as human as anyone else.

"Do you think the police will make the train stop before it reaches the station? Or will they wait until it reaches the city to come look for us?" Jake asked him as he zipped up his own parka. He wasn't cold, but there were appearances to keep up.

"I don't know," Kostya answered. "Either."

"We're leaving big tracks. They'll easily see where we went."

Kostya laughed softly. "You really are from somewhere warm! The tracks will be covered by new snow in ten minutes."

"Ah. Good." In the short time they'd been standing at the bottom of the embankment, the snow they'd disturbed in their fall was already evening out beneath thick, new flakes.

"And have you forgotten, Jake? We can run. They don't know how fast we can move."

Slowly, a smile spread over Jake's face. Barren countryside, snow to protect them, a belly that would stay satisfied for days on the bits of bread and cheese they'd eaten on the train, lungs that would never give out.

"If Anadyr is there," Kostya said, pointing along the railroad tracks, "then east is that way. If we go southeast, we get to the ocean." He outlined their route with his hand. "You know what is on the other side of that ocean?"

"Alaska," Jake said. "And do you know where we can walk from Alaska?"

Kostya smiled.

"Come on, California boy. We're going home."

Am I dreaming? Has the world gone mad—or
have I?

—H. G. Wells, *The Invisible Man*

They have left us far behind. . . .

PART SIX

CURIOSITIES

1. THEY FELL FROM THE SKY

Luck saw one of the sentries fall. Sometimes they swooped through the air intentionally in a way that made her breath catch in her throat. But always, in such cases, the sentries would extend their wings at the last instant, long feathers flaring to full wingspan, halting a dive that looked fatal. And then they would skim along low, above the treetops of the reservation, a hint of a smile on their faces, as if they knew Luck had been worried, as if they were toying with her—stupid Proto—and she'd fallen for it.

That was what usually happened when a sentry appeared to fall—it turned out to be a trick. But this time was entirely different. As Luck stood atop the Rocky Jut, the highest point in the Proto reservation, she watched one of the sentries climb up and up on an early-morning updraft, and then he faltered, his body contorting. The sun was rising and it lit him with a golden light, in which she could see pieces of . . . *something* falling away from him. Luck stopped breathing.

A familiar voice intruded on the moment. "What are you doing up here so early?"

"Look, Starlock!" she said, pointing urgently and unable to spare him a glance. "He's breaking apart!"

The sentry could no longer hold himself up. In a swirling mass of feathers, he tumbled toward the Rez's southern border. The two other sentries on patrol—a male and a female—were racing across the sky toward him, their wings pumping frantically.

"Look! Look!" said Starlock now, swept up with Luck in the drama unfolding in the dawn air. "It's happening to her too!"

The female sentry, her feminine curves quite clear in the sun's early rays, was now struggling as bits of something dropped from her wings—or was it bits of the wings themselves? A moment later, she too was falling. The third sentry dove to catch her, and all three plummeted out of sight.

Luck and Starlock turned to each other, and Luck saw her own astonishment mirrored on his face. The pink and orange sunrise gave the world the flavor of a dream, but this was no dream. The humans had really fallen.

"They could be tricking us," Starlock said, gazing to the south, where the sentries had disappeared. "They could have been holding something and dropped pieces of it, so it only *looked* like parts of their wings. . . ."

"Yeah," Luck agreed, without much conviction, "that could be. But it looked . . ."

"Pretty real," he said, finishing her thought.

Starlock was on morning lookout duty, so he pulled the walkie-talkie from its clip at his waist (the device was more than a hundred years old, but it worked well enough for communication on the Rez), but then he hesitated. "What if they want us to go looking for them so they can laugh at us and throw rocks?"

The sentries had done just that—pretended to be injured and then ridiculed the Protos who showed up to see what was wrong—a year or two ago, although that prank hadn't been done in such a dramatic fashion. There was almost no chance they were really in trouble. And yet . . . who could say? An inappropriate proposition galloped into Luck's mind and formed itself into words before she could rein it in.

"Should we check it out, then, before you report it?" she suggested, keeping her voice neutral. "Checking it out" would require a long walk together, perhaps all the way to the border of the Rez.

She avoided Starlock's eyes but could feel the weight of his gaze, assessing the moment. A walk together was a bad idea—and yet no one could fault them for investigating after what they'd just seen.

When Starlock remained silent, she said, goading him, "You don't want to go check? Even after they *fell*? Report it, then—and I'll go look myself."

Luck turned to go but had made it only two paces when Starlock caught her arm, surprising a gasp from her. She looked at his hand on the bare skin of her forearm, dark against light.

They weren't supposed to touch. Sometimes they came into contact fleetingly, a leg grazing against a leg at mealtimes, a hand bumping a hand in a crowd—moments they could both pretend hadn't happened. But this, this deliberate contact, was different. Startling. He let go immediately.

"No, you're right, Luck," he said, avoiding her eyes in turn. The sound of her name on his lips stirred something in her that she knew was best left untouched. "We can get there as fast as anyone else. We should go look."

. . .

They set out immediately, walking toward the Rez border in the direction the sentries had fallen. It was a long way, and as the sun pulled fully above the horizon and lit the distant Rocky Mountains, they passed through fields of wheat and millet and corn, by the hydroponic greenhouses and the fish hatchery buildings and the sheep pens, all the while keeping well apart from each other. But when they crossed out of the cultivated land and into the wilder area of brush and trees, where no other Proto was likely to see them, Luck noticed that Starlock moved closer, so that their hands almost touched from time to time, and each near miss caused a sensation like an electric current in her fingertips. She had gone to the Rocky Jut to watch the sunrise alone, but this was better.

Every Proto teenager knew the rules: Pairings were made by the humans, in accordance with the Legal Covenants of the Protohuman Gene Pool, and Pairings were based on how you looked, essentially. The humans expected Protos to keep all of their distinctive colorings, all of their "unaltered genetic variation," so that humans might study and catalog that variation. It was the price of the Protos' life here on the reservation, protected from whatever the world had become.

Starlock was seventeen, a year older than Luck was, his skin a deep, rich brown, as rich as the bark of the great oaks in the Rez forest, his eyes so dark they were almost the black of an obsidian stone, and his hair as dark as his eyes, its tight curls cut close to his scalp. And Luck was as light as Starlock was dark, her eyes the pale blue of a clear, early-morning sky, her skin the color of milk, her hair blond with hints of red when the sun shone upon it. There was no possible way that the two of them would ever be Paired—and this meant that they were no longer allowed even to touch.

When their eyes met for a moment too long, he looked away and asked, "What are you reading now?"

"Another Dickens book," she said. *"Dombey and Son."*

"Tell me."

"It's about love and hate and family and regrets," she explained, "and hardly any parts of it are missing."

For pleasure, Starlock preferred to read engineering textbooks, but in earlier days he'd been an eager audience for Luck's descriptions of novels, and they fell easily into that old rapport—just as, Luck thought, they had fallen easily into this walk, on a flimsy excuse, after years of avoiding anything like it.

They discussed the book while the shimmering outline of

the Rez fence grew steadily closer in the distance below. With each step, Luck became more convinced that the sentries had been tricking them. Of course it had been an elaborate prank, one clever enough to scare her and draw them in. She kept glancing over her shoulder to see if the humans were lurking somewhere nearby, in a tree maybe, watching the two stupid Protos who'd taken the bait.

When they were within a quarter of a mile of the Rez fence, they began to hear its hum. The nearly transparent fence, which appeared as a blurred distortion of the air, was forty feet tall, and it marked the limit of Luck's world. The fence drew a line around the reservation, a line that Luck, years ago, had figured out was about sixty miles long, because the Rez formed an approximate circle of forest and river and farmland at least twenty miles wide, and math books were available at the town hall library. Protos were permitted to know geometry and even calculus, and the sciences up to a point, including enough biology to train the Rez medics. Even some history could be gleaned from the allowed novels, though of course any references to politics and war had been removed. (Or rather, one could assume the missing parts referred to politics and war, based on the context of the stories. Probably a host of other topics had been deleted as well.) But all of the books and all of the technology in the Rez library and school halted at the Age of Computers, at the time of the Great Shift, as the humans referred to it, when Protos had made way for the new dominant species.

Just inside the Rez fence was a ring of forest, an inner, concentric circle, which they reached after almost an hour of walking. Once they were inside this wooded strip, the vibration of the fence field filled the air, reminding Luck that the border would fry you in three seconds if you touched it (though it had been years since anyone had been stupid enough to do that). They would have to locate the sentries on the Rez side of the border, of course, or give up the search.

"Keep an eye out, in case they're throwing rocks," Starlock muttered as they made their way through the trees.

The illicit pleasure of their walk was forgotten now. Luck was on edge, expecting the rest of whatever trick the sentries had planned. But where the trees died out into tall grass, only yards from the Rez fence, they discovered there was no trick at all.

"Are you calling them?" came a voice, very close, and clearly in pain.

Starlock lifted an arm to stop Luck from walking beyond the trees. And now Luck saw it: in that tall grass between the trees and the fence, not ten feet away, was a sentry—and he was badly wounded.

"My goodness," she whispered as Starlock raised a finger to his lips.

The sentry looked hardly older than Luck and Starlock. Somehow his wings had held out long enough to break his fall and keep him alive, but they were torn and lay around him in a ragged nest of enormous crimson and silver feathers. One of his wrists hung backward limply. His legs, sticking out at unnatural angles, were obviously broken, though his stretchy black suit of clothing was holding them together.

"They're not answering!" came a different voice, this one frightened and desperate.

Starlock pointed and Luck followed his finger. Beyond the grass, on the other side of the smudged air of the border fence, were the two other sentries, a male and a female. The male was standing, his magnificent purple wings tucked close to his body but apparently intact. He was the one who had caught the female in midair, Luck realized, and he seemed to have landed with her outside the Rez border, while their comrade had fallen inside. The male was tapping at his chest—where the sentries kept their radios—without result. The girl was curled on the ground like an infant in her tight black suit, her wings missing entirely.

"Keep trying," said the sentry in the grass, who could not properly see his companions because of the tall stalks around him. "Come on!"

"My radio's not working at all now!" the sentry outside the fence called back, his voice rising with panic. "It's gone completely dead."

"Then fly over and get me," the nearby boy begged.

"I can't fly over!" the far sentry cried. "It happened to you and then Christine. What if it, like, happens to me while I'm in the air? And I fall—boom—and die?"

"Don't leave me in here with the Protos, man! Could Christine do it? Is she—"

"She's broken up like you. Wings and both ankles," the far sentry said. "Why do you think it took me so long to find you? I had to carry her on foot. And her radio's not working either!"

Luck had never been so close to sentries before. Though their bodies—other than their beautiful wings—looked similar to Protos' bodies, their skin, hair, and eye coloring were as lovely and strange a mix as Luck would have expected: golden hair, shining copper hair, jet-black hair, skin that was the perfect shade of bronze, or that graduated from light to dark beginning at the right hand and ending at the left, with a metallic sheen that glowed in the sun. Luck wondered if humans were permitted to mix with each other however they wished.

"But I heard you reach them on the radio when we first landed." That was the girl beyond the Rez fence, speaking for the first time, in a voice dulled by pain.

"They told me to wait!" cried her companion beyond the fence.

"So—they're coming, then?" the nearest sentry asked, lifting his head hopefully, but still unable to see over the grass. "Thank Tadd! My legs are killing me. . . ."

"No, they—they told me to wait before they could take my report," the far sentry explained. Luck could hear his struggle to keep his voice steady. "It sounded like, like there was an emergency on base. They didn't even let me finish explaining!"

"Should we do something?" whispered Luck. They had come to find the sentries, but she hadn't expected to find them in need of help; it was unprecedented. The rules they would break by getting any closer gave her pause—being reported to the Proto Authority seldom turned out well for any Proto. And yet, if the sentries' radios weren't working, surely Protos would be expected to offer assistance, as they would to anyone in pain?

"It sounds like their radios were working a few minutes ago," Starlock whispered. He looked just as uncertain as Luck felt. "Other humans must be on their way here to help them."

But when the sentry in the grass muttered, "I'm so thirsty," his misery made up the Protos' minds for them. Luck and Starlock shared a look and then emerged from the trees.

"Hey!" the sentry on the other side of the fence called, spotting them immediately as they waded through the waist-high grass toward his fallen companion. "Stay away from him. He's hurt!"

"We saw you fall," Starlock said calmly, holding up his canteen. "I was going to give him water. Is that all right?"

"Oh, thank Tadd," the near sentry said.

"Just—you know the rules!" the sentry beyond the fence said, and not kindly. "Keep your paws away from him!"

Luck bit back an angry retort—Protos did not argue with humans—and Starlock knelt and poured water into the injured boy's mouth. The sentry drank and drank, but his eyes, an unusual gray that contrasted starkly with his bronze skin and golden hair, stared at them defensively all the while, as if they might bite him. (Gray eyes, Luck thought. Like her friend Skylark's grandmother. And his skin had coloring like that of her friend Riverbend and her family. Up close, in this human at least, she could see the distant relationship between their two species.)

Where the sentry's enormous wings had attached to his back, where his muscles for flight should have been . . . there was only a frothy sort of paste, like reddish whipping cream that had dried. Luck thought the paste might once have *been* his muscles—perhaps only an hour ago when he was flying—but now even the paste was breaking up, leaving gaping holes in his back and along his shoulders.

When he'd finished drinking, the sentry's eyes fell halfway closed, and he began to moan.

"I have a radio," Starlock said, holding up the walkie-talkie so the sentry on the other side of the fence could see it. "Can I call someone for you?"

"How far can that thing reach?" the sentry asked dubiously. "Forty feet? You might as well send a smoke sig—"

But he stopped speaking and started yelping as a large piece of his left wing fell off. It was followed by a cascade of flesh and feather from both wings, until, only moments later, his wings detached from his body entirely and landed on the ground with two heavy thumps.

"What's—what's—" the sentry cried, hysterical as his body fell apart. He cried out incoherently, and his lower jaw opened wider and wider . . . and then it fell off. When he tried to keep speaking, his tongue lolled freely, horribly long without the jaw to confine it.

"Oh, that's bad," whispered Luck, appalled. "It's so bad."

Starlock, with his usual focused alertness, cycled briskly through channels on the walkie-talkie, but Luck couldn't wrest her eyes from the sentry. The boy—for he truly looked like a boy now, maimed and terrified—whimpered and grabbed up his fallen jaw. Like the wings, it appeared to be disintegrating, the white teeth becoming more and more prominent. And though he was clearly experiencing pain, Luck was fascinated to note that it was not as much pain as she would have expected. It was as though humans had evolved beyond agony.

"Shit, shit, shit, shit," cried the girl on the ground. "Is my face going to fall off too?"

The sentry near Starlock and Luck croaked, "His face fell off? He had his jaw done . . . so he could taste things on the wind."

"So our mods are failing?" the girl asked.

"Duh," the near boy said. He had given up trying to see his companions and seemed to be curling in on himself.

"Help is coming," Starlock told the wounded sentries as he clicked off the walkie-talkie.

All three looked at Starlock hopefully, which gave Luck a pang of unease. She had heard him reach the town hall, and it was the Rez medic who was coming, not a human doctor.

"But how will we get to those two?" Luck whispered, indicating the sentries outside the border of the Rez.

Studying the shimmering energy field, Starlock said matter-of-factly, "We have to turn off the fence."

2. THEY UNDRESSED BY THE LAKE

We have to turn off the fence.

The words filled Luck with a nervous charge. Throughout their childhood, when lying in a field, or sitting up in the branches of a tree, or wading in the river, Luck and Starlock had imagined turning off the Rez fence. That fantastic act had been the start of dozens of imagined adventures that took the two young Protos off the reservation and out into the wide world beyond.

"Really?" Luck whispered.

"How else are we going to get them?" Starlock asked her.

There was no recognition in his face that they were about to enact a childhood daydream. His expression seemed to say: *I'm only doing what the circumstances demand.* Fence posts stood every fifty yards, tall, gray steel, and Starlock was all business as he looked up at the nearest post.

"We'll take you inside the Rez until someone from your base comes to get you," he told the three humans. "Do you know how the fence works?"

The sentry without a jaw shook his head (tongue lolling) and shrugged: *Not my job.*

It took effort not to flinch from the boy's disfigured face, but Starlock was mostly successful. "There will be power controls at intervals along the perimeter—on your side," he explained, pointing at the line of fence posts which disappeared in both directions. He'd begun his training as a Rez engineer and had learned more than enough to understand this— though in truth, Starlock had been speculating on how the Rez fence worked since he was a small boy. "You find one of the controls and use it to turn the fence off."

The maimed sentry looked for support to the girl lying at his feet with two broken ankles. Luck could read the thought passing through the boy's mind: *We are not supposed to let the*

Protos out. But the girl roused herself enough to mutter, "Go. We need a doctor and we don't have radios." So the boy with no wings and no jaw walked off to the north.

. . .

The sentry in the grass had lapsed into a fitful sleep, and Luck and Starlock had retreated some distance from him to wait. Starlock was looking through the fence at the landscape beyond, and Luck, who had trouble guessing his thoughts these days, followed suit, gazing at the forests and mountains beyond the Rez, as she had done every day of her life.

"Do you think we ever would have done it?" she asked.

"Snuck off the Rez to explore?" he whispered, knowing exactly what she was talking about. He shook his head. "The fence is forty feet high; the sentries were always watching."

"But if we'd found a way over the fence, like we used to imagine. A human slingshot. A glider. And if we'd found a way to avoid the sentries. Would we have done it? Just to see?"

"Probably not," he said, considering. "I mean . . . what's out there? And how long would it take the Proto Authority to find us? And what would they do to us when they found us?"

"Yeah," Luck agreed. Those had always been the questions. They'd asked them all the time when they were younger, but at some point they'd stopped asking, because there were no answers.

After three quarters of an hour, no humans had shown up to rescue the wounded, but the voices of other Protos began to float out from the forest. Luck and Starlock stood, and when they did, Luck caught a fresh look at the sentries. The skin of both—the boy inside the fence and the girl outside—was beginning to wrinkle deeply.

"Starlock, look," she whispered. "They're getting worse."

"By the minute," he agreed, alarmed. It appeared that they might shrivel away altogether.

The Proto voices were getting louder, and now Luck could make out a large group of people walking through the trees. Soon a crowd began to emerge into the grass near the fence. There were four hundred forty-seven Protos living on the Rez and about fifty had put down their work—planting and fishing and building and sewing and teaching—to follow Alderwoman Twinfate down to the border, responding en masse to Starlock's urgent call. This was not surprising—fallen humans were an unheard-of occurrence.

The crowd of Protos, which displayed all of the differentiated skin colors, eye colors, hair colors, bone structures, and facial features that made them so interesting to the humans, had gotten loud and boisterous, but once the group caught sight of the wounded sentries, everyone fell silent.

Each person on the Rez, down to the smallest child, had gazed up at the magnificent humans flying overhead and had thought, *Beautiful, but arrogant.* Now two of those perfect creatures were falling apart before their eyes, and no one knew what they were supposed to feel.

"Has anyone reached the Proto Authority yet?" Starlock asked. "Their own radios are dead." He was gesturing at the closest sentry and took several steps away from Luck as he spoke. Luck soon saw why: there was a girl in the newly arrived group who was staring daggers at both of them. That was Moonlight, of course, the girl with whom Starlock was to be Paired.

"The Authority isn't answering me on the radio," Alderwoman Twinfate said, finding her voice, which sounded flustered. The alderwoman was more than a hundred and twenty years old and nominally in charge of the Rez. "I've tried to reach them several times with no success, which has never happened before."

"There's a third sentry," Luck added, keeping her gaze pointedly away from Moonlight. "He's turning off the fence, so we'll be able to get him and the girl from outside."

At the words *turning off the fence* a murmur traveled through the Protos. Alderwoman Twinfate took a few reluctant steps toward the border. She rubbed her weathered chin, looking uncomfortable as she surveyed the injured humans. "What did you say the other one was doing?" she asked, peering at Luck.

There was no need to answer because, at that moment, the steady hum of the fence went silent. Every set of Proto eyes—dark brown, light brown, golden brown, blue, gray, and green—turned toward the Rez border. Where there had been shimmer and heat and distortion, there was suddenly nothing. The fence was off. The tall metal posts were still in place, but the world on the other side was no longer *on the other side*. It was right there.

"The Proto Authority will be here any moment," Alderman Twinfate warned, as if her people might immediately run off, though no one showed any disposition to leave the safety of the Rez. "Probably by evening they will be back. This is a strange day, but tomorrow everything will be as it always is."

No one could have thought anything different. And yet when Luck stepped over the scorched line where the fence had been, to retrieve the sentry on the other side, her eyes automatically sought Starlock's, and she discovered his eyes searching for her. She understood at once: he had been wearing a mask of indifference earlier to keep himself from becoming too hopeful about crossing over the border of the Rez. Now their eyes met and she saw that this moment meant as much to him as it did to her.

Luck braced for loud sirens heralding the immediate arrival of Proto Authority vehicles. But the world was quiet.

• • •

The boy with no jaw came back. Once he was in sight of the gathered Protos, he fell to his knees in complete exhaustion. Luck and a few other Protos helped him onto a stretcher. She avoided the sight of his gaping jaw but couldn't help noticing that his skin was withering, just as his companions' was.

All three humans were carried away on stretchers by Protos, while Alderwoman Twinfate continued to say "I don't know what we can do for humans" over and over. Starlock didn't walk with Luck as the crowd headed back to the center of the Rez. Moonlight had laid claim to him, as she always did when Luck was anywhere nearby, and was holding his hand at the far edge of the group.

Moonlight was almost a year older than Starlock, and thus two years older than Luck. At nearly eighteen, she was womanly in every way it was possible to be womanly. Her breasts were large; her hips were shapely, and they tapered to a slender waist. She had full lips and small, dainty hands, but worst of all, she matched Starlock: rich brown skin; large, dark brown eyes; and tightly curled black hair that she wore longer than Starlock's and brushed into an impressive halo around her head.

Moonlight and Starlock would be Paired as soon as Moonlight turned eighteen, which was only a few months away. (*No, not months. Five weeks, three days away,* Luck thought.) Everything about Moonlight screamed that she would bear Starlock a dozen children; she would make him love her no matter what; and their children would be beautiful and faithful to their particular genetic traits, which meant they would be able to keep their babies. Of course that was ridiculous—no Protos were allowed to have *twelve* children. The Rez would be overrun in a few generations. But still.

"Luck, Luck! There you are."

A boy with carroty locks and bright freckles ran up to her, out of breath. This was Rocky, who, though his hair was redder than Luck's and his eyes were slightly lighter, had a complexion similar enough that the two of them would almost certainly be Paired, at a point in the future that was not nearly distant enough for Luck's liking.

"Did you just run here?" she asked. She hadn't seen him in the group by the Rez fence. He must have heard what was happening, belatedly, and rushed to join the party as it hiked back to the town hall.

Rocky put a proprietary hand on her shoulder and smiled. "Yes," he said, catching his breath as he walked with her. "Why didn't you tell me you were going to the fence?"

"Why would I?" Luck asked.

It irked her that Rocky, who was a year younger than she was, assumed they would be spending their lives together and treated her accordingly.

"They're falling apart," Rocky said unnecessarily, nodding at the sentries being carried on stretchers and pulling at the crotch of his pants—another distasteful habit. Luck suppressed an urge to slap his hands away from his body. Then he chuckled and said, "Especially the guy with no face."

"Don't laugh at him," she admonished. "If that were you, you wouldn't want to be laughed at."

"But it's not me," he said cheerfully. "This makes five humans I've seen up close, Luck. How about you?"

"Six," Luck grudgingly answered. She was interested in the topic, even if Rocky was the one bringing it up. "But mostly just Mizter Caldwell."

Mizter Caldwell was the Proto Liaison Officer, the human who visited the Rez every month to perform the official examination of each resident and take DNA samples. Mizter Caldwell's skin was a vivid aqua-blue. His arms and legs were overly long and elastic, so that it took serious effort for him to hold himself fully upright. His neck had two inconspicuous gills near his collarbone, and his long-fingered hands were slightly webbed, which made the Protos conclude that he must spend a fair amount of time underwater.

"Plus these three sentries," Luck told Rocky, adding up her close encounters with humans, "plus two others who came once with Mizter Caldwell." She described those last two: a woman with a head so large it threw off one's sense of perspective when looking at her, and a man with four arms and four legs, arranged peculiarly so he walked in a spiraling path. Whatever evolutionary split had separated humans from Protos had allowed humans to continue to evolve in many separate streams—flying sentries, amphibious Proto Liaison Officers, extra-limbed visitors, and who knew what else.

Rocky was suitably impressed with Luck's list. "You saw that one with four legs in person?"

Luck nodded. "We walked right by each other in the Rec Center. Each of his hands had a different number of fingers."

"Like how many?" Rocky asked. "Or how few?"

Luck shrugged. "I couldn't count exactly, but at least ten on one of his hands and maybe only two on one of the others."

"Why, do you think?"

She shrugged.

Rocky looked both delighted with this human tidbit and eager to get away—probably to share it with his friends. For one paralyzing moment, Luck thought he might try to kiss her, but before it occurred to him, he ran off toward a group of boys his own age.

She congratulated herself on getting rid of him so quickly. Alone now, Luck slowed her pace until she'd fallen back to the tail end of the group, where she couldn't see Starlock and his future wife. She drifted until she was near the edge of the woods that covered much of this section of the Rez. There, shadows alternated with warm sun and the breeze was full of the scents of wildflowers. She turned and walked backward, staring down the gentle slope toward the place where the fence was no longer shimmering. The world was there. Just *there*.

Without warning, a hand took hold of Luck's elbow, startling her. It was Starlock, who, in former days, had often snuck up on her like this. He pulled her into the woods, and in a few quick steps, they were on a narrow trail used by deer, out of sight of the others, who in any case were now far ahead of them.

"You're touching me," Luck said, looking down at his hand on her bare arm. Starlock automatically let go, which made her sorry she'd said anything.

He turned left when the deer path forked, and Luck followed as naturally as breathing, as if no time had passed since the days they'd pulled each other all around the Rez, as if their unsanctioned walk together that morning had erased the last three years.

"You know I don't have a choice," Starlock told her quietly, when they'd walked in silence for a long while. "I didn't choose Moonlight."

Those were words they'd both avoided for so long, because

there was no point in speaking them out loud. Why was he doing it now?

"She's beautiful," Luck responded, trying not to sound bitter. "You're lucky, Starlock. It could be much worse. For me, it's going to be worse."

"Stop. Luck, why are you trying to hurt me?"

Luck fell silent again. In another few minutes they were by the river, moving upstream along the bank. The Proto group carrying the humans was still visible in quick glimpses, beyond the forest, but she and Starlock were hidden.

"I've stopped caring," she forced herself to say after a while. She had been working so hard to make those words true, but they nearly burned her throat as they came out. "It took a long time, but I know there's no reason to keep caring."

"Please, Luck," Starlock whispered. "There's every reason."

She stared at her feet, but she continued to follow him without question. When they'd walked a bit farther, he came to a halt on the river's bank so abruptly that Luck almost bumped into him.

"Do you see where we are?" he asked.

She hadn't been paying attention, but now she looked. Ahead of them, at the side of the river's main course, was a deep, cool pool where the water found its way between rocks to create a secluded swimming hole. Trees overhung the bank, but the sun shone between the leaves, so its rays reached all the way to the sand in the pool's depths, inviting one in.

Tears sprang to Luck's eyes.

"Why would you come here?" she asked hoarsely. "I don't want to be here."

She stepped from the path to get away, but she was brought up short by the sight of a tree at the edge of the pool. Carved into the trunk was *L + S,* though lichen was starting to grow over the letters.

Starlock was directly behind her. He didn't touch her, and yet she could feel the warmth of him only inches away. He was looking at the tree, and Luck knew that he was—just as she was—remembering that day, three years ago, when they'd come to this spot together. Their last and only intimate afternoon.

On that day, by this very pool, they had been sitting back to back, so that Luck had felt the rise and fall of Starlock's rib cage against her own as he spoke.

"I turn fourteen tomorrow," he'd said.

Luck was peering at their reflections in the unruffled surface of the water—a reminder of why the two of them would never be Paired. Starlock's birthday was all she'd been thinking about for weeks; fourteen was a cutoff point. After his birthday, he and Luck would be expressly forbidden physical contact and unsupervised time alone. So the era of Luck and Starlock wandering the Rez together was over.

"Maybe they won't find out if we spend time together," Luck said.

"Yeah, sure," Starlock responded. "Like my sister."

Everyone over fourteen was checked every month, and

if you had someone else's DNA on you, you might be taken away. No one knew exactly how much DNA would be too much—because of course Protos ended up touching incidentally all the time at gatherings and at work—and yet common wisdom was that any significant exchange of bodily fluids with an inappropriate person would be enough to get you removed. This had happened to Starlock's sister when she was fifteen years old. Starlock had been nine at the time, and Luck had been eight. His sister, whose name had been Mist, had sworn to her parents and Mizter Caldwell that she'd only kissed a boy a few times, but that had been sufficient for her life on the Rez—and the boy's as well—to be over. Someone was taken away every few years.

Even if she and Starlock somehow escaped detection, if Luck ever had one of Starlock's children, a little baby with light brown skin, and Starlock's eyes, for instance . . . that baby would be taken away. Mixed children of Protos went to live with the humans, no exceptions—they were improperly blended examples of primitive and pure gene patterns. "Do you think your sister is dead?" she asked.

Starlock shrugged against her shoulders. "Sometimes I think she's not," he whispered, "and I wonder what her life is like."

"Me too," Luck said.

"But mostly I think she is."

Luck dropped a leaf onto the surface of the water and watched tiny ripples spread. "If we *all* did it," she reasoned, "if we all disobeyed at once . . . they couldn't take all of us."

Starlock turned to her and took hold of her shoulder. He was more upset by mention of his sister than Luck had realized. "Luck, they *would* take all of us, or punish all of us. It would be so easy. If we make trouble, why not separate the Rez into a dozen reservations, each one with people who all look the same? Or stop teaching us anything useful? The Covenants are what keep us all together and alive." Starlock, who was almost never frantic, was grabbing Luck's shoulder frantically. "I don't want them to take you away," he whispered. "I couldn't live with that."

Slowly, Luck nodded. Her daydreams of disobedience were only daydreams. The consequences of acting them out would be too severe.

"But what are we supposed to do after tomorrow?" she had whispered.

"I can't imagine," Starlock had said. "I don't want to think about it."

Knowing it was their last day alone, they'd made the most of it. They'd undressed each other completely, giggling with embarrassment, but then growing serious as they slid into the cool water of the pool. Shyly at first, but then more and more naturally, they'd touched each other all they wanted. They had both been only thirteen, and nothing serious had happened, but Luck remembered it as hands gliding across each other's bodies, smooth and chilled from the pool, chests pressed together, arms embracing, and a long, sweet kiss with both of their heads just above the surface of the water.

Now in the same clearing, three years later, Starlock closed the space between them and pressed himself against her. Luck's breath drew in sharply at the weight and warmth of him. His hand ran down her arm, and he intertwined his fingers with hers. She studied their fingers, locked together, dark brown and creamy white, alternating. Perfect opposites.

"The sentries falling, no humans answering the radio," he whispered, close to her ear. "The two of us crossing the fence line. It was like we stepped outside our lives for a minute, Luck. Just for a minute, but maybe there's hope that—"

"There isn't," Luck breathed, her heart pounding in her chest. "The Authority will come to the Rez and everything will go back to normal." She unlaced her hand from his. Walking alone together to the fence had been a mistake, and this walk in the woods had been a bigger mistake. She couldn't keep her voice steady as she said, "It would kill me if they took you away. And it would kill both of us if they took our children." She stepped away and refused to look at him. "You should wash your hand extra well when we get back," she told him, knowing this instruction was cruel and unnecessary, "so they can't detect any traces of me on you."

Then she walked back to the others.

3. THEY IGNORED THEIR ELDERS

At the Rez medical center, the Protos did whatever they could for the sentries, which was not much. Their broken bones seemed to have no relation to their overall condition, and all three of them continued to wither up. They were dead before dinnertime. And no one at the Proto Authority was answering the radio.

At dinner in the Rez dining hall that night, Alderwoman Twinfate launched into a meandering speech that sounded like every other speech Luck had ever heard from an older person on the Rez, all of which could be summed up this way: *Life is good, our Rez is beautiful. Let's keep it that way.*

". . . everyone will continue ordinary daily work as we wait patiently to hear from the Proto Authority," Twinfate was saying, her croaky voice fading in and out as she swayed slightly around the microphone. (Luck supposed she was tired after the walk to and from the border that morning.) "Naturally, all of the Covenants are to be followed, and no one is allowed to approach the fence line. . . ."

Alderwoman Twinfate had the features of the South Pacific Islanders, though her once-black hair was now mostly white. She was of the first Rez generation, one of the founding orphans, who had been drawn from different locations all over the world, just as the Great Shift was happening. She and the others of that first group had been raised by humans who were committed to keeping a population of Protos alive. That first generation of Protos had grown up and intermarried—according to the Covenants and their physical traits, of course—and the Rez population had increased over a hundred years to what it was now.

The curriculum of the Rez school had been established for that first group of Protos and had shaped the understanding of all subsequent generations about the world—the world that belonged to humans now, and in which Protos were no longer allowed to live. It was a world no Proto could quite imagine, except for the forests and fields and the mountains that were visible around the Rez, and except as marks on old maps, showing cities that no living Proto had ever set foot in, and except for descriptions in novels, which were often hundreds of years old and might detail a world of carriages and horses and coal smoke or a world of belching automobiles and lumbering airplanes, but most certainly did not describe the actual world as it was now. Set against this unknown, the Rez, with its three hundred square miles of fertile countryside, was an oasis of comfortable life.

For Alderwoman Twinfate, and for most Protos, that was enough. Luck, on the other hand, had made the library her second home. When you'd read Dickens, and Dickinson, and you'd read selections of Greek mythology and stories by a woman called Brontë and even a few by a man called Vonnegut—or at least, when you'd read the parts of those books that made it through the Proto Authority's redaction process—you sometimes thought about a different sort of life.

Of course the teachers on the Rez had explained to Luck and her classmates early on why there were no Protos in their novels and textbooks. When the writers said *people* and when they said *humans*, they *meant* Protos, because *everyone* had been a Proto in those days. That was what *human* had meant. Then had come the Great Shift, and the humans had taken the word *human* and made it mean something *more* than human, or perhaps, Luck thought, something *in*human. They had evolved and taken the word with them.

"Why can't we live with the humans?" Luck had asked her teacher once, to peals of laughter from the other children.

"Think, Luck," her teacher had said. "You've read about Neanderthals. They had much in common with Protos, and yet if there were still Neanderthals, you wouldn't make them live with us on the Reservation. They'd want their own life, and it wouldn't be safe for them on the Rez, with electricity and farm equipment and things like that."

"So the world out there isn't safe for Protos?" Luck had asked.

The teacher had explained about the treaty then. The new species, in its many forms, had spread over the world, but they had given Protos an ideal place to live, and protection. And the Covenants were not much of a burden.

In the Rez dining hall, Luck's reverie was broken when Alderwoman Twinfate was loudly interrupted.

A young, resolute voice said, "You know the Rez isn't self-sufficient, don't you?"

That was Sunchance, a man in his twenties, who took the microphone from the alderwoman without asking for permission. A murmur of indignation rose from the long table of the oldest Rez inhabitants, but he ignored this and explained the only thing that mattered—that the humans supplied thirty percent of what the Rez needed to survive. If the humans didn't show up for months, the Rez would eventually run out of food unless they made some drastic changes.

"Of course they're coming back," said Alderwoman Twin-fate, trying to recapture the microphone.

Sunchance dodged her, kept the microphone, and said, "We need to go out into the world and find out what's happening. So we can plan. Who's with me?"

"They're coming back!" the Alderwoman cried, her voice rising above the hubbub.

But no one was listening to her anymore. People were volunteering. Luck and Starlock, who were sitting across the room from each other and avoiding each other's eyes, nevertheless raised their hands at the same moment.

4. THEY DID NOT SHARE A TENT

"Luck, look! There's something down there!" called Rocky from farther up the trail.

Luck was hiking in a party of four, but she had fallen behind. They'd been heading northeast all day, in the direction their maps told them would take them to the city. Of course, the Proto maps were quite old, but you didn't move a city, did you?

Luck had relished every step taken outside the Rez—at first. But now she was beginning to feel that the world outside the Rez was a lot like the world inside the Rez. They'd seen nothing but empty countryside, and Luck was having a hard time keeping herself focused.

There were many Proto search parties, each one of which

had been assigned a slightly different route to the city, to raise the chances of encountering humans along the way who could help them contact the Proto Authority or perhaps explain why the Authority wasn't answering. By chance (or, more likely, by request of Starlock's mother) Starlock and Moonlight had been assigned together to another group, on some other path. Even though Luck had pushed Starlock away, her mind strayed again and again to the two of them hiking together for hours—

She was jerked out of these thoughts by Rocky, who was pulling at her arm. "Luck, there's an air transpo down there! Just up ahead!"

She suspected her mother had arranged for Rocky's inclusion in her own search party as part of a campaign to wear down Luck's aversion to him. With a show of annoyance, she removed her arm from Rocky's grasp, but she still followed him eagerly. They emerged from the trees to a valley spread out below them. In the center of this valley was a crashed air transpo, its insect-eye windows shattered, its propellers bent, its cabin partially crushed. It was the first sign of civilization they'd yet seen.

"Is that the transpo that comes to the Rez each month?" Luck asked.

"Looks like it," said Rocky. "Let's catch up!"

The two other members of their party were halfway down the hill. Rocky made a grab for Luck's hand, which she quickly drew out of reach. He didn't seem to mind or even notice this rebuff, because his hand was already straying to his crotch. Luck stopped herself from slapping it. She wondered if she would be resisting the urge to slap him for the rest of her life . . . while Starlock would lose all sense of resistance to Moonlight.

"Come on, Luck!" Rocky urged as he trotted down the valley's slope.

Luck followed suit, trying to retrieve her thoughts. Why did she care so much about Moonlight? She'd come to terms with Starlock being Paired with her—mostly—ages ago. Yet she did care. Very much. And Starlock—why had he brought her to that pool by the river, a place she avoided going even in her mind?

"Stop," Luck said aloud.

"What?" asked Rocky.

"Not you," she said. "I was talking to myself."

"Why are you talking to yourself?" Rocky asked.

"Why shouldn't I be?" she snapped.

"Let's not argue," he said magnanimously, as though they'd been Paired for years and he were used to her moods.

As they neared the others, the leader of their search party, a man in his forties called Larkspur, peered through the transpo's broken windows. He called out to them, "It's Mizter Caldwell! And he looks dead."

Luck and Rocky ran the last distance to join them. The transpo's passenger door was partially crushed, but working together, they managed to wrench it upward. Inside, limp against the straps of the passenger seat, was the blue-skinned Proto Liaison Officer. Mizter Caldwell was hardly recognizable. His beautiful skin had shriveled everywhere, though in some places it had expanded into a loose sort of foam, so that there were patches of what looked like fluffy, sparkling mold. His long arms were no more than ropy strands. His mouth was open in a skull-like smile, all of his white teeth prominent. He appeared mummified, and a sweet, chemical smell wafted up from his body.

He was obviously dead, and yet Larkspur, out of a sense of duty, touched the man's neck to feel for a pulse, and then he shook his head. The Protos were not sure how to react to the circumstance of this man's death—this man who had had the power to remove Protos from the Rez, who had frequently inspected Protos' private sleeping quarters to check that nothing inappropriate was happening, this man who had taken DNA samples of Proto children to double-check their parentage . . .

"He came to our classroom once," Rocky said. "He wasn't very nice."

"I remember," said Luck.

That day Mizter Caldwell had told the teacher that he wanted to "observe the Rez's curiosities at play." When the teacher had politely asked him what that meant, since the students were not playing but studying, he'd explained that he was referring to the children *learning*. Protos were, of course, a library, he said, and each Proto child was a book in that library. But their minds were simply curiosities—quaint side effects. As much as Luck loved library books, she hadn't liked the idea of *being* one.

A shuddering breath from the other seat startled all of them.

"The pilot's alive!" said Larkspur.

Pulling the opposite door open, they found a woman slumped over the controls. She drew long, rasping breaths as her half-closed eyes studied the Protos standing in front of her. Luck could not be sure, but it seemed as if the woman was not at all happy to see them. There was something malevolent in her stare.

"Did you get . . . what you wanted . . . then?" the woman croaked.

No one knew what to make of this question.

"What happened?" Larkspur asked her. "Are you sick? Is this a sickness?"

"You would know . . . ," the woman said venomously.

Along her upper chest, a necklacelike ring of skin and muscle had dissolved to her rib cage. Luck caught a glimpse of light pink lung tissue, inflating and deflating as she spoke. The rest of the woman wasn't mummified like Mizter Caldwell; quite the opposite: her skin gave the impression of a solid mass of motion. On closer examination, Luck saw paintings, like living tattoos, wriggling and leaping and slithering across the woman's flesh. They looked obscenely alive on the skin of this dying person.

"Look!" whispered Cloud, the young woman who was the fourth member of their search party. She was pointing at the pilot's arms. The woman's muscles were disintegrating inch by inch, as if a burning fuse were eating her up. In the wake of this "fuse," her tattoos were frozen and blurred over bones that stood out in stark relief. As they watched, the decay spread to the scalp beneath her multicolored hair.

"Should we move her out onto the ground?" asked Cloud.

"Don't . . . touch . . . me," the woman rasped. She tried to reach a golden pendant, some sort of good-luck charm that was hanging from the controls, but she had no strength left.

Luck untangled the gold chain to put it into the woman's hand, and for a moment she herself was transfixed by the image on the pendant. It was a delicately rendered holograph of a human with flowing black hair falling over his forehead on one side, and curly brown hair on the other. This man had one black eye and one green eye in a face mottled by different skin textures and colors. A beautiful golden light radiated from his head as he lifted his many-colored arms toward her and smiled.

The pilot murmured, "You Naturalists . . . standing there . . . watching me go . . ." She drew in a long, wet breath. "This is his world, not yours. . . ."

These last words were hardly audible. The woman's mouth fell open, and her eyes sank back into her skull as she died.

Rocky retched and turned away. All of the Protos stepped back from the transpo in disgust.

"Why does she think we did this?" Luck asked, feeling ill. She'd never seen this particular human before, and yet she felt the woman's intense hatred. Was it the mere fact that they were Protos?

"Are they all dying?" Cloud asked.

"There are too many of them," Luck said. "They can't *all* die."

"But, Luck, every human we've encountered has been affected," Larkspur pointed out. "And doesn't Mizter Caldwell live in the city? If he was flying from there, people in the city must have it—whatever it is."

"Or if they don't, they will soon," Cloud agreed. "It must be everywhere."

Luck could see where this discussion was heading. The others wanted to go back. Trying to sound logical and not eager, she said, "We should still go to the city. Think about it. We need to find out for sure what's happened to the Proto Authority. We'll never know unless we keep going."

Larkspur hesitated, weighing her argument, but he shook his head. "It's true. We need to find out about the Proto Authority. But we've seen enough to know that the humans are in trouble and we'll have to figure out how to feed ourselves, at least for a while. We should go back to the Rez and tell them that."

• • •

That evening, before the sun went down, they set up camp on the ridge above the valley, from where they would walk back to the Rez the following morning. As Luck collected wood for the fire, she had a clear view to the north, where she spotted Starlock's search party, setting up their own camp.

Hours later, after a simple dinner and another argument

about pressing on to the city—which Luck lost—she lay awake in the tent she shared with Cloud, staring up at the tent fabric, thinking first about Starlock and then about the humans. They had always presented themselves as perfect and invincible. Benign, mostly, except for the occasional practical joke by a sentry or a cutting remark by Mizter Caldwell. Benign strength—that was their nature. Luck could scarcely imagine that anything, even a plague, could overcome them.

When the others had fallen asleep and her camp was quiet, Luck pulled on her jacket and boots, scooped up her sleeping bag and the small bundle of provisions she'd stashed away after dinner, and quietly let herself out of the tent.

She saw the wisdom in Larkspur's plan to go home, and if she hadn't been the one to see the sentries fall or the one who had found them, and if she hadn't set her mind on reaching the city, or at least seeing and understanding a larger piece of the world, she would have accepted his decision. But as it was, Luck was not ready to turn home yet.

The night air was perfectly still and, though the moon had not yet risen, she could see a long distance by the light of the stars. She began walking north, toward the faint glow of a dying campfire.

By the time she reached Starlock's camp, more than an hour later, Luck was tired and cold, and the new camp's fire had long since gone out. She crept quietly between the two tents and listened, thinking she would find the one that belonged to the girls and sneak in for the night. In the morning, she would have another chance at convincing her fellow

Protos to keep going to the city—or she could tag along with them if that was already their plan. She was sure that Starlock, at least, would not want to turn back.

Hearing nothing from either tent, Luck quietly unzipped the flap of the closest one and peeked inside. Her eyes had long since adjusted to the night and she could make out the interior quite easily. Two shadowed figures lay inside. One figure opened its eyes, saw her, and sat up. In the dimness, its features resolved into Starlock's face.

"Luck," he whispered. "How—how did you get here?"

"Starlock—" she began. But the rest of the sentence died in her mouth. She had recognized the other figure in the tent, who was still fast asleep, an arm thrown across Starlock's midsection, a leg draped over his legs: Moonlight.

Luck was dimly aware that she was acting out a scene from countless novels as she stood outside the tent, her mouth forming an O of surprise while she watched Starlock hastily remove Moonlight's arm and get to his knees.

"We're only—she wanted—" he began, continuing to follow the script Luck had read before. "Luck, I couldn't say no when—"

She didn't need to hear any more. Luck shut her mouth, let go of the tent's open flap, and dashed away from the campsite.

She ran until she was quite out of breath, and then she walked as fast as she could. Her heart was pounding, and yet it seemed to communicate no warmth to the rest of her.

"It doesn't matter," she whispered.

It would have happened eventually. They were going to be

Paired in five weeks, and Luck had told him no. And yet . . . and yet the world had been unbalanced for days. She'd begun to think these last weeks might be . . . she didn't know what she had thought they might be. Different. But Starlock had given himself to Moonlight—or Moonlight had taken him. It was done.

Luck stumbled on until she was too tired to go any farther, and then, feeling as desolate as the countryside, she unrolled her sleeping bag beneath the wide canopy of an oak tree and slept alone.

5. THEY WHISPERED IN THE DARK

When she woke at first light, Luck found that her emotions had clarified into a grim determination. She decided to press on to the east alone. If the Proto Authority found her and punished her, so be it. What exactly was left for her on the Rez anyway?

At midday, Rocky caught up with her. Luck had known she was heading toward the main path, where all of the search parties would eventually converge, but she'd thought she was far ahead of everyone else and so was entirely surprised when he came puffing along the trail to join her as she sat on a rock eating jerky and looking out to the horizon.

Rocky dropped to the ground, sunburned, winded, his sleeping bag and pack of provisions bouncing against each other as he dumped them onto the dirt. After he'd caught his breath, he ran a hand through his sweaty hair and smiled up at Luck as though nothing could have been more natural than him following her.

"You're going to the city anyway," he said. He took a long drink from his canteen.

Luck nodded. "You read my note?" She'd left a note in the tent for the others to find so they wouldn't waste time looking for her.

"Note? No. I—I woke up really early and I saw you were gone. But I guessed where you were headed." His tone suggested that this was the cleverest conclusion imaginable. "I had to go so fast to catch you! I'm glad you stopped for lunch."

"I wasn't really looking for company, Rocky."

Rocky smiled as though he could see right through her. "Course you were. No one would want to be out here alone. It's practically my job to protect you, Luck. And I'm dying to see what a city looks like."

"There might be a lot of dying people *in* the city," Luck told him, turning his words around in an attempt to discourage him from coming along. "It's not going to be fun."

Rocky shrugged and wrinkled his nose and said, "So what if they're dying? They're just humans, Luck. We don't have to be sad for them. There's thousands of them. Or millions. And I don't think they care about us as much as the teacher in school said they do."

She had no intention of overtly agreeing with Rocky about anything, but privately Luck thought this last idea might be true. And it seemed, to her irritation, that she'd now inadvertently agreed to him coming with her. Though she would never have admitted it to herself, she was relieved to have a companion.

"Do you think there will be horses?" Rocky asked.

"In the city? I don't think so. Not for hundreds of years."

"Cars, then?"

Luck shrugged. "Maybe."

They walked through hilly, forested country all that long spring afternoon and stopped to eat dinner when the sun was going down. They had built a fire, over which Luck was heating a can of soup, when branches were pushed aside and Starlock walked into the clearing. Luck felt a surge of happiness when she saw him (he had come for her!), which quickly died when Moonlight appeared a few moments later, looking slightly disheveled but generally beautiful.

There was a pause that lasted for what felt like half an hour. During this time, three things took place: Moonlight realized where and to whom Starlock had been leading them; Luck digested the fact that Starlock had brought his lover with him; and even Rocky participated with visible disappointment in Starlock's arrival—because of course every young person on the Rez was aware of what Luck and Starlock had once felt for each other.

"Where's the rest of your group?" Luck finally asked, breaking the silence. She turned back to the fire and her soup, which was nearly boiling.

"They're coming," Starlock answered. Luck was pleased to note that his temper sounded frayed. "We found some dead humans this morning, and the others in our group stayed to bury them."

"More dead," Rocky said with a knowing sigh.

"The ones we found were teenagers who'd been climbing a cliff," Moonlight explained. She seated herself right next to Luck, as though the two of them were the best of friends. "It was kind of a mess." She produced a piece of jerky from a pocket and took a bite. Somehow even eating jerky was a feminine activity when done by Moonlight.

"They fell when their limbs began to wither," Starlock told them in a more subdued fashion. He was still standing, as though paralyzed, at the edge of the clearing. "Only one was still alive, because he hadn't started climbing yet. His legs just sort of crumbled beneath him."

"But he died while we were there," Moonlight said, taking back the narrative. "He talked to us for a little while, but then—" She mimed a dead face, mouth sagging, eyes closed.

"His heart finally went," Starlock explained. "Whatever makes them wither happens pretty quickly, but it seems to take longer to get to the internal organs."

"Why did you guys come on ahead?" Luck asked indifferently. "Are you both so eager to see the city?" She put a slight emphasis on the word *both*, hoping that Starlock would contradict her and protest that he hadn't wanted Moonlight along, but of course he didn't.

Nodding at Starlock, Moonlight said, "This silly boy made up his mind that sooner was better. He wanted to get to the city immediately." Moonlight patted the spot next to her, calling Starlock over to the fire. He approached but didn't sit. Luck saw all this without removing her gaze from the soup. She had no intention of meeting Starlock's eyes. "It didn't make any sense for him to go alone—that's so dangerous!" Moonlight continued. "So I came too." She warmed her quick-moving, nimble hands over the fire and the image came to Luck's mind, unbidden, of that right hand draped across Starlock's chest. She could imagine the girl's fingers sliding beneath his clothing. . . .

"Why did you go on ahead?" Starlock asked Luck.

Still looking at her food, Luck said, "Because I intend to find out what's happening."

. . .

After they'd all eaten, Starlock set up the tent he'd brought. The four of them and their sleeping bags fit snugly inside. Moonlight preemptively placed herself and Rocky in the middle with Luck and Starlock on opposite sides. Then Rocky said, rather gallantly, "I don't want you to be cold, Luck, so I'll take the outside." Which meant Luck was lying between him and Moonlight. Luck's skin was almost crawling with the awkwardness of it as silence settled over the tent.

She felt herself drifting off when she was startled awake by a voice coming directly into her ear: "This is the first time we've slept together." It was Rocky, mercifully speaking in a whisper low enough that neither of the others would be able to hear.

"We're not sleeping together, Rocky," Luck whispered back. "We're just sharing a tent."

"Would you like me to kiss you?" he breathed. "We won't get in trouble. Everyone knows—"

"No," Luck hissed.

"What if *you* kissed *me*?"

"That's the same thing, so *no*." She struggled to put sufficient force into the nearly inaudible words.

"Why not?" Even through the whisper she could hear a whine in his voice.

"We're not Paired," she whispered back.

"We *will* be."

"Maybe," Luck allowed. "But not for years."

"One year and seven months," Rocky murmured, as if the calendar of Luck's life were written inside his eyelids and he referred to it all the time. Then, breathing into her ear canal, he suggested, "I could touch your breasts. Girls like that, don't they?"

"Go to sleep!" Luck hissed, moving her arms up to cover herself.

Rocky lapsed into silence then, and in a short while she could hear him breathing evenly in sleep. Yet Luck fancied there were shifts and movements in Moonlight's and Starlock's sleeping bags, the sound of hands seeking each other out, of lips touching. . . .

For the second night in a row, she wriggled out of her bag and climbed out of the tent, moving as silently as she possibly could. Once outside, Luck was cold, but glad of the distraction provided by the sharp air. Their campsite was at the base of a forested hill, with tall fir trees all around. The night sky hung above the trees' pointed crowns, magnificent with stars.

She walked to the small brook near the edge of the clearing and knelt down. Her reflection greeted her on the surface, blurred and dark. She splashed cold water over her face for a long while, reveling in the biting chill. And then she jumped in alarm when a hand grasped her elbow. It was Starlock, of course, crouched just a foot away.

Luck, in no mood to appreciate his talent for sneaking up on her, pulled her arm away and stood. He placed a finger to his lips, took hold of Luck's arm again, ignoring her reluctance, and stepped across the stream. Starlock led her quite a distance into the trees, far enough that they could be sure of their privacy.

"I didn't sleep with Moonlight," he whispered.

"You obviously weren't sleeping," Luck said, tearing her arm away from him again.

"She—she kept saying how scared she was to sleep out in the wild. The others got annoyed and made me stay in the tent with her."

"Starlock, I saw her all tangled up with you." She almost spat the words.

"I was fully dressed!"

Luck paused. That was true. He'd been clothed when she'd seen him, but—

"No. I *saw you.* You were holding each other. I'm sure the two of you are clever enough to work around clothing." Her voice rose above a whisper.

"Shhh! Do not wake her up, please! Luck, she's worried about me. She's worried about *you.* I'm supposed to be her mate, and now things are . . . *confused,* and she wants to keep me with her."

"So you slept with her to make her feel better?"

"I *didn't*— Look, she kissed me a couple of times and I didn't push her away, okay? That's the truth. But they were childish kisses."

"Wonderful." The word felt like acid in her mouth.

"You told me to leave you alone, and you were right!" Starlock said in exasperation. "You know I probably have to spend the rest of my life with Moonlight. I can't be rude to her— I can't tell her that I don't want her. What happens when the humans get the Rez back under control, Luck? Even if it takes a few months? If they don't send all of us away for crossing the border, then I'll be Paired with Moonlight and she'll make me sorry for rejecting her till I'm ninety."

It was the longest speech he'd given her in years.

Luck turned from him, frustrated and shivering. "I know," she said eventually. Because she did know. It was why she hadn't ordered Rocky to go away; it was why she put up with him even though he irked her deeply. She was going to have to live with him eventually. "It's just—imagine you had found me like that with Rocky."

"I would break his neck," Starlock said without hesitation. "I'd punch his freckled nose into the back of his head."

"Then it's good you didn't hear him trying to get under my shirt earlier."

"What?" hissed Starlock. "I'm going to snap that carrot in half."

Luck smiled, but the smile felt like it was floating on the surface of her face and reaching no further inside. Now that her anger was fading, she was excessively aware of Starlock's closeness. There was a magnetic pull between them, so that it took effort to remain where she was. She whispered, "I've started to hope. . . ."

"Me too."

"I have to stop hoping, Starlock. Because it makes me feel like you're mine. And if nothing is actually different . . . It was awful last night when I saw you two."

"Nothing happened."

She nodded, believing him now. In truth, she'd already known. It had simply been easier to be furious than to dwell on how much she wanted to be the one tangled up with him inside that tent.

"You're shivering," he said. He took off his coat and draped it around her. She tried not to look at him, but it was hard. He was *right there.*

Starlock stood away from her for several moments, and then, as if he could hold out no longer, he came closer and wrapped his arms around her. They hadn't embraced in three years and

Luck had forgotten how good it felt, your whole body pressed up against the other person. He was taller than he'd been the last time they'd done this—taller and stronger and warmer.

"How could I sleep with her?" Starlock whispered. "Since we saw the sentries fall, all I can think about is that something might change. I imagine taking you back to that pool by the river—"

"Stop, please stop."

But he didn't stop; he leaned down and his lips found hers. For a moment, they were kissing, actually kissing, and it was startling how good it felt.

Luck turned away, pushed him back to arm's length.

"We have to find out first," she whispered. "Please. Or I won't be able to stand it."

Starlock nodded, stayed away from her, though Luck could feel that magnetic force trying to pull them back into each other's arms.

"It's good Moonlight and Rocky are here," he whispered. "If it were just the two of us, I'd never stop."

6. THEY FOUND MORE THAN THE WALLED CITY

They emerged from the forest the following afternoon to find themselves on an open ridge above a broad valley. But Luck and the others noticed nothing in the landscape except for the city. It was a mile or more away, encircled by a high wall.

She had read about cities in old books, imagined what cities must be like . . . but in real life this one was immense. Tall glass buildings grew up from the city center, elbowed each other for room as they rose high, high above the wall and speared the sky. These buildings were of every shape and color imaginable, sharing only height and glass as common traits. There was a pale blue cylinder that swayed on currents of air; a tall white column covered all over with sharp crystal facets like bristling diamond armor; a sort of changing geometric tower with rect-angles and hexagons and trapezoids interlacing and shifting in and out of relief as though moved by the wind. Another tower reflected the sky and the city in every hue of the rainbow, the colors creeping across its faces in an ever-changing display. A dozen other buildings were connected by arching walkways to form a silver lattice that spread throughout the city. Luck had once read a book about a place called Oz, and the city within the wall reminded her of that.

It took a few moments for her to notice the smoke rising from dozens of locations within the wall. Black plumes hung thick and almost unmoving in the air.

"Buildings are burning," she said.

"I think those are power stations." Starlock pointed to three of the nearest plumes. The buildings beneath the smoke were just visible over the top of the wall. All three were like blocks of shiny, braided pipes with the most enormous round chimneys Luck had ever seen. "I've seen pictures in our en-gineering books," he explained, because of course at the Rez they used only solar panels and diesel generators.

"Are the humans fighting?" asked Rocky.

"And what's that smell?" asked Moonlight.

The breeze had just shifted, and an overwhelming odor had washed up from the valley below. It was a scent that had been slowly building in the air for the last hour of their hike, Luck realized, but only now, with the wind in their direction, did it fully make its presence known. Luck took several steps closer to the edge of the plateau, bringing the valley into view.

"Oh, goodness. Look," she said to the others. The words were hopelessly inadequate, and yet they were all she could manage when she saw the scene spread out beneath her.

The other Protos joined her at the lip, so that all four of them quickly understood that the burning power stations were the least of the city's problems. The real horror was below them. A mass exodus.

Their plateau overlooked two enormous roads that issued from tunnels through the city's wall. One of those roads came straight toward them, curved just beneath the hill on which they stood, then continued on to the south. This road was choked with land-going vehicles and dead humans. Withered corpses lay inside every car and littered embankments all along the roadway.

"It doesn't look like there was fighting," Starlock observed. He looked physically ill as he surveyed the devastation.

"They tried to get out of the city when the sickness—or whatever it is—hit," Luck murmured.

"And they kept going until they started to die," Starlock

said. "The fires . . . we're seeing what happens when all the workers collapse at once."

It was quite clear where one vehicle had stopped suddenly, causing others to slam into it. This had happened again and again as some vehicles had gotten through, only to stall out farther down the road.

"The ones who were still alive tried to get away on foot," Luck whispered, looking at the corpses sprawled in the open. They were of every shape and size and color—not all of them with anything you could reasonably call a "foot." Farther away were countless crashed air transpos.

Luck had known that humans numbered in the millions, but that number had been meaningless to her before this moment. She was seeing more living creatures than she had ever seen in her life. Except that they weren't living anymore.

Pulling the collar of her shirt up over her nose, Moonlight whispered, "It smells awful."

The corpses had been dead for days at this point, and the fetor rose from the road in clouds and rolled toward them on the breeze. And yet it was not the stench Luck would expect from a dead animal.

"It's like death and toffee," Rocky gasped, throwing an arm over the lower half of his face.

This description was exactly right. It was, Luck thought, as if someone had mixed the scents of dead rats and butterscotch. She pinched her nose, fighting not to be sick.

"Look!" Starlock said.

An air transpo had lifted above the city wall. It made an erratic, swooping turn and then flew directly toward the four Protos standing on the plateau.

"They're coming for us," Moonlight hissed, clutching Starlock's arm. She tugged him toward the edge of the forest. "We have to go. They're going to take us for being off the Rez."

"Do you think that's true?" Rocky asked, looking to Luck. "Should we hide?"

Luck was scared that Moonlight was right, but she refused to agree. "I didn't come this far to run away now." She said it to Starlock and saw her own feelings echoed in his eyes.

"What are you looking at her for?" demanded Moonlight.

Starlock took both of Moonlight's hands in his own and said, with all the calm he could muster, "The humans have other problems right now, Moonlight. You hide if you want. I'm not going to."

• • •

The very dented transpo landed, rather hard, just yards from Luck and Starlock, kicking up a dust storm and forcing them all to crouch down and cover their eyes, even Moonlight and Rocky, who had retreated several yards toward the trees. The engines were cut abruptly, and a rear door came crashing open. Three figures in T-shirts and trousers in a pattern Luck recognized as "camouflage" spilled out onto the grass. Only—

"They're Protos!" Starlock said quietly. He looked to Luck for confirmation. "Aren't they?"

Luck watched the newcomers closely. There were no odd colors or improperly sized heads or extra limbs, though all three were so wobbly on their feet that it took them a while to stand up straight, and one of them never did. That one was coughing so much from the dust still swirling in the air that he clutched his knees and rocked back and forth to try to stop the spasms. The other two, also coughing, approached Luck, Starlock, Rocky, and Moonlight with something like amazement.

"Hello, Fellows!" called the first one. He and his companions were young, perhaps in their early twenties, and all very dirty. With effort, he pulled himself fully upright and clapped a hand to his chest. "I'm Matt, and these are Jason and Raul. We greet you in the form Nature intended."

"I'm Starlock," said Starlock.

"And I'm Luck," said Luck. "And you're Pro—"

"We—we greet you in the form Nature intended," the newcomer repeated.

When the Protos hesitated, the one still on the ground crawled forward and asked, "Aren't you—aren't you Naturalists? He says, 'We greet you in the form Nature intended,' and then you say the other part."

"Do you not learn the greeting in your bloc?" the first one asked, perplexed. "You're supposed to say, 'We are all Fellows in the Natural.'"

Tentatively, with a glance at Starlock, Luck began, "'We are all Fellows—'" but she was interrupted when the one who hadn't yet spoken grabbed the shirt of the one called Matt in a fit of emotion and practically shouted, "It's because they're not, they're *not*. Look! They're, they're completely black and completely white. And orange," he added, with a nod to Rocky.

The faces of the other newcomers fell into something like shock.

"You don't think they're . . . ?" began one.

"For real?" asked the one still on the ground. "You're saying they're—for real?"

Matt pounded his own chest for a moment as though to jump-start his lungs, and then he addressed the Protos with formal courtesy. "We are *Naturalists*. We don't get mods, because it's, like, a terrible thing to do. But you don't have mods because—" He paused to pound his chest again.

"Because you're Protos!" the other standing one said, taking over. "Holy fucking Daughter, you're Protos!"

Luck and the others nodded hesitantly, while Luck mused on his use of the word *fucking* (she'd read swear words in many books, but no one on the Rez ever used them). The three Naturalists—whatever that meant—hollered and punched each other's shoulders and one even pulled up the fellow on the ground and put him into a headlock with affectionate amazement. All of this gave the impression that they had just been granted their most cherished wish. The Protos were baffled by this display.

Eventually one of the newcomers broke off the roughhousing to cough for an entire minute straight. The other two sat on the ground in silence, catching their breath. Luck was reassured by their apparent harmlessness, though their coughing was troubling—coughs were rare on the Rez, unless someone got a lungful of smoke from a bonfire.

"You're not Protos?" Luck asked.

"We wish!" said the one called Matt. "We're just basic humans, a mix of everything." He gestured at his own face and hair and then at his closest companion's. The features of both men were rather unremarkable to Luck, except for a general appearance of having been drawn from many parts of the world and combined.

Matt went on with joyous incredulity. "I saw you through the telescope from our lookout post, and I only thought about your *shape*, you know?" he said. "And whether or not you were armed. I wasn't thinking about your color, or where you could have come from. Honestly, I wasn't even sure that Protos were real. Miz Babbidge is going to flip."

. . .

"I am *not* going inside that city," Moonlight objected in a low hiss that was intended to keep her words private but carried quite clearly to Luck, "and neither are you, Starlock."

The Naturalists had excitedly demanded that the Protos come with them into the city, where they would be fed and briefed and maybe even celebrated, they said, by the rest of the Naturalists. ("You're, like, hope for mankind," the one called Jason had told them. "You're what we all believe in.") The Protos had retreated to a private spot among trees a good fifty yards from the transpo to consider this offer.

"Do you think it smells this bad in the city?" Rocky asked.

"It's going to be much, much worse," said Starlock. "However many people got out to the road in their cars, there might be ten times as many inside."

"And if they all died days ago . . . ," said Luck. She shuddered.

"I'm *not* going," Moonlight said again, not bothering to lower her voice this time. "The rest of our search parties will be here soon, and they can go. Starlock, I forbid you—"

"Moonlight," he said, cutting her off, "you knew I was going to the city. That's why we came. The others will get here eventually, but we can find out what's happening *right now*."

Moonlight gestured wildly at the road far below. "That was the plan before we saw all the dead humans. One or two isn't a big deal, sure, but this is going to be . . . it's going to be awful."

"It *is* awful," said Luck, finally allowing her impatience with Moonlight to show. "It'll be the worst thing any of us has ever seen. But I'm not turning back."

The breeze kicked up again, bearing the scent of death and sweets. Rocky retched. He was looking green beneath his freckles.

"I don't think you should go, Luck," Rocky told her. "It's so disgusting. It's like I'm *breathing in* their dead bodies. Did you know there were that many humans? We should go home."

"No," Luck answered, evading Rocky's arm. "If I go home, I'm just a Proto teenager, waiting to be told what to do. I don't want to wait. I want to know *now*. What if the Proto Authority is still there, fully operational, in some kind of special quarantine zone? Or what if it's not?" When she saw Rocky's blank face, she added, "Haven't you ever thought of anything outside the Rez, Rocky?"

"Jeez, Luck," said Rocky, stung. "I'm just saying it's gross."

Moonlight looked from Starlock to Luck and then back again. "You want to go be with *her*," she said in a stage whisper that was full of anguish she'd obviously been fighting to keep in check.

Luck averted her eyes, but she could not deny the thrill it gave her to hear Moonlight say this out loud.

"I have to find out what's in store for us," Starlock said gently. He put a hand on her shoulder. "Don't you want to know?"

Moonlight picked some dirt off her pants and didn't meet his eyes. "I don't have to know *right now*," she said.

"Then you should wait for the others to get here," he told her softly.

"All right," Moonlight said at last. "You find out *our* future and then come back."

She kissed Starlock on the lips, but Luck observed that Starlock kept himself just a little too far away for the kiss to connect properly. With that, Moonlight glared at Luck and turned her back on the two of them.

A tug on Luck's sleeve reminded her of Rocky's presence. "Good-bye, Luck," he said earnestly. Emulating Moonlight, he leaned forward to plant a kiss on Luck's mouth, but she stepped back, so his kiss landed somewhere in the region of her shoulder. Rocky didn't mind—he looked delighted that he'd managed to get his lips to connect with any part of her.

Starlock and Luck turned to the Naturalists. He put a hand cautiously on Luck's back—neither of them sure what the men might think of such contact—and walked toward the waiting transpo.

7. THEY ENTERED THE LAND OF HUMANS

They'd never been in an air transpo before, so they had no way to judge whether this particular vehicle was airworthy or not. When they'd all strapped themselves to seats—Luck and Starlock and the Naturalist called Raul in the back, and the other two up front at the controls—the transpo's engines spun up into a whispering torrent of wind. Luck clutched her seat as the vehicle lifted into the air in a cloud of dust. Its engines rattled and thumped as it cleared the edge of the hill and carried them over the wreckage on the road below.

In a wide sweep, Luck saw the cropland that surrounded the city. The sun was going down to the west, and in the golden light were fields stretched to the eastern horizon, full of brown, withered grain. Then the transpo swerved, showing her dead humans instead of dead crops.

The pilot was coughing as they went. Every time he coughed hard, the controls jerked, so the transpo was jumping around in the sky. Raul, sitting across from Luck in the back, was not coughing, but he kept his eyes closed, as if concentrating on each breath.

"Are you all right?" Starlock asked him.

He nodded without opening his eyes. "The fumes from all the dead bodies are getting to us. Makes a burning in your lungs."

"How did they all die?" Starlock asked.

"Quickly," Raul answered. "Starting six days ago, this cata-strophic . . . withering." He made little half coughs as he spoke.

"There are so many," Luck whispered as she looked out the window.

"Yeah," Raul said, his eyes still closed. "Denver had, like, one and a half million people inside the wall a week ago."

One and a half million was such a staggering number Luck couldn't wrap her mind around it. Riding in a vehicle through the sky, meeting these Naturalists who could almost be Pro-tos, catching glimpses of the devastation below them on the ground—she was losing her sense of reality. She managed, "Are they all dead?"

"Most of 'em. They tinkered with nature, didn't they?" Raul drew a gasping breath. He placed a dirt-encrusted hand on his chest, as if to monitor the motion of his lungs. In the confines of the transpo, Luck could smell that he hadn't washed him-self in some time. "We Naturalists have been saying for years that it couldn't last. It *wouldn't* last. Their arrogance has, like, brought the human race to the brink of extinction. Miz Bab-bidge will explain better. She's more scientific."

Studying Raul, Luck said, "I didn't know humans could look so much like Protos."

"Most don't," he answered. "But Naturalists do, because we don't get mods. Which is why we're not getting this disease."

"Mods," Starlock whispered, trying out the word.

Luck remembered that the sentries at the Rez fence had used that word too. The female sentry had said, *So our mods are failing?*

"When you say mods, do you mean things like wings and gills?" Luck asked.

"Mods. Modifications." Raul opened his eyes and regarded Luck with quiet astonishment. "You don't know about mods."

"We—we do know that humans are different, and they're different in lots of different ways," Luck said, looking to Starlock for support, who nodded his agreement. "But they're born different, aren't they?"

"Some mods are programmed into DNA. Eye color, height, reflexes," he explained, drawing a cautious breath. "But big stuff—legs, wings, whatever—that comes later. Pick and choose, add it on."

"So, so . . ." Luck was at a loss for words to fit his statement into what she knew of humanity.

"But humans are a new species," said Starlock.

"There was the Great Shift," added Luck.

Raul was looking at them blankly. "The what?" he asked.

The Protos turned to each other, feeling their world alter. Humans had evolved. Or had they?

"Are you saying there's no difference, really, between us and humans?" Starlock asked, turning back to Raul.

"Of course not," Raul said simply. "The only difference is arrogance."

"But . . . ," Luck began, with no idea how to finish the sentence.

"Hey!" Starlock yelled suddenly, pointing through the front window. "Watch out!"

Instead of the carnage of humans and vehicles, they were looking at the city's wall looming huge in front of them—and they were headed straight for it.

Suddenly Raul was yelling too. "Jason! You're way too—" But he was overridden by Matt in the right-hand seat.

"What the hell are you doing?" Matt yelled at their pilot. "We're going to crash!"

In the driver's seat, Jason was clutching his chest. "Can't breathe . . . ," he gasped.

Matt laid both hands on him and hauled him up. The transpo bucked and banked dizzily to the left. Matt climbed into the driver's seat, wrenched the controls. The transpo soared in a long, steep arc toward the road. Luck and Starlock pitched forward against their seat belts and grabbed each other's hands as they plummeted. She and Starlock would be two more corpses no one would ever find . . .

. . . and then the transpo righted. Matt was cursing at the engines in language as colorful as any Luck had ever read. They were gaining altitude. The transpo's engines whined and shook, but at last they were above the wall, and the city was spread out before them.

Luck had glimpses of smoke, of stalled vehicles littering

roads, of a fire burning in the distance. Then the transpo was dodging lower buildings and bouncing to a stop in a huge concrete courtyard at the center of a complex of low buildings.

The three Naturalists kicked open the door and stumbled outside. The odor hit Luck as soon as the doors were open—rot and butterscotch, far more intense than the smell outside the city. The air felt thick with it.

"Welcome to Denver," Matt said, offering his dirty hand to Luck.

She and Starlock unclipped themselves from their seat belts and stepped out of the transpo. Luck's legs were shaky as she stood on the concrete. Heaps of equipment were piled everywhere—boxes and cans of food stacked twenty feet high, clothing, radio parts, medical supplies. Their three escorts were waving to a group of people—Naturalists, Luck supposed, since they looked like Protos—approaching from one of the buildings.

Starlock whispered, "Let's not say much until we understand what's happening."

Luck nodded. The sense of having stepped out of the known into the entirely unknown was overwhelming. She felt like that girl Alice, when she'd tumbled into Wonderland—except this wonderland looked and smelled awful.

In a moment, the new group had arrived and Luck and Starlock were surrounded by people wearing scarves and paper masks to keep out the pervasive odor of human death. An older woman, clearly the leader, pulled the bandana off her nose and mouth, revealing a face of weathered tan skin beneath light brown eyes. Almost ceremonially, this woman knelt in front of the Protos and took their hands in her own.

"Noble Protos," she said to them. "How beautiful you are. And exactly what we need."

8. THEY WERE EXCESSIVELY ADMIRED

The woman introduced herself as Miz Babbidge. She looked about sixty years old, by Proto reckoning, though Luck had no idea how age manifested itself with Naturalists (other humans, like Mizter Caldwell, had never seemed to age at all).

"I'm the Chief Fellow among the Naturalists," she explained. "Now that we're all that's left, I suppose you could say that I'm running Denver. Were there only two of you? I thought the lookout said four."

"The others decided to wait for us outside the city," Starlock answered.

Luck wondered if the other Proto search parties had reached the promontory yet, or if Rocky and Moonlight were still there alone, perhaps complaining about their future spouses. They felt immeasurably distant now.

Miz Babbidge directed a look of irritation at the three Naturalists who had flown the Protos into the city. "I had hopes you would bring everyone," she said. She spoke with a funny wheeze, as though her lungs, too, were bothering her, so this sentence sounded like "I had hopessss you would bring everyone-huh."

Matt coughed and asked, "You want us to go back?"

"Later, maybe," Miz Babbidge answered brusquely, and then she looked toward the sinking sun and added, "Or maybe tomorrow." ("Tomorrow-huh.") She turned her attention back to Luck and Starlock and gave them a sympathetic smile. "We'd love to have all of you here, of course. Come."

With a gesture, she dismissed everyone else and the other Naturalists dispersed. Miz Babbidge shepherded the Protos through the concrete yard, around stacks of supplies, toward the buildings at the east end of the complex. The whole of the complex was encircled by its own high wall, isolating it from the streets outside.

"Are there many people still alive in the city?" Starlock asked.

"It's impossible to know, but there can't be many," Miz Babbidge answered, as though this was an unfortunate though not unexpected fact, and not to be lingered over. "In there, we've set up our sleeping quarters," she said, indicating one of the buildings. "We'll find a place for you two, of course. We don't have running water just yet, but maybe in a few days." She called their attention to the small, low building toward which they were headed and said, "There's where we've set up the kitchens, and a lab."("Kitchenssss" and "lab-huh.")

"What sort of lab?" asked Starlock. "Are you studying the sickness? Could there be a way to stop it?"

"No," she said. It was a decisive *no*, like a chop with a knife, so forceful that she stopped walking when she said it. "The modifiers have gotten their due punishment. But it delights me that you're interested," she said sweetly as she continued walking. "I would love to show you what we're doing in the lab. And then some food?"

"Sure," said Luck. It was late afternoon and she was famished.

"Food is the one thing that's not an issue." (With the wheeze it sound like "issue-hum.") "Denver's filled with enough food for a million people. Canned goods will keep us supplied for months or even years."

She was fiddling with a bracelet on her wrist, to which Luck's attention was drawn as they walked. On the bracelet was a three-dimensional image of a young girl with mismatched eyes and hair of different colors. Her arms were crossed in front of her chest in a warding motion, and she was gazing out at Luck sadly.

"Why are there so many babies?" Starlock asked, drawing Luck's attention back to their surroundings. A loose gathering of twenty people was visible in an open area to the side of the courtyard. These people were all wearing camouflage, as every Naturalist had been so far, and each one was walking about with a small baby on his or her shoulder.

"Our future!" Miz Babbidge said. ("Future-heh.") When one of the enormous roll-up doors along the complex's perimeter wall began to clang open noisily, she clapped her hands together in delight and said, "Look! Such good timing. A rescue patrol is arriving now."

As the door lifted open, a truck with huge tires and a long, long passenger section rolled into the complex, allowing a glimpse behind it of a street and buildings already in twilight as the sun went down. The door was rolled shut behind the truck so quickly that the metal shook the ground.

A stream of Naturalists poured out of the vehicle, each one carrying a small child or baby—some had one in each arm. A few of these little ones were crying with great gusto, but most looked weak and exhausted.

"Our future," Miz Babbidge said again, looking rather pleased with herself, as the baby-minders began to disappear into the building near the kitchens. "Some have been without food or care for days, so we have to get them fed immediately."

Luck followed the parade of children with her eyes, thinking that they looked just like Proto children, except for the mixed variety of their skin tones.

Perhaps Miz Babbidge guessed what Luck was thinking, because she said, "They haven't been modified, you see. Big mods happen after children are two years old. So the little ones . . . well, we are Naturalists, and they are *natural,* like you. We have patrols out, going block by block to find every one of them still in the city. Their parents and older siblings may have died in this plague of their own making, but we'll try to save the tiny ones." ("Onessss.") She added darkly, "There are others who wouldn't do that, who think even their children shouldn't be saved."

Luck and Starlock shared a glance at this unsettling statement, and then they followed the direction of Miz Babbidge's gaze. For the first time, Luck noticed the large number of armed guards standing atop the buildings of the complex, looking outward. Starlock's brow creased, and Luck could read his thought: *If everyone out there is dead, who are they guarding against?*

Luck took a leap and asked the question that had brought her and Starlock to the city in the first place: "Is . . . is the Proto Authority still running?"

Miz Babbidge let out a short laugh, like a bark, which turned into a fit of coughing. Then she scanned the buildings of the city, visible above the complex's outer wall. She pointed viciously at the tallest building Luck could see, a structure covered in sharp crystal facets like diamond armor.

"There!" she said, her voice hoarse. "The source of this plague. The Bureau of Modifications and its departments, the Proto Authority and the Cellular Crop Authority. One can only hope they were the first to go!" ("Go-huh.") Miz Babbidge's pleasant demeanor, inconsistent as it had been, was now beginning to fall apart in earnest. But at least, Luck thought, the woman's anger was not directed at them.

They had reached the low building that was their destination, and Miz Babbidge guided them inside. On their right, the hallway opened onto a public dining area full of other Naturalists, many with weapons. Miz Babbidge led them past this area, saying, "Let me show you our lab."

Farther down the hall was a set of double doors. She threw these open to reveal a makeshift laboratory. It reminded Luck of the medical observation room on the Rez, though this space was more crowded and much less clean. Inside were several Naturalists wearing surgical gloves and masks. One was testing the straps on a gurney.

"Dinner soon," their hostess said pleasantly, "but first we need a few samples of your cells"—("cellsssss")—"from your lungs and other organs, to help us rebuild our own."

At first Luck thought she'd misheard, because the woman's expression remained so friendly. Starlock's sharp voice told her she had not. "What do you mean?" Starlock asked, taking tight hold of Luck's hand.

"You want to operate on us?" asked Luck, suddenly alarmed. Starlock stepped backward, pulling Luck with him.

"Oh, no," Miz Babbidge said, almost cooing. The woman's volatile mix of sympathy and rancor now resolved into a frightening eagerness focused entirely on the two Protos in front of her. "You made that sound awful. We're *Naturalists*. We would never use you as fodder for an experiment. But we need your cells with their unaltered DNA. Through no fault of our own, some parts of our bodies aren't working as they should. Our lungs, for instance." ("For instanssss.") She took a shuddering breath by way of illustration. "With a little electricity, the right enzymes, and a consistent cellular contribution from you, we can make things work again." The group in the lab moved ever so slightly closer to the Protos, and Luck could feel their *need* filling the room.

Miz Babbidge gestured for her guests to enter the lab, but Starlock, holding Luck's hand tightly, turned to leave. They bumped into the solid figures of four men who had come up behind them undetected. Strong hands clamped down on the Protos' shoulders, wrenched their arms behind their backs with professional skill . . .

. . . and the world turned to chaos around them. Beyond the open doors at the end of the hallway, the tornado roar of air transpos filled the air, and everyone outside and inside began to yell.

The men holding Luck and Starlock let go, and the others inside the lab rushed past them, unholstering guns as they went. The dining area emptied as the Naturalists flooded outside. Luck heard bullets ricochet off metal out in the courtyard and then the fast, endless repeat of automatic weapons.

"Go! Go!" Miz Babbidge yelled at the Protos as she too pushed past. "Go farther inside and hide!" she ordered. "They've come to take you! And they will be much worse to you than we are."

"To take *us*?" Luck yelled back, terror and confusion equally mingled in her mind.

"They call themselves Naturalists, like us, but they're killers and crazy!" Miz Babbidge called over her shoulder, and then she too disappeared into the chaos.

"Come on," Starlock breathed. "If she's calling someone else crazy . . ."

He was pushing Luck in the opposite direction, away from the outer doors. They flew wildly down the hall as plumes of dust swirled into the building.

"The Protos are there!" a man yelled from the courtyard. "Get inside!"

Luck dared to glance back. Soldiers from the newly arrived air transpos were fighting their way into the building. A leader of these new arrivals—an unmodified man with a very large gun—was looking right at Luck as he ran through the outer doorway. A gunshot and the man pitched forward, and then there were people fighting hand to hand, and she stopped looking, because Starlock pulled her around a corner in the hallway.

They dashed to the end of this new hall, turned again. When they found a metal door in a side passage, Starlock wrenched it open, pulled Luck through, and locked it behind them with a huge sliding lever, shutting out the sound of the melee. From there they chose a path at random and ended up in a basement corridor, filled with all manner of old machinery, piled clothing, and stacks and stacks of canned food.

"Which way?" Luck asked, when they reached an intersection.

"This way, I think," Starlock answered, pausing to get his bearings and then choosing a direction. "If we go far enough, we might come out beyond their walls."

"Wait, then," said Luck, stopping him by a heap of camouflage uniforms. They pulled these over their clothing and found scarves to conceal their unusual complexions. Then they ran on for a long while until they came to a dark stairwell, leading upward. At the top was a door with a grate set into its lower half. Starlock knelt down and looked through.

"It's the street," he told her. "And it's pretty dark out now."

"But where are we going? Out of the city?"

"Look," he said.

Luck peered through the grate. Framed against the sky in the distance was the building Miz Babbidge had pointed out.

"She said the Proto Authority was there," Luck said, understanding.

Starlock nodded. "It's what we came to see."

9. THEY REACHED A NEW WORLD

They emerged into twilight, somewhere quite a distance from the perimeter wall of the compound. Air transpos were spinning up not far away and the noise of gunfire could still be heard sporadically, but before them was a small, quiet street that lay mostly in darkness. Everywhere they looked, buildings were adorned with plants growing around windows, framing doorways, spilling artfully off roof corners. It was as though the humans believed that nature still held sway here.

Starlock led Luck past a few abandoned vehicles to the corner, which opened onto a larger street. Turning back, they could see dust rising from the distant courtyard where they had landed, and in the midst of the dust cloud were two transpos lifting into the air. As the vehicles cleared the outer wall of the Naturalists' complex, there was a deafening boom. The Protos ducked, but Luck's eyes stayed riveted to the nearest transpo as its forward window blew out, followed by the pilot, who dropped, flailing, out of sight.

"Come on!" Starlock said, pulling her down the street as

the transpo spun out of control. Luck couldn't see the impact, but the sound of a crash reached them moments later. The whine of the second transpo continued, growing louder and closer, until it was visible flying low above the street they'd just left, a searchlight sweeping the ground. They hid themselves in the shadow of a vine-covered building as it passed.

"You think they're looking for us?" Luck asked.

"Don't you?"

"Yeah."

The transpo flew off in another direction and she and Starlock continued. On this new street, which was lined with beautiful trees, the vehicles were not empty. Corpses lay against car windows and across seats—colorful faces, withering. Through the back window of a vehicle, three eyes—each a different color—in a neat row across a woman's dead face seemed to follow Luck as she went.

The next street was worse—a dozen vehicles, inside which were arms in odd shapes, shining horns, long folded legs, elongated torsos of bodies that had shriveled almost to skeletons. There were more body types and variations than Luck could have imagined—and all had been overcome as they tried to leave.

The whir of the air transpo grew louder as it doubled back to look for them, and they crouched in a dark doorway as its searchlight flooded the street. In the glare, Luck saw four dead humans—a family—inside an overturned vehicle. Suspended in their seat belts, their matching large heads hung heavily toward the ground with something like antennae curling out of their hair. She wondered fleetingly if those strange curling bristles conferred additional senses, or if they were merely decorative quirks. The rats scurrying through the vehicle and leaving raw, pink bite marks in their flesh didn't care either way. In the last of the glow from the transpo's searchlight, Luck registered that one of the adult humans was not quite dead—a low, hoarse exhale was escaping the woman's mouth.

"Starlock . . . ," Luck whispered, clutching his shoulder.

"Look," he said, "they're going to crash."

The transpo had flown off erratically, its searchlight sweeping in wild arcs. As they watched, it bobbed over buildings and disappeared from sight. The sound of its collision reached their ears almost immediately.

"They're dropping like flies," Luck said.

But the noise of the transpo's engines had already been replaced by a low, deep rumble. An enormous vehicle was rolling onto the street, identical to the truck they'd seen in the Naturalists' courtyard.

"Collecting more kids," Starlock whispered.

The truck plowed down the road toward them, shoving vehicles out of the way as it went. As it passed, they could hear babies crying within.

"Let's hope the fighting's stopped back there," Starlock murmured.

"The Naturalists aren't so bad if they're saving all those kids," Luck whispered.

"If they're actually saving them," he said grimly.

Luck thought of the lab and the gurney with the straps and

the ravenous expressions of the Naturalists when they spoke of taking the Protos' undamaged cells. "We'll keep our fingers crossed," she whispered.

When the truck had gone, they followed the street for a long way until they arrived at what was certainly one of the main thoroughfares of the city. From there they had a clear view of the Bureau of Modifications, which was outlined by the last glow of the sunset, so that the edges of its diamond facets smoldered with reddish light.

"It's pretty close," Luck said.

"And look—there are lights on." Most of the building was dark, but one floor near the middle was fully lit up.

They crossed the wide boulevard, weaving through vehicles full of humans, then passed through a gardenlike strip in the middle of the street where deep rows of flowering trees briefly blocked the scent of decay. The other side of the boulevard was more crowded, the vehicles packed tightly and crashed into each other, so that it was difficult to find their way through. Luck avoided looking directly at the occupants of the cars, but when they reached the far side of the street, it was no longer possible to escape the sight of humans; the pavement was clogged with people who'd gotten out to walk before they collapsed. There had been, at one point, a stampede, which had left bodies piled against each other in waves. Luck tried to keep her eyes slightly unfocused, but flashes of horror got through anyway: faces, hands, legs, in every shape and color, some mummified, some bloated. Rats were scampering over everything but only biting occasionally—she wondered if there was something about the taste of humans that they didn't like.

At last, the Protos' way was blocked by a sidewalk so thickly covered with corpses that they would have to climb over them to continue on.

"I can't do it, Starlock!" Luck cried, stopping in a tiny clean patch of pavement. She leaned over and crushed an arm against her nose, her stomach heaving. "I can't take anymore."

"Just a little farther . . . ," Starlock said. "It's right there."

The high, crystal building was much closer. They could see it above everything, growing darker and darker against the sky, but with one floor still brightly lit.

He wrapped his scarf more tightly around his nose and mouth and did the same for Luck. Then he took her hand and together they climbed over the hill of bodies. Luck tried not to feel the soft give beneath her shoes nor to see the tangled limbs and wings and brightly furred appendages on which she was stepping. Some of the bodies were glowing with bioluminescence. Others had a kind of aura around them, flickering and fading as they bathed themselves and nearby corpses in a ghostly illumination.

If the Naturalists had been telling the truth, these were not humans, a new and varied species; these were humans who could not stop changing themselves. Seeing their grotesque diversity on such a scale, Luck understood that no natural process could be responsible.

"They're still breathing," Starlock gasped beneath his scarf.

Luck said nothing. She could hear labored breaths here and there, but she didn't want to look any more closely.

On the other side of the human barricade, the pavement was nearly clear. From there they ran and did not stop until they had arrived at the diamond-faceted edifice. They came to a panting halt before towering doors of black glass. In small silver lettering were the words *Bureau of Modification.*

Because it was too awful to speak of, they wordlessly banged their boots against the side of the building, knocking off the gore that had accumulated. Then they tried the doors. There were no handles, and the glass didn't budge with repeated attempts to shove it apart. Just as they were about to look for something with which to smash the doors, they came open on their own, gliding smoothly on polished tracks.

"Cameras," Starlock said, pointing out their glass eyes all around the building's entrance. "Someone inside is watching us."

"So the Proto Authority is still here?" Luck whispered.

"Maybe," Starlock answered.

And yet, after seeing the city outside, it was impossible to fear anything in this building. The humans were not in control. Together they stepped across the threshold and entered the lobby. The heavy doors slid shut behind them, closing out the city.

They had arrived into a different world. The space was enormous and fancier than any room Luck had ever been in. Every surface in the lobby was made of crystalline facets fitted together to form sharp, beautiful patterns, like the armor of a horned lizard, done with great sheets of what looked like diamond. The walls reached up in staggered tiers to a vaulted ceiling of the same crystal, which glowed far above with a pale white light.

In the center of the space, drawing them in, was a curving line of glass sculptures, depicting all of evolution. The parade began with a small glass amphibian emerging from a frothy glass wave. From there, the sculptures got larger: early vertebrates and mammalian reptiles, a platypus, something like a mole, then a lemur, then larger creatures recognizable as primates. There were apes then, and stooped and hairy figures that were beginning to look like Man. And then there was a Proto, a tall male with broad shoulders and features that, though rendered in clear glass, made him look like he could be related to Starlock. This Proto was flawless and proud, but something in his expression said that his time had come and gone, he had ceded the world to someone else.

That "someone else" followed immediately in the line of figures; beyond the Proto were the largest sculptures: a human with gills and fins as well as hands, another with wings outstretched, and the final, a woman with legs twice the ordinary length, shown leaping up toward the high, high ceiling. Luck understood the glowing vault above them now: it was meant to represent perfection, and these humans were rising to it.

The Proto statue looked forward at those magnificent human creatures with a stoic mien, informing the viewer that he understood and accepted his vast inferiority.

"There we are, I guess," Luck said at last.

"There we are," Starlock agreed. His eyes drifted back to

the crystalline walls and he said, "The walls are supposed to be cells. Do you see?"

He was right. The diamond facets butted up against each other and repeated, stylized versions of living cells, grouping and regrouping and forming intricate structures. The whole building was an artist's version of the work done by the Bureau of Modifications.

The room was so beautiful that it threatened to mesmerize them, and it was only with great effort that they tore themselves away. There were elevators located down a side passage, but the controls inside did nothing. This was just as well; though Luck and Starlock had both read about elevators, they weren't eager to take their first elevator ride in a mostly dead building in a mostly dead city, after the sun had gone down.

Instead they found the stairs.

10. THEY SPOKE TO A DYING MAN

Up and up they went in the stairwell, until Luck began to imagine that it was infinite, a repeating series of landings that would go on forever. At each new floor they looked through the glass window in the stairwell door, but only darkness greeted them—until they arrived at the fifty-seventh floor. There, they left the stairs into a well-lit hallway that dead-ended at a large, heavy door. When they pulled up on its handle, this door hissed open and then swung smoothly inward as if it had been waiting to welcome them inside.

They found a kind of laboratory when they stepped across the threshold, so large it spanned half of the fifty-seventh floor. Luck's first impression was of a polished white floor and ceiling, windows along two sides giving a view of the city and the world beyond. But her second impression was quite different. Every bit of wall that was not a window was taken up by glass tanks teeming with life. She and Starlock stepped farther inside the room, and Luck saw that each tank contained a miniature Earth environment. The nearest one looked like a tiny rain forest, and it was inhabited by snails with fantastically colorful shells. In the next tank were sand and a tiny artificial sun and a dozen varieties of ocean mollusk with delicate pastel hues, clinging to a small rock. Shimmering butterflies were in the next, frogs and toads in the one after that. And all along the edges of the polished floor were tubs of dirt out of which grew tall stalks of grain. There had been several books in the Rez school with pictures of different ecosystems, but for Luck and Starlock, this was their first time seeing most of these creatures and their vegetation in real life. Luck watched in fascination as a startlingly bright salamander walked across the glass face of its cage.

"I don't believe in God or anything like that," said a hoarse voice, surprising a yelp out of Luck and causing Starlock to jump, "but still I was praying for you to come."

They turned to discover a man sitting in the very center of the room. They had not seen him at first because he and his desk were surrounded by tubs of tall grain stalks. He looked about forty, with two arms and two legs and skin and hair that were both a light reddish brown, which contrasted interestingly with his very light blue eyes. He sat heavily in his lab chair and quite obviously was having difficulty breathing, yet he managed to smile at them. He made a sweeping gesture, inviting them farther inside.

"I'm Mizter Dekkle," the man told them, when they'd come a little closer.

He sat before a round table that gave the impression of having grown right out of the floor. This table was topped with glowing glass, beneath which were any number of minute pieces of equipment.

"I'm Luck," Luck said. "And this is Starlock. We came—"

"—from the Cathedral Proto reservation, I would guess," the man said, interrupting her with an unexpected eagerness.

"Yes," Luck agreed. She'd heard the Rez called "Cathedral" before by Mizter Caldwell. It was the Rez's name among humans, even if no Protos ever used it.

The man pulled an oxygen mask up to his mouth and inhaled from it for a time, holding up a finger politely to ask them to give him a moment. After several slow breaths, he removed the mask.

"How can I help you?" he asked kindly.

"We . . . ," Luck began, then she fell silent. She was hesitant to tell him that they'd come only to find out if the Proto Authority was still operational—and that they had dearly hoped it was not.

"Humans stopped coming to the Rez," Starlock said. "And so we . . ." He too trailed off.

"You wanted to know if we were ever coming back at all," Mizter Dekkle suggested.

"Yes," they both said.

"So. The short answer is *no.*"

The man put the oxygen mask over his face again. His eyes inspected them as he breathed. Luck became aware of how shabby they both looked in the old camouflage uniforms, their hair full of dust, their hands and faces as dirty as the Naturalists'. Mizter Dekkle was surely taking in all of those details, but she sensed that he could see much more. This man *designed* people, and Luck had the peculiar sensation that he might be peering into their minds.

At length, he removed the mask again. "I will explain more, but are you hungry?" he asked.

They had gotten no food from the Naturalists and so were ravenous. Mizter Dekkle pointed them to the far end of the room, where a refrigerator sat beneath a counter. On the way, Luck peered into a tank full of iridescent beetles and another that held tiny starfish.

"You see here some of the things we steal," Mizter Dekkle said, noticing her interest. "The traits we take from you Protos—hair color, eye color, skin color, height, and so on—are added in the womb. Other traits come later, and we borrow those from every creature in nature."

Another piece of the human puzzle fell into place. Of course the humans had not been merely studying and cataloging Proto DNA. They had been using it.

The refrigerator was full of some sort of food that came in

bars wrapped in plastic. They returned to Mizter Dekkle and ate while sitting on the floor in front of him, surrounded by tubs of grain.

"Please, can you tell me who that human is?" Luck asked, pointing to a large portrait standing on the floor, where it was leaning against the glass of the lab windows.

It was an image, she was sure, of the same man she'd seen on the necklace belonging to the pilot of the crashed transpo they'd found on their way to the city. In this portrait, however, the man had made more changes to his body. The wavy black hair on one side, the curly brown hair on the other, the black eye, the green eye—these were the same, but he had, additionally, a yellow eye like the eye of a bird of prey on each of his temples and two extra arms. Each of his four arms exhibited a different skin color.

Mizter Dekkle removed his mask and said, thoughtfully, "That, Luck, is the Reverend Mizter Tad Tadd. Once a rabble-rousing preacher, later the man singularly responsible for uniting the modern world. He . . . well, he spent his life influencing the masses—the masses you have undoubtedly seen as you walked through the city."

"Is it a religious painting?" Luck asked.

Most references to religion had been excised from the Proto library and school curriculum, of course, but there were still hints here and there, in books on art and music. The Reverend Mizter Tadd, in this image, reminded Luck of the poses she had seen in some centuries-old paintings.

"Some would say yes, it is a religious painting, though most would claim it is exactly the opposite—that it pays tribute to a man who set science free from religion."

"And the darts?" Starlock asked, for the portrait had been used as a dart board and was speckled with holes from this abuse. A tight knot of darts had been left in place, piercing the man's chest just where a glowing, enormous heart had been painted.

"I have become somewhat less enamored with the great Reverend Tadd," the man answered, "in light of recent events." He disappeared into his oxygen mask for a time. When he removed it again, he said, "You wish to know what's happened to the humans? The best answer I have is this: we are all dying or dead."

"Everywhere?" Starlock asked.

"That brings up an interesting question. When you say *everywhere,* what do you mean by that word?"

"We mean the whole Earth," Luck answered. "Are humans all over the whole world dying?"

"And by humans you mean *modified* humans?"

They both nodded. "We thought you were a different species," Luck said.

"That was by design," Mizter Dekkle admitted. "But you've figured out the truth?"

"That you just like to make changes?" Starlock suggested.

"Yes," Mizter Dekkle agreed. He continued, "I know you've been given no books on recent history, so you won't know that the rest of the world, apart from the North American Voluntary Federation, has shut themselves off from this country for decades. Their idea of what humans should be and our idea were not . . . compatible." He spoke rather slowly, to conserve his breath, and here he paused to take more oxygen. "Russia and many others didn't like the variety we've given ourselves. To them, manipulating our own genome was unethical, a kind of profanity. And we in the West didn't like the half-mechanical slave laborers they were creating to make their own lives easier. Both sides arguing for human rights from opposite directions."

"So . . . there is no 'rest of the world'?" Starlock asked.

"Oh, it's there all right," the man answered, "though I know very little of it. Occasionally a scientist might break the communications ban to speak illegally to a fellow scientist on the other side of the Genetic Curtain, but this doesn't happen often enough to get a sense of their world."

After a stint in the oxygen mask, Mizter Dekkle continued, "But let's set aside the rest of the world, which may be healthy, for all I know. Everywhere in our country and in the North American Federation, humans are dead or dying. Like the poor souls you have seen on your way here. Indeed, like me."

"You're dying, then?" Luck asked, sorry to hear it. "I thought maybe you just had damaged lungs from the fumes, like the Naturalists—"

"Have you been with that crazy lot?" he asked, a little sharply. This brought on a fit of coughing, which necessitated more time in the mask.

She and Starlock explained their encounter with the Naturalists and the attack by another group, also calling themselves

Naturalists. When their story was finished, Mizter Dekkle removed his mask and said, "Naturalists come in different factions, representing varying degrees of craziness." Their host shook his head. "So . . . they control the city? Hmm. But it's not a lung condition, Luck," he explained. "I may look unmodified, and I am *largely* unmodded. But I was given extra-efficient lungs when I was a child, to extract more oxygen from the air. This gave me increased brain function and a lower sleep requirement. It's a standard mod for a family who wish their child to go into science. My lungs haven't entirely succumbed yet, but they will in time." He paused for a few breaths in the mask, and then continued, "We humans all got modified hearts and lungs of one sort or another in early childhood, but doctors do most basic organ mods automatically and aren't required to tell the parents. Most Naturalists may not even know that parts of their bodies aren't original. They may not understand why they are being affected by this illness. But they will die nonetheless, just as I will. No one modded will be immune."

"They wanted to put us in their lab and take our cells," Starlock said, "to teach their own cells how to grow properly again."

Thoughtfully Mizter Dekkle said, "If they took enough of your healthy cells, often enough, and injected them in the right places in their own bodies . . . it's possible they could put off death for a time. An interesting thought. But it would not be pretty for you.

"What did they tell you about this sickness? That we created it right here in the Bureau of Modifications?"

Luck answered, "Miz Babbidge said this building was the source of it."

Their host looked amused. "That's an easier story than the real one. But the truth is that we've all been killed by crop blight."

"Crop blight?" asked Luck, trying to understand the connection. The Protos were familiar with blight, of course—they were farmers, after all.

"Do you mean that your food supplies failed?" asked Starlock.

Mizter Dekkle shook his head and gestured to the tubs of grain all along the floor. "No, I mean that we've been building *ourselves* out of food supplies." He pulled up a stalk of grain from one of the tubs. Luck thought it resembled millet, but it was brown and dead-looking, and the head, where all the seeds were, was too large, each seed more like a small fruit than a kernel of grain. Mizter Dekkle split one of the seeds, revealing something that was not millet at all inside. A gray-brown goo leaked from the pod onto his hand.

"What is it?" she asked.

"It's millet—and humans," he told them. "It's both. A hybrid of human and plant cells and the building block of mods. Some are programmed in at conception—hair, eye, skin color, height, gender. But for bigger mods—wings or extra limbs or special lungs—we guide the DNA, often copying other creatures from nature. And these cells"—he was rubbing the goo between his fingers—"are very easy to program. They're the scaffolding for all modification. Do you understand that word, *scaffolding*?"

"Yes," Starlock said.

"Starlock's an engineer and I . . . I read," Luck told him.

"Ah, scholars. That is fortunate for me. But then again, I am one of the few who campaigned to keep enough science in the Proto curriculum to give you some control over your world, even if it was only the world of the Rez." He pointed out to them several tubs of millet, all of which were dry and brown. "The Naturalists attacked the modified millet crops—to stop people from creating mods. They did it publicly. Do you see all the withered stalks? Those plants died a few weeks ago. But the virus does more than attack the human crops. It goes after any cells derived from these plants—which means all of our added mods, all of us. And it spreads faster than anything I've seen."

"We saw one Rez sentry catch it from another in a few seconds," Luck told him.

"Yes," said Mizter Dekkle, "I was here in the lab early on the day it crossed from plants to humans. I watched people in neighboring buildings catching it from each other almost instantly. Our population lives entirely within city borders, so the spread was . . . cataclysmic. I will give the Naturalists the benefit of the doubt and assume that they achieved more than they intended. But they will succumb too. And soon."

They were all silent for a while, until Luck whispered, "Who will take care of those children when the Naturalists die? And will they try to take the children's cells?"

They explained the long trucks gathering up infants from all over the city. Mizter Dekkle grew increasingly upset as he heard this. He spent a long time in the mask, staring at the floor. Eventually, he said, "I am too slow. You see that some of the plants are still green. I've gathered varieties from the greenhouses downstairs that are not as susceptible to the blight." The tubs behind his desk were full of healthier plants. "And see . . ."

They rose to look at the table in front of him. Beneath the lighted surface were several round glass dishes, each with a slimy and spongy sheet of something vibrantly pink alive inside it.

"Healthy tissue from the healthy plants," Mizter Dekkle said. "If I could culture them more rapidly . . ." He gestured helplessly at his failing body.

"Could we help?" Starlock asked.

He regarded the two of them as he breathed through his mask. After several breaths, he said, "We kept you on a reservation for our own convenience, taught you that you were inferior. Did you really come here to help us?"

"No," Starlock admitted. "We came to see if you were still watching us. But now . . ."

". . . we've seen the city," Luck finished for him, "and all of those children."

Mizter Dekkle nodded, visibly moved. "How many other Proto reservations have gotten free?" he asked them. "If I had all of you to help—"

"Are there other reservations?" asked Luck.

"Are there more of us?" asked Starlock at the same time.

After a moment's confusion, the man understood. "Of

course," he said. "You haven't found each other yet. It's only been a few days." Seeing how startled the Protos were, he explained in a gentle voice, "There are reservations dotted all over Colorado. Most are exactly like yours. A few are where we keep the Protos who get kicked off their original reservations or who managed to sneak past their border fences. But even those are much like your reservation."

Starlock swallowed, and with a painfully hopeful look he asked, "Do you mean that . . . that all . . . ?" but he wasn't able to put his question into words.

Luck asked it for him. "When Protos are taken away for breaking the rules, they're not killed?" she said. "Or thrown in prison or something? They're just moved to another reservation?"

"Yes," Mizter Dekkle agreed, looking contrite. "I'm sorry that we led you to believe the worst. You can understand that there had to be consequences for breaking our Covenants? We wanted to keep you diverse."

Tears had sprung to Starlock's eyes. "My sister and her boyfriend were taken. So . . . ?"

"She is very likely safe, within a few hundred miles of where you're standing now."

Starlock stood there quietly, overwhelmed.

"How—how many other Protos are there?" Luck asked.

"Several thousand," their host told her. "If I can slow our deaths enough to help all of you . . ."

He studied the two of them again as he brought the mask to his face. Luck's right hand hung by Starlock's left, and he appeared to be appraising those two hands, so different in color, but so much the same in every other way.

When the mask came off, Mizter Dekkle was looking past them, toward some vision only he could see. "We took all inherited disease out of the human genome. At least we did that for you," he reflected. "Then we took your strawberry-blond hair, Luck, and your brown skin, Starlock, for nothing more than vanity. But for someone like me, who is supposed to take the long view of our race, you Protos were always a backup plan, our safe-deposit box, our genetic repository."

His eyes came back and he gestured for them to move closer to him. When they did, Mizter Dekkle took one of their hands in each of his. Then he put their hands together.

He looked from Luck to Starlock and said, "You came here to see if you were still our pets. You're not. You are free."

11. THEY SHARED A DREAM

Mizter Dekkle asked them to bring him into a back room for the night. They pushed him there in his rolling chair, down a long hallway. Their destination was a space that had been a break room, with tables and chairs, and one long couch. Rumpled blankets on the couch showed them where he'd been making his bed each night.

"No, it's all right," he said, waving away their help as he transferred himself onto the couch and arranged his oxygen tank so it was in easy reach. He allowed Luck to straighten out his blankets and pull them up over his chest, though. "The fifty-seventh floor is nearly self-contained," he told them, pulling the mask aside. "You'll find showers down that hall to the right. And a bedroom beyond that."

Luck was mortified that this man was concerning himself with their sleeping arrangements. Her cheeks burned hotly, but Mizter Dekkle only smiled at her as he closed his eyes.

"It's for you now," he told them.

"What is?" Starlock asked.

"All of it," he murmured.

Mizter Dekkle fell into a fitful sleep only moments later. And Luck, watching him, fell into a kind of reverie. What was it like, she wondered, to be the last of everyone you knew?

She was roused by Starlock's warm hand taking hers. He led her down the hall, toward the lighted room at the very end.

"My sister," he said, in a voice that told her he couldn't quite believe what he was saying, and yet his dark eyes looked more awake somehow. "And maybe everyone who was ever taken." Luck squeezed his hand.

They found the showers and also a small adjacent laundry, where they slowly undressed. Since that day long ago in the woods, Luck had imagined undressing in front of Starlock again so many times, and she'd always pictured the moment as wildly romantic, a chapter in a novel that she would savor because she'd waited so long to read it. This was something else.

"I don't feel . . . ," she began as she stripped off her shirt. They were both filthy, and she was aware of all the death just beyond the walls.

"It's all right," Starlock murmured. "I keep thinking about those children in the truck."

"I keep thinking about all the people I stepped on along the way. And the *rats*."

They removed all of their clothing. Luck stared at Starlock's naked body, unashamed. It was as beautiful as she had remembered it—more beautiful. He was three years older than the last time she'd seen him unclothed. He was a man, strong and lovely. He was studying her as well, but the look on his face was more sad than anything else.

"You're beautiful," he whispered.

"So are you."

They didn't touch each other. The weight of the walled city had settled between them. Instead they stuffed their dirty clothes into a washing machine and watched as water and soap darkened the material. Luck wasn't sure the machine could wash away the smell.

The shower room had several stalls. Starlock turned on the first one, and they both stared in awe at the gallons of warm water that came flowing out. There were showers on the Rez, of course, but they were usually feeble and lukewarm.

"The humans were frivolous," Luck whispered. "And arrogant. They treated us like . . . like monkeys or something. But . . ."

"They didn't deserve this."

"No."

"Come here," Starlock whispered.

He pulled her under the spray with him. They washed and washed. Luck watched dirty water flow off them and down the drain, until at last the water ran clear and they were absolutely clean.

Still, they did not touch. Luck kept seeing those people with antennae, hanging upside down in their overturned car as rats scurried over their bodies. When she thought about the world outside, she felt as if her body weighed a thousand pounds, as if her heart were so heavy it would fall to her feet.

"You're crying," Starlock said.

Tears had begun to flow down her face, and even though the water washed them away, more came, as though she might cry out her whole body weight until nothing was left.

"They were just like us," she told him, when she could speak. "They pretended we were different, and we accepted it. But we were the same."

"I know."

Starlock pulled her to him and held her as the warm water ran over them and Luck sobbed against his shoulder.

. . .

When she was all cried out, they wrapped themselves in towels and found the bedroom. It was a small chamber on the interior side of the hall, so there were no windows. A light came on automatically when they opened the door, revealing several bunk beds, with bottom bunks that were wide enough for two people. They unfolded a blanket across one of these and crawled beneath it together.

The walls were covered in a mural that depicted a meadow full of flowers, with a yellow sun up in the corner of the ceiling, spilling warmth over everything. Among the flowers and grass, human children in their many, many forms leaped and played. Luck saw golden arms raised to catch a ball, long ears twitching to listen to something far away, and a boy with four legs jumping higher than any Proto ever could. But over by the door, there was an ordinary little girl, sitting beneath a tree, playing with a doll. Humans and Protos were in this painting together, she realized, as though Mizter Dekkle and his colleagues had claimed otherwise, but they had known all along that everyone was equal.

Starlock turned off the lights and settled next to her. "Do you know how many times I imagined sleeping in a bed with you?" he whispered. "Thousands. But I never imagined this."

"How could we ever imagine this day?"

They lay in silence for a while, Luck curled into him, Starlock holding her tightly.

At length, he said, "When we find a proper radio, we can call the Rez. And the other reservations. We'll get all the Protos to come and we'll find a way to take the children somewhere safe."

"There might be hundreds of kids," Luck whispered, "or thousands."

"But there are thousands of us too," he pointed out. "And

Miz Babbidge said there's lots of food in the city. Think, Luck, there are libraries here. You can read whatever you want."

That was something Luck hadn't considered. "We'll know what happened in all the years after our books end."

"And what to teach all of those children."

"And there's the rest of the world," Luck said. "Maybe people across the oceans."

They thought about this for a bit as Starlock tucked his chin against her neck.

Then Luck said, "Thank you."

"For what?"

"You know."

"Yeah," he said. "Thank you too."

They drifted off that way, pressed together so tightly they might have been one person.

• • •

In the middle of the night and half asleep, they began to kiss each other. Luck was dreaming they were on the Rez and also on the highest floor of the building with diamond armor. They were together, in her dream, in both the safest place in the world, and also the most frightening. They were at the pivot point of everything, with the world revolving around them.

She kissed Starlock and kissed him and kissed him, in the dream and in real life, enough to make up for three years apart. They woke just enough to pull the towels off each other. There was nothing between them then, and Starlock was warm and strong and everywhere, the weight of death and the dead city banished for a little while.

Pain brought Luck fully awake for a few moments. She sensed the dead all over the city looking at her, their varied arms reaching out to grab her. Then the faces were gone, the city was gone. She was back in her dream, with Starlock, enveloped in the all-consuming sense of the two of them together.

At that moment, Luck understood something new. There were horrors and there was death, there was evil and arrogance and apathy. But more than these, there were friends and there was hope. There was her life on the Rez and there was the wide world. And there was love. The bad things collected, but so did the good—and the good, she grasped, were more important than the bad. You could look past the bad if you wanted. Each good thing Luck had experienced, each good thing she had learned, built upon all of the others and added up to one thing she felt completely for the first time:

Human.

AUTHOR'S NOTE

This book began with a revelation. After poring over articles about gene editing, methods of growing human organs outside the human body, changing the body's structure and function using bioelectronic interfaces and microscopic mechanical devices, and all manner of coming wonders, I thought, "This is it. Soon we'll be able to eradicate disease, extend our life spans, turn humans into superhumans!" A few minutes later I had a very different thought: "We will definitely find some way of messing this up in spectacular fashion."

The stories in this novel were born in the space between my first thought and my second thought.

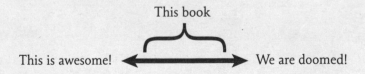

As we are increasingly able to live without disease, modify our bodies, and change what it means to be human, how will these capabilities alter our view of each other and of the world? What will it be like to grow up, to fall in and out of love, to choose what you believe in, when the very essence of "you" might be changing?

I don't have the answers. All I have are the six young people who inhabit this book, and I've tried very hard to set their stories down properly. I hope I've succeeded.

ACKNOWLEDGMENTS

These six stories, and the single novel they create together, were, to me, a kind of dragonfly: savage, iridescent, and unearthly. I want to thank the people who saw their grimness and their hopefulness and decided to make them into a proper book.

Krista Marino, firstly for tearing through the manuscript over the weekend so we could talk about it at lunch on Monday. But secondly, and mostly, for all her care with this book and her love of the characters.

Ray Shappell, for the eerie and wonderful cover. Ken Crossland for the lovely look of its pages.

Colleen Fellingham and Amy Schneider for the copyediting, without which no author should go out in public.

A huge thanks to the many, many creative and wonderful and caring people at Penguin Random House who worked to make this book and share it with the world, particularly Jules Kelly and Joshua Redlich.

To Jodi Reamer, whose gut instincts are uncannily accurate

and whose excitement over this book was infectious. (Incidentally, her love of Disneyland is just maybe possibly starting to rub off on me, but I will deny it if questioned.)

To Kassie Evashevski, for keeping an eye on me and this story, even when she was on the other side of the country.

To Cecilia de la Campa at Writers House, for bringing my books to every corner of the world.

To Helen Russell, for helping me translate dialogue into Russian, including many swearwords.

To Sky Morfopoulos, Alexandra Meldal-Johnsen, Jennifer Anderson, and Michael Doven for being my beta readers.

To my family, and particularly my husband, Sky Dayton, who is a pretty great husband and who puts up with and possibly even enjoys the strange things I like to read and talk about. Also to my children, who make it hard to relax or concentrate or finish things or keep a clean house but who make me laugh and look at the world with fresh eyes and feel happy to be alive. I love you all very much.